THE SONGBIRD AND THE SURVEYOR

THE TWENTY-NINERS OF THE GEORGIA GOLD RUSH
BOOK ONE

DENISE FARNSWORTH   WRITING AS   DENISE WEIMER

WILD HEART BOOKS

Cover design by Evelyne Labelle at Carpe Librum Book Design.
www.carpelibrumbookdesign.com

ISBN-13: 978-1-963212-40-2

CHAPTER 1

JUNE 1832
AURARIA, NORTH GEORGIA

Gold Digger's Road that ran through the boom town of Auraria, Georgia, beckoned many toward their dreams, but Jesse Holden was fated to follow it out of town and keep right on going until he ran out of freedom. That his line of thinking offered a sad commentary on the joys of matrimony did not bear examination in his current state. Right now, all he wanted was a bath and a shave, followed lickety-split by a meal that hadn't been salted, smoked, or cooked over a campfire.

He had to get himself cleaned up before he contemplated a return to Gainesville. As he was, his sweet bride-to-be would run on sight of him. Which would not please Jesse's mother. Or his fiancée's family—especially her brother, Wade Coulter. Even the fact that Wade was Jesse's best friend wouldn't save him.

And then there was the fact that after five months apart, his yearning for Emma ought to overpower every other sensibility.

That it did not gnawed a hole in his midsection worse than his hunger pangs. What was wrong with him?

He'd think on that after a night of rest in a real bed—preferably, one without bedbugs. The infernal pests were one of the many reasons Jesse preferred his bedroll and a blanket upon a pine bough. But Nathaniel Nuckolls's hotel was so new that maybe the ticking was yet insect free.

Jesse spoke over his shoulder to his four-man crew. "We'd best hurry if we want a room." His surveyor's tripod in hand and rifle strapped to his back, Jesse picked up his stride toward the buildings rising from the ridge like a skinny cur's backbone. He spared not a glance to see if his crew followed.

Word was that upwards of six hundred surveyors with crews like his—a pack man, two axe men, and a cook—had descended on North Georgia like a massive flock of pigeons— or maybe more like vultures—darkening the green hills, tromping about on land that rightfully belonged to the Cherokees, dividing it into 160-acre farming plots and 40-acre gold lots. It had all started when Benjamin Parks kicked up a nugget in twenty-nine, on his way back from salting his cattle's lick log.

Since then, the state had yielded to pressure to divide the Cherokees' land. Well ahead of the lottery, which was to begin this fall, prospectors flooded the narrow neck of land between the gold-rich Chestatee and Etowah Rivers, spreading out to placer mine along the feeder creeks and into adjacent counties. Georgia Guards stationed at Scudder's Trading Post attempted to prevent altercations and protect the natives until their removal to Oklahoma could be completed. They weren't always successful.

The job Hall County had elected Jesse's crew to do was done now, and he couldn't say he was sorry to get shed of them. Not that they were bad sorts. But even the best of men could wear on your nerves when you spent that much time together.

"We should be fine. I heard Nuckolls built more rooms on

his hotel." Lean-as-a-sapling Taylor Jones nearly matched Jesse's pace despite the leather supply pack riding his back like a turtle's shell.

The ringing of hammers ahead seemed to validate his statement. Men squeezed the last bit of the twilight hour to toss up lumber and slap a sign on the front. A salesman broadcasted the merits of his cradle rockers and sluice boxes from a wagon at the end of the main thoroughfare. Farther along, outside a tavern advertising a nightly game of *vingt-et-un,* two aged miners argued over some papers. Casting them leery glances, a woman in faded linen hurried her toddler from the back of a wagon into a general store. The scent of roasting meat drew Jesse past them.

"I say we've earned a pint at the Boom or Bust first." Taylor panted along beside him. Jesse's frowning glance intercepted the glow igniting in the nineteen-year-old's eyes. "Some miners back at that last camp we came across said the Songbird of Auraria is goin' to perform tonight at the saloon's grand opening."

Jesse made a blowing sound as he stepped around a red clay rut. The water in the bottom that remained from yesterday's rain reflected the coppery rays of the sun sinking to their left. A bank of clouds in an otherwise-clear sky illuminated in vivid peach, promising a glorious goodbye to the day from Auraria's clear-cut ridge. Soon as dark fell, he'd be fast asleep. Thoughts of women could wait for his wedding next month.

"I heard they're chargin' five dollars for admission," one of the Loudermilk brothers said from behind. Zeke? The burly axe men weren't twins, but most folks couldn't tell them apart. Jesse couldn't tell their voices apart.

Their cook, Rook Anglin, snorted. "Who'd pay five dollars to hear a gal sing?"

Jesse's thought exactly. Five dollars was two days of pay at a professional job. A week of meals.

"I would," said the other Loudermilk, Malachi. "'All I want in this creation is a pretty little wife and a big plantation away up yonder in the Cherokee Nation.'" He sang the ditty Jesse had heard countless times in the past few months, the one expressing the same craving for land that had frustrated Governor Gilmer's noble plan to use the goldmines to finance road improvements and education. "Besides, the money's not just for admission. They're doin' a drawin', and the winner gets a kiss from Miss Genny."

Zeke wended his way around a swaybacked nag hitched to a post in a cabin yard. "A kiss on the *cheek*."

"It'd be worth it." Taylor's sigh made Jesse roll his eyes. "Everyone who's seen her says she's the purtiest gal in North Georgia. Hair the red-gold of that sunset."

Rook's tin cup clanked against the frying pan hung from his pack as he chortled. "Even if that's true, your mama will be none too pleased if you squander your pay on a saloon girl."

"She's not a saloon girl." Taylor snapped his response with so much vigor, you'd think the man had insulted his mama. "Charles Martin is her guardian. And they say she can sing good as that English soprano who's tourin' the big cities."

"Right. Because we know you're there to hear her sing." Zeke gave Taylor's arm a shove, causing him to stumble into one of two large turkeys a Cherokee hunter carried upside down.

Taylor's hand shot out in an entreating gesture. "Sorry." Most Cherokees dressed like the European settlers now, but the glare the man gave Taylor was fierce enough to slow his steps. Once the hunter had blended into the traffic, Taylor expelled a lusty breath. "Sheesh...this place. I need a drink. I'm goin' to the Boom or Bust."

The boy didn't wait for Jesse's permission before veering toward the biggest white clapboard building in town—far finer than the hewn-log Nuckolls Hotel across the street. Like a fine lady staring down a backwoods spinster. Jesse didn't need to read the sign emblazoned with the establishment's name above the double doors to know they'd reached the famed Boom or Bust. He started after his crewman, but a rickety wagon passed between them with a loud rumble of wheels. "Taylor! You've got the pack!"

The pack with most of the money and with Jesse's prized Young's Improved Compass, the most valuable thing he owned. Without that compass, he wasn't a surveyor.

He threw up his free hand as he turned to the others. "Well, let's go get him. The first thing we need to do is secure rooms, and we can't do that without our money."

At the mention of the money, Malachi's face lit with realization, and he scuttled after Taylor—only to join him on the saloon's veranda as the boy paid the doorkeeper.

Zeke cast Jesse a sheepish glance. "My brother's a lightweight. Better make sure he don't do something foolish." So saying, he hurried past a miner pushing a wheelbarrow and joined the others just before they entered the Boom or Bust.

Rook sighed. "Sorry, boss. I was in favor of a good meal, myself."

Jesse ground out a sound of frustration. Trouble was, as of today, he was no longer the boss. And those men were bound and determined to celebrate the completion of their assignment. "I'll get that pack back. But I'll be hog-tied if I pay five dollars to do it." He handed the gray-haired cook his tripod, then jerked his head to the far side of the porch. "Wait there. I'll be back in a few minutes."

The saloon had to have a back entrance. Jesse slipped down the narrow alley between the building and the neighboring tailor's shop which still smelt of fresh-cut yellow pine. His passage disturbed a stray dog gnawing on the leg of... something.

In the back, there was no cover, the townsfolk having cut

the trees that would have offered shade. Jesse peeked around the corner as a dark-skinned man in a dirty apron finished a smoke, dumped out the contents of his corncob pipe, and disappeared through a back door. Jesse waited a few minutes and followed.

He found himself in a rear foyer with the kitchen to his left, beside a narrow hallway blocked by a massive guard with his back turned, his muscular arms straining his striped shirt as he surveyed the noisy main room. Jesse wasn't getting past that man. The only other option—a flight of narrow, dark steps—no doubt meant for servants—ascending to his right. Jesse started up them as a voice rang out from the bar room.

"Gentlemen! Welcome to the Boom or Bust." The speaker broadcasted his greeting in confident and cultured tones. "I am Charles Martin, your host. We're delighted you've come to celebrate our grand opening tonight, and we promise not to disappoint. We have your drink of choice, your game of choice, and your lady of choice."

Whoops and whistles covered any squeak of the stairs as Jesse reached the top. A flickering oil lamp mounted on the wall illuminated a series of doors that opened onto a hallway and ran the length of the two-story main room below.

Mr. Martin chuckled. "The state of Georgia may prohibit public gambling, but it also makes allowances for certain entertainments for respectable gentlemen. You are all respectable gentlemen, are you not?"

Guffaws and hearty agreements answered him.

Jesse inched from the shadows far enough to identify Martin, standing on the balcony at the far end of the passage. To be someone's guardian, he was surprisingly young. At the most, he had five years on Jesse's twenty-four. Halfway between them, a broad set of stairs descended before splitting in two directions at a landing and connecting to the crowded main floor below. The light of the candelabra that hung from the ceiling gleamed on the man's pomaded brown hair, the silk of his russet vest, and the jet buttons of his frock coat.

"I have no doubt you will conduct yourself as such when I introduce this fine young lady who will inaugurate our proceedings. The one you have paid to see tonight..."

"Paid to smooch!"

Martin frowned at the exclamation from someone in the crowd but didn't miss a beat of his obviously rehearsed introduction. "Here to render Samuel Francis Smith's patriotic new song, the angel of the goldfields, the Songbird of Auraria, my *ward*...Miss Genevieve Gillbard!"

No doubt about it, that one little word he emphasized served as a warning. But it was another word that caught Jesse's notice—Gillbard. An unusual name for these parts. Where had he heard it before?

At the roar of applause, a door cracked open. A woman with bright red hair peeked out, then she opened the door fully and stood back. A petite girl—for she couldn't be above eighteen—glided out in a puffed-sleeved silken dress that glistened like fairy threads in a shade between gray and light blue. She held her head with its mass of upswept strawberry-blond curls and loops high. A painted tortoise-shell comb crowned the top. Her dainty hands raised her hem as she descended to the landing. Her ethereal beauty, like a morning glory on the vine, drew Jesse forward. He paused in the shadow of a linen press.

From there, he had a view of a skinny man seated at a square piano—probably the only one in town—as he rippled out the first chords of the song. Men swept battered hats from their heads, and a hush fell over the room.

"'My country, 'tis of thee, Sweet land of liberty, Of thee I sing...'"

Jesse's breath stuck in his throat. Indeed, though the girl's voice trembled as she began, he'd never heard another so rich. Nor, to his practiced ear, so perfectly on pitch.

A movement drew his eye to the foot of the stairs—a barrel-chested man with a dark beard elbowing Taylor Jones to the side. The one who had shouted earlier? Jesse had completely forgotten about the bag, the money, the compass. Now he couldn't retrieve them until Miss Gillbard finished singing. But somehow, that was no longer a hardship.

"'I love thy rocks and rills, thy woods and templed hills; My heart with rapture thrills...'" She clasped her skirt in her hands, her tone swelling with intensity and raising the hair on the back of Jesse's neck.

That was exactly how he felt when he was out in God's creation. Could she share the same joy of nature, the same love of freedom? That was something he feared his betrothed would never come to understand. Indeed, quite the opposite—she seemed to fear setting foot outside town.

Was that where Jesse was destined to spend the rest of his life—in a town? Working for his father-in-law as a bookkeeper? Could he truly do that...give up adventure and fresh air and mountain vistas forever?

When Miss Gillbard finished the anthem, disappointment flooded him. But before the crowd could stir, the pianist moved into a solemn tune. Everyone would recognize the favorite Scottish ballad with words by Robert Burns, "Highland Mary."

"'Ye banks, and braes, and streams around the castle o' Montgomery, green be your woods, and fair your flowers...'" The Songbird of Auraria rendered the opening verses with even more conviction. Was she Scottish? She sang as though she were, even with the accent. And another song of nature... and love. Jesse didn't like where it took his thoughts. Ought a man to sacrifice one love for another? Should he not tarry for both?

And thinking of love...Charles Martin watched his ward with an intensity that blocked out everything else in the room, so he likely didn't notice when the burly miner edged to the front of the crowd. When Miss Gillbard sang of rosy lips that "I aft hae kiss'd sae fondly," the man fell to one knee and bellowed, "I beg of ye, Miss Genny! One wee kiss!" He tapped his bearded cheek, and a number of the miners broke into laughter and whoops.

Jesse stiffened. How dare the man? This was no doxy, but an innocent girl, one who clearly took her singing seriously.

The songbird stepped back. She closed the stanza with decidedly less enthusiasm. Nevertheless, the men clapped loudly. The obnoxious patron rose but kept his foot on the bottom step.

Miss Gillbard turned as though to flee, but the redheaded woman who had been in the room with her earlier descended and hooked her arm around the girl's waist. Her emerald gown shimmered in the light. She held up a brass pot and spoke over the commotion. "Gentlemen, I have here your tickets. We've come to the moment you've been waiting for. I will draw one lucky winner who may then ascend and claim a kiss from Miss Gillbard."

Whoops and catcalls broke out. Even from his position partially behind her, Jesse could tell the girl had gone pale. Her fingers dug into the folds of her skirt. Had she any say in this indignity?

Her guardian looked on, cigar smoke wreathing his amused expression. Did he care nothing for his ward's reputation? Allowing her to sing at such a venue was bad enough. The opportunity to cash in on her skills must outweigh any personal regard he might hold for her.

She cast an anxious glance over the gallery as if searching for the man. She didn't seem to note Jesse beside the wardrobe, but he drew in his breath at the full view of her face—the wide eyes, softly rounded nose, and rosebud lips. He knew where he'd heard her name—at Mt. Olivet School for Girls in Gainesville. He'd even glimpsed her on the property once or twice when the school had held socials. She'd been a year behind Wade's sister.

What was an educated girl doing here, serenading this rough-and-tumble crowd? Surely, her guardian would heed her distress. But to Jesse's astonishment, the man merely winked at her.

The older woman—who must be around thirty—raised her hand. "On the cheek, of course!" She smirked at the chorus of groans and cries of "aw, Miss Mattie!" and plunged her hand into the pot. Around the room, men held their breath and raised their ticket stubs. She came up with a ticket, held it high, and paused dramatically before reading it. "Forty-two."

"That's me!" No doubt about it—it was Taylor Jones who crowed the response. He surged forward, but the bearded miner planted a beefy hand on his chest and shoved. As Taylor stumbled, the larger man vaulted up the steps. No way was his goal a buss on the cheek.

Miss Gillbard grabbed onto Miss Mattie.

Jesse's legs started forward without any conscious decision on his part. He was at the top of the steps when the miner lunged for the girl. He grabbed a fistful of her skirt as she attempted to flee. Fabric ripped.

Jesse thundered down the stairs. For one moment, her face tilted up toward his. Her lips parted, and her green eyes rounded. Then he put the women behind him, extending his arms. He faced the ruddy-faced roughneck. "Back off, or you'll deal with me." Never mind that the guy was twice his size. His mother might have done everything else wrong, but she'd raised him to respect women. His intervention allowed the two behind him to scurry up the steps.

The miner's face slackened with surprise for only a second before it twisted with a sly grin.

Jesse braced himself.

The man lowered his head like a charging bull and aimed

his bulky shoulder at Jesse's midsection. Just prior to impact, a large object hurtled over the balcony and shattered against the miner's head. The man staggered and fell backward onto the landing, falling amongst the pieces of what had been a painted porcelain vase.

Jesse looked up, expecting to find that Charles Martin had launched the missile. But the Songbird of Auraria met his startled gaze from where she stood beside the railing. Martin was hurrying to her side. Just as he grasped her arm with a concerned expression, Miss Gillbard gave Jesse a nod. And his heart went right out of his chest.

Martin wrapped his arm around his ward and intercepted Jesse's gaze. Who knew what his expression looked like in that moment? Probably as love-struck as Taylor's had. The saloon owner addressed Jesse in a grave tone. "Thank you, young man."

The felled miner gave a low moan.

Martin's attention shifted to the oaf, his lips twisting in distaste. He spoke to the muscular employee who had guarded the back entrance and was now shoving his way toward the stairs. "Larry, get rid of him."

"My pleasure, boss." The man's bass voice rumbled through the room.

The saloon owner broadened his gaze to include everyone present. "Let it henceforth be known, I will tolerate no boorishness in this establishment. Especially toward those I hold dear." He drew Miss Gillbard closer to his side, tucking his chin as he turned a possessive gaze on her. "The next man who presumes to touch my ward leaves in a coffin."

Jesse's stomach soured, and not at the threat. That wasn't the look of a trustworthy benefactor. And while Miss Gillbard's lips tipped up for the briefest of moments in response, she quickly looked away. Back at Jesse.

But someone was tugging on his arm, threatening to

unsettle his balance on the stairs. Mr. Striped Shirt. Larry. The dark-haired man glowered. "Come on, Romeo. Just this once, I'm not gonna ask how you got upstairs. But don't ever let me catch you up there again, or you'll get the same as this guy." He jerked his thumb toward the miner, who attempted to sit up but sagged back on the landing instead.

"I have to speak to her." The words came out of Jesse's mouth with the same disobedience his feet displayed earlier.

"Who? Miss Genny?" Larry exploded in a rude laugh. "Fat chance. Nobody gets close to the songbird. She belongs to Mr. Martin." He bent and lugged the semi-conscious miner downstairs by the shoulders, boots thumping behind him.

Taylor was gaping at Jesse from the bottom—holding the pack he'd come in to retrieve.

Its contents no longer seemed important. But the balcony was now empty. The saloon guard's words sickened him more than the owner's look. *Belonged* to Mr. Martin? Something wasn't right here. But what could he do about it? His life waited for him down in the Piedmont. What happened in these mountains was no longer of concern to him.

All the same, Jesse left the Boom or Bust with the uneasy sense that he'd failed in the rescue that mattered most.

CHAPTER 2

TEN MONTHS LATER
APRIL 1833
AURARIA, GEORGIA

Genevieve Gillbard stood in a small storeroom behind the Boom or Bust's bar and straightened the flowers in her hair. The few minutes afforded her until the magician finished his act wouldn't be enough for her to rally. Not after her conversation with Charles.

How had she ended up back here? She knew how. She'd sung here before. And that was all that needed to be pointed out to the principal of Mt. Olivet School for Girls for Genny to be handed her dismissal. Things had gone so well until the Christmas concert. Teaching at Mt. Olivet as autumn robed the foothills of Hall County had offered a measure of freedom for the first time in her life. Her students loved her—probably because as a recent graduate, she was only a year or two older than most of them—and the concert had been the culmination of her efforts as a voice instructor. Until that snobby parent—

Mr. Culper—recognized her. She'd been left with little choice except to return to the Boom or Bust.

At first, she'd sent out multiple inquiries every week, applying for teaching positions in the adjacent states of North and South Carolina, Tennessee, and Alabama. But her missives always went unanswered. Surely, her infamy as the Songbird of Auraria hadn't spread that far.

The possibilities seemed endless when Charles invited her to sing at his saloon's grand opening. She'd thought of it as the first step into a career that might eventually allow her to make her own choices. Life with Father had meant that surviving under the thumb of a controlling man was nothing new. At first, when Charles lured Jago Gillbard away from the goldfields near Charlotte, North Carolina, for the expertise he'd gained in the copper mines of Cornwall, Genny had hoped for a new start. Especially when Mr. Martin—as she called him then— had taken an interest in her education. Father accepted her tuition money as part of his compensation. Genny never dreamed he would entrust his boss with far more than her schooling. But there was little she could do when Father's will named Charles Martin her guardian.

Even less had she expected to become Charles Martin's bride. But it seemed that was what he intended when he brought her home at Christmas. Home...if such a place could be called that. The monthly trips to Atlanta since—when he spoiled her with pretty boughten frocks, fine cuisine, and voice lessons with Madame Coublet—offset the indignity and tedium, promising broader opportunities once she was Mrs. Martin. That Charles's demonstrations of affection increased apace with his generosity and flattery made protest nigh impossible.

But then he'd grown silent, withdrawn. Because she withdrew from his kisses that one time? And today he'd said—

"Where's Genny?" The question from the other room,

spoken in the oily tones of Larry Jones, stopped her musings cold.

Given that his voice carried to the storeroom above the sprightly piano tune accompanying the musician's routine, he must be standing near the door that stood open to the bar. Genny backed up a step and rubbed her arms. What was he doing here? Last she'd heard, he was mining for Rupert Hanks.

Walter Shoemaker, Larry's older and kinder replacement, snorted. "You'll be lucky if she shows tonight. Though you'd best keep your distance."

The man Charles initially hired to provide saloon security had himself been thrown out after he'd cornered Genny on the back stairs a couple of months earlier.

Larry grunted. "I ain't afraid of a dandy like Charles Martin."

"You ought to be. He's the type of dandy what carries a blade in his boot." A glass clunked on the bar. The men fell silent as the crowd laughed and clapped at something the musician did on stage.

When the room quieted down, Larry spoke again. "Why wouldn't she show? She's supposed to sing tonight, ain't she?"

"I seen her storm off all ruffled earlier when Mr. Martin said he wouldn't be takin' her to Atlanta with him this month. Told her too much business needed his attention while he was there. Little does she know what business that is."

"What business is it?" The question Larry posed gave Genny her first occasion to be grateful to the man. She leaned forward, angling her head to one side.

Walter barked a laugh. "His engagement to the rich little belle his family wants him to marry."

Engagement? Genny swayed and covered her mouth with both hands lest her horror escape audibly. Walter couldn't be right. Charles had promised he'd always take care of her. Could he have meant that only as a guardian? But the way he looked at her...and the liberties he'd taken, hinting that they were not only his right as her guardian, or for her protection, but a prelude to a greater commitment...

The saloon guard continued. "He's been courtin' her while Miss Genny had those singin' lessons she prizes so much. He's leavin' tomorrow and stayin' in Atlanta until the wedding, then he's off to New Orleans for his honeymoon."

Genny's stomach lurched. She moved her hand to the front of her tight-laced bodice and turned for the back exit. Then a dark figure blocked the light from the main room, and she whirled around, her pulse hammering. Larry's familiar bulk had risen from his stool. He plunked his bottle on the counter and leaned forward—presumably to clap Walter's arm as he stood behind the bar.

"Leavin' tomorrow, is he? That gives me time to abscond with Hanks's gold and get a head start with the girl...should I decide to take her with me. And I've half a mind to. That would serve old Charlie right."

Genny stifled a cry. With his skulking presence and lascivious glances, Larry had always made her skin crawl. But to think that he would go so far to have her! Was there a man alive who didn't look at her with lust? Even her father had treated her like a commodity, bargaining for their betterment by allowing Charles to pay for her education, then leaving her to his care when Father's weakening heart finally gave out. And now that Charles was leaving, she would be shiny pickings for Larry or any other miner greedy or bold enough to take her.

Holding in her sobs, Genny fled up the back stairs. She darted past a saloon girl on the arm of a grizzled prospector, ran into the gold-toned room that served as both a retreat and a prison, and slammed the door. She hesitated only a second before locking it. Charles didn't abide locked doors. He said every room in this establishment belonged to him, and anyone within was answerable to him as well. But little did it matter if she set off one of his black silences, not when he was leaving to wed his Atlanta fiancée. And Genny would be leaving soon after that. She would take the stage as far from this miserable rat hole as possible.

She flung open the trunk that sat at the foot of her cannonball-post bed and began to fill the bottom with shoes and books.

But...where could she go? Her mother lay at the bottom of the sea, a casualty of their 1829 Atlantic crossing. Any distant relatives in Cornwall would have forgotten her—even if she found the means to return. The only two people who had been kind to her here were Miss Mattie and Mrs. Agnes Paschal, a local innkeeper and respected healer.

Of the two, Mrs. Paschal seemed the most trustworthy. But the older lady, a widow from Oglethorpe County, had only just arrived in town with her lawyer son. They had barely exchanged words in the general store when Mrs. Paschal invited her to the Baptist church she was organizing. But there had been something about the concern in her eyes... maybe that Genny hadn't seen the like since her mother passed. Or maybe it was because Mrs. Paschal seemed to sense how lost Genny was in this town. In her life, if she was being honest. Yet that was hardly enough to presume favors upon. And the Paschals were busy renovating the old Nuckolls Hotel.

That left Miss Mattie. Despite her common ways, she acted as something of a mother figure to the saloon girls...and to Genny. More than once, she'd chided Charles about his familiarity with Genny, reminding him he made a promise to her father.

Then again, if Mattie hadn't been such a guard dog, maybe Charles would have married Genny despite what his parents wanted.

She would relieve him of his responsibility to her. She

would be twenty-one in October. After that, she could do as she pleased. But what? And where?

Terror of the unknown assailed her like a summer storm on the unprotected ridge, and for a few minutes, she gave in to tears, sinking into her feather mattress with its finely embroidered coverlet.

God, if You ever cared about me, help me now.

The unbidden prayer mushroomed from a place in her soul fertilized by her mother's instruction and example. Genny once eagerly listened to Bible stories at her knee. Her first songs had been hymns of the old country, duets with Mama's soprano. She could hear it even now, faded and sweet, echoing through the years.

Rock of Ages, cleft for me. Let me hide myself in Thee...

Genny wiped her tears. She would talk to Miss Mattie.

Sudden knocking hammered against her door. Her spine went straight as a fresh-strung wash line. That wasn't Mattie. Or God. Indeed, it might be the devil himself. And everyone knew what was said about opening the door to the devil.

"Genny?" Was that genuine concern in Charles's tone? Could he feel bad for hurting her? Maybe what she'd heard below was nothing more than gossip.

"I'm sorry, Charles." She strengthened her voice. "I'm not feeling well. I cannot sing tonight."

Or ever again in this place.

"Genny, let me in." His wheedling tone posed more of a challenge than anger would have. "I know you're upset about Atlanta. Let's talk about it."

Much as she might wish to tell him to go away, she never displayed such boldness with her guardian. And the bigger part of her always yearned to please him, to avoid his ire. "I-I'm not ready to." She hated the waver in her voice.

The knob rattled. The silence that followed only served to accentuate the galloping of Genny's heart. She rose from the bed and drew her hands to her chest. She never defied Charles, not directly, not like this. One must use flattery, placation, and avoidance as diversionary tools.

What would he do? Would he give up and go away, intending a lack of goodbye tomorrow to serve as her punishment? She could only be so lucky. Today might well be the day his brooding flared into rage.

A key turned in the lock. Of course, he had a key.

The open trunk! He must not know she was planning to leave. What he would do, she had no idea, but something warned her she didn't want to find out. She raced to the foot of the bed and closed the luggage just in time.

The door opened to reveal Charles in his black evening attire, set off by one of the jewel-toned vests he favored, his straight brows slashing even lower than normal over his emerald eyes. "Why is the door locked?"

Her knees weakening, she sat on the trunk. "I told you. I am unwell."

"And that necessitates locking the door?" He stepped inside and closed the portal behind him. "Do you think I'm here to drag you from your room?" The teasing edge to his voice caused her to waver—emotionally and physically—and either at the change in her expression or the sight of tear tracks on her cheeks, his expression softened. He strode toward her, opening his arms. "Come here, my sweet."

Engaged—she need only remember that one thing. He had played her for a fool. Her hand shot out. "No." She nearly choked on the word, so foreign was it to her vocabulary.

He stopped, his eyebrows shooting up, and took a step back. "All right, then. If that's the mood you're in..." A palpable force of coldness emanated from him. He turned as if to exit—betting, because her whole world hinged on him, that she would have to make things right. But this time, she must have an answer.

She got to her feet. "Is it true? You're engaged?"

Charles froze, then turned slowly back to face her. "Who told you that?" The heaviness of his brow threatened a brewing storm that would break in fury upon the guilty party.

"I...I overheard some people talking." Walter didn't seem a bad sort, and she might need another friend in her corner before this was all said and done.

"What people?" His dark tone harkened back to all the times he'd drawn her closer by implying others were against her. Against them being close.

"It doesn't matter." She lifted her chin. "What matters is if it's true. Were you courting a girl in Atlanta while I was with Madame Coublet?"

His back stiffened. "You are my ward. I'm not obliged to reveal my personal plans to you."

"Very well. As my guardian, what are your plans for me?"

"Are you not fed? Are you not comfortable?" He flung his hand out to indicate her room with its plush Oriental rug and walnut furnishings. "Are you not educated? Have your lessons not prepared you to pursue a career, should that be what you desire? What more could you want? And yet, all I hear is complaining. Demands."

"I'm not complaining." Though Charles had accused her of doing so any time she raised questions or concerns. But too much was at stake now not to ask. She spread her hands open, doing her best to explain her needs, to seem reasonable. "I just don't know what to do, Charles. How am I to pursue a career if no one will have me? Would you have me stay here forever?"

Charles scoffed, rolling his eyes. "Of course not. But we could hardly waste such talent on some rustic girls' school, now, could we?"

Genny angled her head. He couldn't be saying what she thought he was saying. "You mean, all my letters...were not even delivered?"

He drew his shoulders back. "*Naturally*, I'm referring to Mt. Olivet." The emphasis he placed on the first word reminded Genny he was always one step ahead of her. And he was never wrong. "As for a career, I'm working on a connection in Atlanta. I didn't wish to tell you until it was secure and the time was right."

Indeed...one step ahead. He practically glowed with his benevolence, though the edge in his voice scolded her for doubting him.

"The time was right for what?"

"For a surprise." Exasperation laced his tone. "I'm always working behind the scenes for you, Genny, even when you don't see it."

Just like God. As if Charles was god in her world. Anger lanced through her. "So you can keep me close to you and your flam-new bride?" Sometimes, especially when she was betwattled, the old Cornish sayings from her youth popped out, despite her father's determination that her schooling should drill them out of her.

Maybe Charles took her disgust for hurt, for he stepped forward and took hold of both her arms, drawing her closer. "Genny, I have no choice. I come from an old family and am expected to marry well." His fingers bit into her forearms through the puffed sleeves of her cotton dress.

"You always have a choice." Her own words, once spoken, gave her pause. In how many ways had she not been given a choice? But he was a man, a wealthy and powerful one.

"It may seem so in Auraria, but not in Atlanta. There, my father is the master. You know how he is." He dipped his head. Was that a flash of tears in his eyes?

Genny bit her lower lip as her heart tugged. Indeed, Charles once confided the cruelties he'd suffered from his father as a youth.

"I know we dreamed of a future together. I haven't given up

on that." He pressed his forehead against her temple. His breath always smelled of peppermint—his cheeks of after-shave. She turned her face away from the familiar scents lest they weaken her. He pressed a kiss against her cheekbone. "I must have you in my life. And not from afar. Your sweetness makes life bearable."

This wasn't about his father. It was about his betrothed. As he drew her closer, Genny planted her hand on his chest and pushed. "This sweetness you have milked from me is the type intended for a fiancé—and you are not that." She had been naïve and foolish to grant it.

"You know we belong together, Genny. It's what your father wanted. I can still make mine see it as well." He tipped her chin up and covered her mouth with his. These were not the neat kisses of months past with his lips carefully molded to hers, testing her resolve, but the kind that devoured forbidden fruit.

Genny pushed against his chest, turning her head away. "Stop, Charles. This is not right."

He wasn't letting go. "Come, now." His breath hot on her skin, he dragged his mouth over to her neck and ear. "You've teased me long enough."

"I let you kiss me...because I thought you were going to marry me!" Shame filled her.

"And it can still be." His fingers tugged at the laces at the back of her gown, untying the bow at the top. "I'll make you mine. For once, my father will not win."

Oh, God, help. She had to get to the door.

When she wrenched away, he wrapped his arms around her and lifted her by the waist, carrying her to the bed while she futilely kicked her legs. "Don't be afraid, my sweet." His voice, like honey. "Everything will be all right."

"No!" The cry wrung from her as he dropped her onto the mattress with a poof of the feather contents. If he had his way with her, she'd be utterly ruined, and not just for marriage.

Someone pounded on the door. "Genny?" Miss Mattie's call carried an urgency Genny rarely heard from her.

She managed a strangled reply. "I'm here!"

Charles yelled over her. "Not now!" He'd just turned toward the door as if realizing he hadn't locked it when it flew open.

Mattie's wide-eyed gaze swung from her employer to Genny on the bed, her arms akimbo and skirts askew. "What is going on here?"

Genny scrambled upright. She scooted to the edge of the mattress as fast as she could.

Charles's chest expanded. "What gives you the right to barge in like that?"

"A missing singer and a houseful of paying patrons, that's what. Can you hear them down there?" Miss Mattie opened the door wider, admitting the sound of boots stomping in an impatient rhythm. "They're calling for the Songbird of Auraria."

When Genny got to her feet, Charles moved between her and Miss Mattie. "She's not singing tonight. She's unwell." Was that chagrin in his voice? Something Genny had never heard from him. But then, she'd never witnessed him getting caught before.

"I'm recovered." She practically ran around the man who was supposedly her guardian and darted for the exit.

Before she could escape into the hallway, however, Miss Mattie caught her arm. On the pretext—or, more likely, the necessity—of fixing Genny's hair, she leaned close to whisper, "Come to my room after."

Genny straightened and gave the barest nod. She'd gained an ally. Now for her last performance at the Boom or Bust...

CHAPTER 3

*J*esse straightened from shoveling another scoop of creek bottom into the sluice box and paused to rub his lower back, aching from a month of spring planting on Wade Coulter's land. Back in February, his best friend had helped him clear from the cabin to Baggs Branch, where Jesse now stood. The music of the shoals that meandered down to the Etowah River broke the stillness of dusk. White blossoms upon dogwood and pear trees studded greening woods, glowing softly in the golden light.

No doubt about it—Wade was one of the lucky ones where the lottery was concerned, drawing not only a prime gold lot but one also well-suited to farming, located as it was in the fertile union of creek and river. Not to mention, the Cherokee family that lived here earlier had left a sturdy single-pen cabin, a shed, and a corncrib. And they'd actually gone west without a fuss after being paid for the improvements to their property, unlike many Indian families the government might eventually face evicting. A shameful situation, to be sure, but that hadn't stopped Wade from entering the lottery on the chance of securing his own future. He didn't want to be sheriff forever—a sentiment shared by his wife, who'd just delivered their first baby. After they lost Emma just prior to Christmas, Wade suggested Jesse take over the farm until Wade could hang up his gun. The change would be good for both of them.

At first, Jesse had agreed. From the time he'd returned to Hall County last summer, the mountains beckoned, visible on clear days from high ground. The walls of his father-in-law's accounting office near squeezed the breath from him—or maybe that was due to the excessive clinginess of his new bride. So much was that the case that when he'd seen the advertisement for surveyors of the new townships of Mississippi Territory, he'd put in his application and been accepted. He'd barely gotten settled and started on his new assignment when the express letter came, calling him home.

As it turned out, the solace he'd once craved now only mocked him. He'd gotten what he wanted—but at what cost?

Guilt was a bitter companion.

Jesse set the shovel aside, grabbed hold of the cradle's handles, and rocked the contraption, the goal being to capture any gold on the bottom of the trough as the silt moved through the transverse cleats.

A bark from the tree line where Toby was nosing around brought to mind his only companion. His Irish setter—*Emma's* Irish setter—tore off into the woods. Jesse grabbed his rifle from beside the corncrib and ran after him. Sure enough, brown-speckled wings fluttered in the thicket.

Jesse brought the loaded rifle to his shoulder. "Whoa, Toby!"

The dog halted and assumed his pointing stance, indicating a pheasant now roosting on a low-hanging limb of mountain laurel. He sighted the gun and fired. When the puff of smoke cleared, he let out a chuckle. The bird lay on the ground, unmoving. Fresh meat for dinner.

"Release."

At his command, Toby darted to retrieve the pheasant, then dropped it at Jesse's feet and looked up with tongue lolling. The exuberant expression so closely resembled a smile that Jesse laughed. He wasn't the only one best suited to field and forest.

He bent and petted the dog's silky russet head. "Good job, boy."

Jesse returned to the cabin yard with his canine companion at his side and his heart a bit lighter. The solitude and staying in one spot might make him maudlin at times, but he felt at home enough here that maybe he could figure out what to do with the rest of his life—if his application to resume his job in Mississippi failed to pan out.

After removing the pheasant's head at the chopping block, Jesse tied Toby's catch upside down to the corner of the shed and tousled the dog's ears. "What do you say to a quick splash in the river, old boy?" The mountain runoff was sure to be bracing, but the setter would welcome the opportunity to frisk about. "Might as well get cleaned up while the bird's draining. Then I'll pluck it, and we'll feast tonight. Tomorrow, we'll get a bigger dose of civilization than we want, won't we?" If one could call Auraria civilization. His overly bright tone must have translated to a promise of roasted pheasant in dog lingo, for Toby licked his lips.

While the boomtown now boasted a population of a thousand with maybe twenty stores, a dozen offices opened by lawyers advertising their expertise to settle property suits, a handful of hotels, and even a newspaper, its very nature was as destructive as a rabid coon chasing its own tail. Land disputes, horse thieving, conflicts at the mines—especially between whites and Cherokees, and the regular appearance of wild-eyed miners showing off nuggets they'd found in the waterways made for a rowdy environment.

It also made for a shortage of supplies—which was why he'd be taking his yams and potatoes in to town to sell and then meeting Wade there to get the wheat seed he'd purchased for a more reasonable price in Gainesville. Plus, Wade wanted to look at a new machine for washing sediment touted as much more efficient than cradle rockers or sluice boxes. He encouraged Jesse to spend all the time he could spare from farming in panning for gold. So far, he'd found enough dust to fill a couple of goose quills—the preferred method of payment in Auraria.

Thought of town brought back memories of the girl he'd left at the Boom or Bust. She'd entered his mind more often than he'd care to admit over the past year. He was concerned for her—that was all. It ate at him that he'd not found a way to help her. She'd seemed to have so few options.

Could he find an excuse to stop in at the saloon in hopes of catching a glimpse of her?

~

"You foolish girl." The manager of the Boom or Bust's saloon girls stared at Genny with her arms akimbo, a flowered Chinese wrapper fluttering over her corset and undergarments.

Genny blinked at her. She couldn't decide which stung worse—the insult or the pity in Miss Mattie's eyes.

She'd rushed to the older woman's room the moment she finished the final stanza of "Home, Sweet Home" and spilled a breathless recounting of the conversation between Walter and Larry—all except the last bit, which had gotten lost in her angst over Charles.

The other woman let out a huff of breath. "So you

confronted him. Demanded to know how he could do this to you. And that's what led to the situation I found you in."

"Why, yes." She'd finally found the courage to speak up for herself, only to be berated for it? She'd thought a woman of the world like Miss Mattie would validate her resolve.

"And you actually look surprised that I called you foolish…" Miss Mattie whirled in a swirl of silk and slid with jerky movements onto the stool in front of her dresser, where she removed her black jet earrings and placed them in a small jewelry chest.

Genny took a few steps closer to her. "Do you not agree that Charles has behaved in a way that led me to believe he planned to marry me?"

The older woman chortled. "Oh, yes. Indeed, I do. That you fell for it is what I find incredible."

Genny dipped her chin as the filthy bathwater of shame deluged her. It was as she'd come to fear even before this evening's assault. "He only ever intended to make me his mistress."

Miss Mattie screwed open a pot of cold cream and caught her gaze in the mirror. "And surely, after today, you realize he won't give up until he does." She dipped her finger in the lotion and smeared a liberal amount over her décolleté, then rubbed it in. "Thankfully, he's leaving tomorrow. You can stay in here tonight." Her benevolent expression faded as Genny's brow wrinkled. Before Genny could tell her why that much-appreciated offer would be insufficient, the madam jerked her chin. "Oh, don't be too hard on yourself. Once upon a time, I was as naïve as you, and Charles is very good at his game. Which is why I will help you now.'"

Genny clasped her hands in front of her waist and moved to Miss Mattie's side. "I'm relieved to hear it. I was planning to ask you for that very thing, but I'm afraid I must get away from here d'reckly. Tonight, even."

"Tonight?" One finely plucked ginger eyebrow quirked

upward as Miss Mattie closed up her little pot of promised youth. "Charles will be gone for weeks. No, I must make arrangements." She turned down the wick of her oil lamp. "I have a sister who works at a hotel in Pendleton. You can take the stagecoach to South Carolina, but first, I should write so she can prepare a place for you."

"Miss Mattie, that is better than I even hoped, but..." She ventured to touch the older woman's shoulder. Miss Mattie flinched but refrained from frowning at her. Genny withdrew her hand quickly. She had always sensed a silent resentment from the manager that kept her at arm's length. Word was that despite her Southernized title, Miss Mattie was a widow. Perhaps she envied Genny the opportunities youth and talent afforded. "I have yet to tell you all."

Miss Mattie swiveled in her seat and gestured toward the chaise lounge in the nearby corner. "Sit."

Genny did so, leaning forward and speaking in a low voice. "As I was leaving, Larry said something to Walter about skipping town with Rupert Hanks's gold while Charles was away... and taking me with him."

Miss Mattie's brown eyes rounded. "That does put a different spin on things." She sat back and tapped her chin. "What do you know about the Hanks mine?"

"Only that Charles once owned it...in addition to his half share of the other mining company. That was the one my father was brought down to work."

"That's right. Charles drew the Chestatee River parcel in the lottery, but he'd had men secretly placer mining in that area for some time. Don't ask me how he got lucky enough for his ticket to be drawn." Miss Mattie paused to press her lips together. "He hired Rupert Hanks to work the claim. At first, it didn't produce as expected, so he sold it to Hanks. Not long after, Rupert found a sizeable nugget. Charles accused Rupert of deceiving him, and they got into an altercation down in Gainesville at the end of last year."

Genny nodded. Tales of swindling, stealing, and even planting false evidence in order to sell claims at inflated prices abounded in Lumpkin County. "That doesn't surprise me. But obviously, they both survived."

"They did. The sheriff's sister didn't."

Genny's mouth fell open. How had she never heard about this? "What happened? Was Charles at fault?"

Miss Mattie gave a casual shrug. "The details don't matter now, except to say that for once, I don't think Charles intended to hurt anyone. She happened along at the wrong moment."

"So when Larry was fired from here and he went to work for Rupert..." Genny flattened both hands on the chaise. "He was doing it to get back at Charles?"

Miss Mattie rose and jerked her wrapper back up on her shoulder. "That's what folks assume. And if he's been siphoning off gold and is planning to abscond with it, taking you would heap on an extra layer of insult. And it's very possible he would do it. For whatever reason I can't understand, both seem besotted by you."

Besotted wouldn't be the term Genny would choose, but more important matters were at stake—such as avoiding her own kidnapping. "What do we do? Can you send a letter of introduction with me on the stage? I can be ready to leave tomorrow after Charles is gone." She stood, yearning to run to her room and pack right now.

"Yes, you will leave tomorrow, but if Larry and possibly even Walter are up to no good, it won't do for you to be seen getting on the stage." While Miss Mattie patted her hands together, Genny held her breath. Then the older woman snapped her fingers. "I'll put it about the place that I'm sending you to use your pretty face to haggle a good price from the drovers outside town. You'll go on my horse in the afternoon—only, you'll ride to Gainesville instead. You can pick up the stage to Pendleton there."

It was a good plan. Everyone knew how much they needed meat, and with chickens running up to eighteen cents a pound in the hard-pressed boomtown, the hundreds of wild turkeys drovers would bring from the Appalachians were highly anticipated. Plus, the fact that the recent rains would make their camps less accessible would drive down prices. "The drovers' camp is north of town, so I'd need to circle back."

"You can take the lane that runs parallel to Gold Digger's Road, to the west. It rejoins the road to Gainesville south of town."

She nodded. "What about my trunk?"

"I'll ship it later in the week." Miss Mattie reached into her pocket and withdrew a key, then held it out to Genny. "Lock the door behind me. This is the only key that works. I saw to that myself."

Genny accepted the piece of cool metal with a twinge of unease. "Where are you going?"

"Your room." She wiggled her brows. "If anyone tries to pay me a visit, I'll enjoy giving them a nice surprise."

A soft huff of a laugh escaped Genny despite her dire circumstances. She didn't even want to ask what the surprise might be. Gratefulness swelled within her, and she couldn't help it—she reached out and hooked Miss Mattie in a hug as she passed by.

"Thank you, ma'am. I don't know why you're doing this, but thank you for being a friend to me."

"No need for that." The saloon manager brusquely disengaged from Genny's embrace. At the door, she paused with her hand on the knob and turned her face to one side. Not all the way to look at Genny, but enough that she glimpsed a rare moment of vulnerability. "I wish I'd had a friend when I needed one. Now get some sleep. You've a big day tomorrow."

Yes. The first day of true freedom.

CHAPTER 4

The next afternoon, Genny left the livery near the Boom or Bust on Miss Mattie's mare, Belinda. Genny blinked her weary eyes in the bright light and shifted her biggest-brimmed bonnet lower.

She had laid awake until the wee hours, and not because the singing, swearing, and shouting in the street disturbed her. No, she had long ago learned to tune that out. It was smaller sounds she listened for...furtive footsteps or the picking of a lock. But all remained relatively quiet within.

Shame at being caught in his inappropriate behavior must have prompted another smoldering withdrawal from Charles. No doubt, he was lying awake, too, thinking of ways to punish her. Blaming her for not providing what he was due and deciding what he might withhold from her in return. Thank the Lord he generally preferred concocting plots designed to produce mental and emotional turmoil to physical attacks. Then again, if he had resorted to assault earlier, she might have already found the strength to leave.

But d'reckly, she would be gone, and she could only pray his bride interested him sufficiently to refocus his attention.

Though...she would miss those moments he joked with her and gazed at her with adoration in his eyes. And the way he said, "Whatever makes you happy, my sweet" when he was pleased with her...

The saddle seemed to shift a bit beneath her, and Genny caught onto it with one hand while tightening her grip on the reins with the other. The rugged countryside cradling Auraria did not lend itself to a novice rider, so horseback outings were not a pastime she partook of with Charles. Probably just as well since it was doubtful he'd have taken a chaperone. He considered *himself* the chaperone.

She'd best focus her attention lest the mare get away from her on the busy street. 'Twas clear Miss Mattie prized the animal, which the ostler had instructed Genny to lodge at a particular stable in Gainesville for her to retrieve. The stable hand was accustomed to serving Boom or Bust clients and knew Mattie, Charles, and Larry well.

She passed the new office of *The Western Herald*, the editor's name, A.G. Fambrough, over the door. The fresh coat of paint on Mr. Ware's confectionary provoked a memory of Charles buying her sugared plums and chocolate creams. That might have been after one of their fallings out. He'd kept an account at McLaughin & Company Dry Goods, where she could shop to her heart's content for turkey-red print calico, books, chintz shawls, and Irish linens— so long as she hadn't done anything to vex him. Indeed, now that she thought of it, so many of even her good memories were tainted.

Agnes Paschal waving to her from the front of her hotel as a workman installed a sign provided Genny's one regret at leaving town. The woman was the closest thing to a true believer Genny had seen since her mother passed. She waved back and swallowed a lump in her throat.

As she reached the end of businesses lining Gold Digger's Road, she glanced back to ensure no one was following her. It was hard to tell amid the horses, mules, varied conveyances, and foot traffic, but no familiar face caught her eye. That wasn't a surprise since she knew so few people in town. But they knew her. She'd do well to remember that.

Nevertheless, her heart beat a little easier as she reached the lane that cut back to the southwest. Checking behind her again, she made the turn, then drew the mare alongside a well next to a log cabin. She waited a few minutes. When no one she recognized passed by, she clicked to the horse and resumed her journey. The houses were soon spaced farther apart, and she felt comfortable nudging Belinda's sides for a trot. Cool shade enveloped her as she rode beneath a tunnel of softly fluttering spring leaves and out of town.

Then—mud splattered and horse hooves thudded behind her. She jerked around.

A man in dark clothing with his hat worn low and a kerchief over his mouth and jaw seemingly appeared out of nowhere astride a brown stallion and quickly gained on her. Had he been lying in wait in the forest? Whatever he intended, it couldn't be good.

Fear frazzled every nerve as Genny leaned forward in the saddle. "Ha!" She switched Belinda's neck with the ends of the reins, and the startled mare surged ahead.

Genny squeezed her thighs as tightly as she could. The forest became a blur of green and brown on either side. The rider edged closer. His horse huffed inches from Belinda's haunch.

God, please help me. When she prayed the night Charles assaulted her, it did seem that the Almighty had sent Miss Mattie. *Please send someone now.*

How much farther to the main road? Was that it ahead? Plenty of travelers should be on the route to Gainesville at midday. One of them would help her.

When a figure on a gray horse rode their way, Genny's heart leapt with hope. Had her prayer been answered? But no...

The man also wore a bandana over the lower half of his face.

She'd never fallen from a great height, but she could imagine this was the feeling—that absolute paroxysm of mingled terror and helplessness, knowing impact was unavoidable.

And then—a route opened to her right, leading down the ridge. No wider than a deer trail, but it might as well have been the highway to heaven paved in gold. Genny jerked Belinda's head toward it, and the mare swerved onto the muddy path.

Here, the trees grew close to the narrow lane. While the branches weren't in full leaf, plenty hung low enough that Genny maintained her crouch. Her thighs began to tremble and burn. Her breaths wheezed in and out past her corset. But at least one of her pursuers continued the chase.

Had she made a mistake? Ought she to have attempted to veer around that second man and taken her chances within shouting distance of the road, rather than being robbed and ravished in the wilderness?

If she stood a chance of evading them, she must get off this path.

As soon as she sensed an opening in the trees approaching to her right, she directed Belinda across it. Thankfully, the underbrush was not yet prolific. She headed toward a ravine and out of sight. No sound of pursuit. Praying hard and frequently scanning her environment, Genny directed Belinda to follow the shoulder of the ridge at a steady pace for about ten minutes until it dropped into a gulley where a creek burbled. Perfect. Even she knew the wisdom of hiding one's tracks in the water.

"Come on, Belinda." She steered the horse into the small stream, following it southwest at a cautious walk. Water splashed as the mare's hooves overturned round stones and clopped on flat ones, then sank deeper into sandy purchase. Occasionally, they swerved around noisy shoals.

Genny frowned as she surveyed the woods spreading on either side with no sign of a trail. How was she to find her way out? First, to evade her pursuers.

How had Charles already learned she left? He must have someone watching her. Or it could be Larry and one of his cronies.

She had been traveling downstream for several minutes when a shout carried on the wind. Her head jerked up, and she pulled on the reins. Time to make a break for the other side.

The western shore sloped gradually down to the water, but scaling it could expose her to anyone on the ridge on the other side. She'd have to take that risk.

Genny clicked her tongue and pressed her heels into Belinda's flanks. The mare scrambled out of the creek. Genny couldn't resist a glance over her shoulder as they climbed the side. The saddle shifted beneath her. She faced forward again in an attempt to right herself.

Smack! A leafy young branch hit her face.

With a cry, she and the saddle slid from Belinda's back. A splintering pain shot up her shin as she landed and rolled down the rocky embankment.

~

"*H*ey!"

The unfamiliar voice that shouted from the ravine brought Jesse upright in his saddle. He was still on Wade's land, riding the trail to town on his brown stallion with Toby at his side. No one should be out here.

A glimpse through the half-bare trees revealed a flash of a man in an ecru-colored shirt about a hundred yards away, bent in examination of something by the creek, his untethered brown horse behind him. He was facing away from Jesse, so the intruder hadn't been summoning him. That meant there was at least one more. And Wade didn't pay him to work his land for nothing. Jesse was also responsible for chasing off squatters and swindlers—the term favored for those who sneaked to prospect land not their own. It wouldn't be the first time. He slid his rifle from its sheath on his saddle and turned Perseus into the forest.

Be with me, Lord. He didn't pray often these last few months, but this seemed a needful occasion.

As his stallion crunched through winter's dry leaves and Toby leapt over rocks and logs at his side, it was Jesse's turn to shout the greeting—more of a demand. "You there!" He pulled up on Perseus's head.

With the briefest of glances over his shoulder, his face shadowed by his wide-brimmed hat, the man came to his feet.

"What're you doin' at that creek?" Jesse brought his firearm to a horizontal position but refrained from sighting it.

Rather than answer, the trespasser pulled a kerchief over his mouth, stuck the toe of his boot into the stirrup, and vaulted onto his horse's back. A quick swipe of his arm directed another rider atop a gray stallion on the ridge, and with a "ha" and a kick of his heels, he took off after his companion toward the crest.

Jesse pursued, letting Perseus have his head until they rode the swell of the land and he could make sure the men were leaving. Their mounts skittered down the opposite side and picked up a game trail. He thanked the Lord they hadn't drawn on him and obliged him to use his rifle on anything besides supper. He didn't relish ever learning what it felt like to shoot a man. No doubt, the men were checking for signs of gold in that section of Baggs Branch. But why skedaddle like murderers rather than playing dumb and making up some story about being on the wrong claim, as the last interlopers did?

What was even stranger...why hadn't Toby chased them? Jesse glanced back toward the creek and frowned. The dog was sniffing the ground, anxiously circling a sandy spit, as though he'd picked up a scent.

With a final look to confirm that the riders had passed out of sight, Jesse turned Perseus back to the creek. When he reached the Irish setter's side, he dismounted. "What is it, boy?"

He knelt to study the ground. The prints of the trespasser's stallion approached the stream from the northeast but stopped a few feet shy of the water. Yet on the other side, smaller, lighter hooves had left a semi-circle of indentions in the sand. A mare, perhaps. Had the men been following someone?

Jesse raised his head to find Toby in locked position, pointing downstream. Jesse's sharp-eyed glance swept down one bank and up the other, but nothing seemed out of place. "Somebody down there?" he asked the dog in a low voice.

Toby retained his point.

"Lead me to them." He prayed he wasn't sending his dog into danger. "Release."

Toby bounded along the bank. He took the path of least resistance, whether it be by land or water, jumping over roots and launching off large rocks. Jesse mounted quickly and followed, his rifle at the ready. When the setter rounded a bend in the creek and let out a bark, Jesse urged Perseus up the shore. No sneaking up on this prey. Could he be riding into an ambush? There was nothing like the lure of gold to bring out the devious and devilish in men.

But when he made it to the turn of the creek, he let out a huff of disbelief. On the western shore, lying in a heap of brown calico and white petticoats atop a patch of blue wood violets, with Toby snuffling about her head, was a woman. Her face was turned away so Jesse couldn't see past her bonnet brim, her arms were flung out to the sides, and her one leg was bent in a manner that brought his brows down. A few feet away from her lay her saddle, and a few feet beyond that, a brown mare noisily ripped up long grasses.

Jesse rode closer and swung down. Was the woman alive? He knelt and took hold of the arm extended in his direction, then pressed his fingers to her wrist. Yes. A faint pulse.

He nudged Toby back as he moved closer and balanced on one knee. "Sit." When the dog obeyed, Jesse ventured to touch the woman's chin. "Ma'am? Can you hear me?"

A faint moan came from the delicate throat, and though her eyes remained closed, the lady turned her head enough for him to glimpse her rosy lips, softly rounded nose, and the straw-berry-blond hair escaping from her bonnet.

He sat back and gaped. The Songbird of Auraria had landed on Wade's property.

CHAPTER 5

Fire kindled in Genny's lower leg. It pulsed from the outside of her right calf down into her ankle. She couldn't feel her foot.

She groaned and attempted to open her eyes, but bright sunlight flashing between tree limbs quickly forced them closed.

"Easy, miss." The admonition in a man's deep, rich tones made her anything but.

Genny jerked and attempted to sit up. One arm flailed. The other was trapped. Her legs kicked in the air, causing a shriek of pain and panic to escape her. Her heart raced like a runaway thoroughbred. Her last memory was of hitting the ground after crossing the creek on Miss Mattie's mare, yet she was not sitting —or lying down—but being carried.

The men! The riders pursuing her—they had found her.

Genny went stiff and pushed on the broad chest she was mashed against. "Let go!"

"Please, miss." The arms holding her raised and tightened, keeping her steady. "I won't hurt you, but if you attempt to stand, you could injure yourself worse. I think you've broken your leg."

Genny gasped and stilled long enough to take in the hat-shadowed face. Strands of blond-brown hair were visible below the brim, and stubble of the same hue sprinkled a strong jaw. Eyes the color of the toffee in Mr. Ware's confectionary met hers, but it was the concern in them that confused her. "So you've been hired to bring me back, then, not to kill me?" There was something familiar about him. Probably she'd seen him about the Boom or Bust.

The man's mouth fell open. "Kill you? Mercy, no. I found you thrown from your horse by the creek. Your saddle came loose."

How convenient her accident made this for him. And to think, she'd almost gotten away. But...her saddle had come loose. Had someone made sure it did so?

Genny sucked in a shuddering breath. She might as well prepare herself to meet her fate. "Who am I going back to—Charles or Larry?"

Her captor's brows shifted closer together. "I'm not taking you to anyone. If you'll lie still, I'll carry you to my cabin. I checked you over for injuries the best I could, but I can't promise—"

"No!" Genny attempted to right herself again but only succeeded in offsetting the man's grip, forcing her to throw her arm around his neck so he didn't drop her. "I'm not going to any cabin with you."

His face darkened. "Trust me, I'm no happier about this than you. But I could hardly leave you in the woods."

She lifted her chin. "Good, then. If you'll kindly help me mount my mare, I'll continue on my way."

The pain wasn't so bad that she couldn't make it to Gainesville if she avoided bearing weight in the stirrup. She could endure that far, couldn't she? That seemed a safer bet than allowing a stranger to carry her back to his hideout in the woods. Maybe he'd double-crossed Charles or Larry. Maybe he planned to hold her for ransom...or keep her for himself. She shuddered.

"Didn't you hear me?" Impatience edged his tone. "I said, your leg's broken. Do you want to never walk again? No, we'll go to the cabin, then I'll ride out for the doctor."

Genny clamped her lips shut. Maybe she could leave while he was gone. She twisted to look over his shoulder. "Where is my 'oss?" The Cornish eeked out of her when she was most flustered.

"Your horse? I tethered her by the creek. I'll go back for her once you're settled."

There was a horse behind them, though it wasn't Belinda. The man had tied the leather lead of a brown stallion to his belt. The animal's intelligent eyes met hers as if to ask why she didn't trust his master. At the same moment, something wet swiped her hand, and she looked down to find an Irish setter capering at her captor's heels, the damp fur that flapped from his legs and underside attesting to a recent foray into the water. "Well, hello, there." A man whose dog and horse loved him couldn't be all bad, could he?

He redistributed her weight, and this time, she didn't fight him. He started walking forward—or rather, resumed walking forward, for they appeared to be on a narrow forest trail, and the creek was nowhere in sight. "That's Toby. You can thank him for finding you. The horse is Perseus."

"Thank you, Toby." She smiled at the Irish setter, who responded with a toothy grin as he huffed along beside them. Then she glanced back at the man carrying her. Why did he leave out the most important name? Genny raised a brow. "And you are...?"

"Jesse Holden."

Didn't he want *her* name? He didn't even look at her. "Genevieve Gillbard."

His jaw tightened for a moment. "I know."

She let out a little breath. "Then you *were* hired to find me."

"No."

She waited for an explanation that wasn't forthcoming.

"But I saw two men who apparently were."

"Where?" Her eyebrows flew up, and she scanned the woods around them. Nothing but fresh green leaves and sunlight.

"Down by the creek a ways. I chased them off...for the time being, at least." A frown flashed over his features. "Are there more I should know about?"

"Not that I'm aware of."

"Want to tell me why they were following you?"

Genny shook her head, her sight misting over. How could she understand—much less explain—being hunted like wild game, to be brought back like a trophy? She was a commodity, just as her father had said. Her mind, her spirit, her will were of no consequence. Only her face and body mattered to these men. And sometimes, her voice.

"Something about Charles or Larry?" While Mr. Holden pressed her for more information, he'd gentled his tone, though the intensity remained in his gaze. "Would that be Charles Martin, your...guardian?"

So he knew about her situation, though she was not ready to talk about it. "You've been to the Boom or Bust?" She did her best not to stiffen and betray her unease. Men who frequented saloons usually fell victim to more than one vice.

"Only once." He looked straight ahead and leaned into his stride as they began to climb a slight rise.

Had they met? Genny failed to recall an introduction or any conversation with the man, though that could be due to hitting her head when she fell. It was almost as though he avoided the subject. Years of hypervigilance under her father and Charles had taught her to read people fairly well...especially men. But this one kept his emotions close to his vest. And he'd mostly spoken only to question her.

Then again, his breathing deepened with the exertion of bearing her up the hill. How far had he carried her prior to her regaining consciousness? And while the chest and arms surrounding her were solid, he was no muscle man—not like Larry. Before she could decide whether to be concerned or intrigued, he spoke again.

"We're here."

No doubting the relief in his voice.

Genny shifted to take in the rows of young corn they were passing, followed by a garden patch. A couple of plots had been plowed and harrowed but lay empty, like a bed with the covers turned back. The soothing music of water told her a creek ran just beyond the tree line. The same one she'd crossed earlier? And just the other side of a swept-dirt clearing sat a neat log cabin with two shuttered windows and a door opening onto a porch. Not far away were a couple of outbuildings. A handful of chickens scattered at their approach, flying up to roost in the trees.

She'd expected a shack tucked in heavy woods, hastily thrown up for shelter while he panned for gold. "This is a nice spread." Which nudged her like a silent beagle to trust him a bit. "You must've lived here for some time."

"Not really. We broke ground at the end of February and pan a bit on the side."

Oh. Genny brightened. "You have a wife?" Perhaps God had answered her prayer, after all. If a woman waited in that cabin, Genny would feel far safer.

The touch of pride that her compliment about his land engendered faded almost immediately. Mr. Holden's countenance closed off. "No wife."

His reaction warned her not to press, but her safety was at stake. "You said 'we.'"

"My...friend drew the place in the lottery." His boots thudded on the steps as he climbed onto the porch.

"Is he inside?" Genny glanced at the cabin's door. Would that be a bad or a good thing? And why had she not thought to ask Miss Mattie for a pistol? Not that she knew how to fire one.

"He's from Gainesville. But he'll be here soon. At least, I assume he'll come when I don't show up in town on time." Mr. Holden met her eyes, his gaze serious. "I need to put you down so I can untie the horse."

"Oh...yes."

Perseus stood patiently beside the steps, still tied to the back of Jesse's belt. Toby padded over to sit by the door, his tongue hanging out the side of his mouth as he huffed quietly.

"Put both arms around my neck and let me bear your weight as I ease you down. Don't attempt to stand on that foot." He was still staring at her with that same intensity which did strange things to her midsection. What was wrong with her? She'd best not let her guard down, even for a moment. Even though this man might appear kind and caring, so had Charles, at first. And whenever he needed to woo her to his bidding.

She nodded, and Mr. Holden began the measured process of releasing her. He let her body slide down his until her good left foot contacted the floorboards. Genny barely registered the odd fact that the man's face twisted as if in distaste at the contact. Even the act of making her right leg semi-horizontal triggered shooting pain that resulted in waves of dizziness and nausea. She sucked in her breath and stifled a whimper.

"Hold onto me." The gravelly admonition cut through her fog of misery. "I'm just going to let go for a moment, okay? To untie Perseus. But you keep holding on tight."

Despite her resolve to maintain her distance, she clung to his neck. It was all she could do to keep her injured leg immobilized and suspended a couple of inches above the wood. Every move he made, no matter how minute—and she sensed he did his best to be quick and to make only small motions—made her want to burst into tears.

"You all right?"

She opened her eyes, and her stomach dropped clean to her toes. The impatience from earlier had fled. Concern reflected in Mr. Holden's amber-flecked eyes. It terrified her enough to want to skedaddle back into the forest despite a broken leg and two kidnappers—because any similar display from a man always masked a hidden motive. At the same time, she wanted nothing more than to sag against him and trust that he actually was that nice.

Genny settled for a nod.

"Good. You're doing just fine. Now we've got two choices. I can either carry you inside, or you can try to hop a bit with me bearing most of your weight. Which will it be?"

She grimaced at the mere idea of him lifting her, and then putting her down again. "I'll hop."

He gave some completely unnecessary directions for her to keep her arm around his neck as he turned her to face forward and made his way toward the door, bearing most of her weight with her against his right side and his arm wrapped securely around her.

Inside the dim interior, a table with two benches sat on one side of an open room near a hutch displaying creamware dishes. Another two chairs atop a braided rag rug faced a fireplace, while the other end of the space held a simple rope bed with a brightly patterned quilt, a side table, and a trunk on the far wall. It was to that bed he led her.

"No...no, I'll be fine on the chair."

"You're lying down and elevating that leg." The brusque statement left no room for argument. Mr. Holden eased her onto the edge of a mattress that, judging by its girth and crinkle, had been recently stuffed with bedstraw.

Genny sat for a moment, closing her eyes as she panted softly in an attempt to control the pain and steel herself to raise her leg over the bedframe. From across the way came the unnaturally loud sound of Toby lapping up a drink from a bowl.

Her unwilling host crouched by her side. "Take your time." He waited until she opened her eyes. "Would a drink of water help?"

She nodded if only to buy herself a few more minutes.

Mr. Holden swiped off his hat as he rose. He hung it on a peg next to the nearest shuttered window, which he cracked open. Then he went to the sideboard, where he poured liquid from an earthenware pitcher into a tin cup. When he returned to her side, his dog accompanied him. The man handed her the cup while the canine sat at Genny's feet, a droplet of water falling from his muzzle to her free hand as it rested on the mattress.

She patted Toby's silky head. The dog scooted closer as if sensing she needed his support. She'd never owned a pet. Part of her wanted to snuggle the furry body against her and have a good cry. More than a part.

"You should drink it all." Mr. Holden's level statement reminded her he stood waiting. Without his hat, he appeared younger than she'd first thought—maybe five years her senior. And he was handsome in an earnest, boyish way she'd once allowed herself to dream of—hair with a slight wave, nose slightly rounded at the tip, and chin with a slight cleft.

Genny took a long, slow swallow. Despite the water being room temperature and possessing a metallic tang, she drained the contents of the cup before handing it back to him.

Mr. Holden gave a nod and set the cup on the bedside table. "How can I help?"

"Thanks, but you can't." She gritted her teeth and maneuvered back onto the bed, swinging her good leg over the side. But when it came to raising the right one, a groan slipped past her lips.

Mr. Holden was quickly at her side, sliding her skirts under her and supporting beneath her leg just above the knee.

"Please—don't touch me." She gritted out the admonition from between a clenched jaw.

"Don't be daft." The sharpness of his scolding cut through her bravado. "You can't do this without help."

He was right. Her right leg was screaming its protest, her muscles trembling violently. She gave a sharp nod, and he provided the assistance she needed to swivel into position. Just as she panicked about lowering her foot to the mattress, he slid the extra pillow beneath it. That helped, but not enough to prevent a few tears from slipping from her eyes.

Mr. Holden was gone again, back to the sideboard. He returned with a damp cloth, folding it and raising it to her face. Then he blinked, and his hand faltered. He lowered and held out the cloth. "Here."

"Thank you. You're very kind." Genny buried her face in the cloth for a few moments. Its coolness helped dispel the dizziness and nausea as well as wipe away her tears and any dirt she'd accumulated during her jaunt through the woods.

When she returned it to him, he set it aside and asked, "Ready to lie back?"

She took a tremulous breath and lowered herself slowly, conscious of the hand he slid behind her shoulder and the scent of spice and outdoors that came from the pillowcase. More tears threatened. She was completely at the mercy of a stranger. No matter how decent he seemed, in her experience, all decent sorts eventually lowered their masks. Would she be able to escape this one before he did?

CHAPTER 6

Jesse's brief glimpse of Miss Gillbard's shin when he helped her onto the bed revealed that her lower leg was swelling by the minute. If they were in town, he'd see about fetching ice. As it was, cold creek water would have to do. But first things first. "That boot has to come off."

Instant panic arrested her features as she levered herself off his pillow. "No. Don't touch it. Please." Her hand shot out to the side, ready to grip his should he make a move.

Jesse managed to contain his impatience. "I know it's going to hurt, but if we don't get it off now, it won't come off at all."

"And you know good and well I won't be able to get it back on either." Her angelic face hardened, and she propped herself up on her elbows.

"You think this is about me plotting to keep you here? Can't you see I'm trying to help you, lady?" He straightened, a rush of heat flushing his face. "I'm going to the creek for a bucket of water. While I'm gone, you can decide if you want the boot pulled off or cut off—which is what the doctor will do when he gets here."

He didn't wait for her reply before striding across the floor. He whistled for Toby, who looked over his shaggy shoulder. "Come." Jesse waved his arm toward the door.

Toby emitted a high-pitched hint of a whine and did a little dance with his front feet...but remained at Miss Gillbard's side.

Fine. Jesse left the door ajar should the dog change his mind—not likely, as the songbird dropped her hand to the smitten animal's head and stroked the russet waves of fur. Jesse snatched the bucket from the front porch. On the way to the creek, the soft spring breeze whispered a reminder that he had no idea what type of treatment the woman in his cabin had received. His indignation evaporated along with a thin sheen of perspiration.

There was another problem. If Miss Gillbard was indeed fleeing Charles Martin, calling the doctor would alert the saloon owner to her presence in Jesse's cabin. He could send his thugs to take her—by force, if necessary. Was Jesse ready for a shootout?

With the man who had shattered his life...and Wade's? Indeed, he was.

When Jesse returned, he set the bucket beside the bed and pulled a chair over. Miss Gillbard turned her face away from him, but not before he glimpsed tear stains on her cheeks. As much as her unforeseen arrival reminded him of his painful past failings, and as little as he knew about dealing with women—especially one who was convinced he was a bad guy —she was not responsible for this impossible situation. He attempted to gentle his tone even as he spoke directly. "I need to know more about the men who might have sent the riders after you."

Her dainty chin lifted and shifted toward him. "How will I know you won't help them...maybe even offer me in exchange for a bag of gold?"

A mischievous grin broke across Jesse's face. "Not a bad idea. Thanks for the suggestion."

Her expression went slack, and she blinked.

Instant remorse smote him. He ventured a quick touch to her arm. "I'm teasing. But I shouldn't do so given your situation. Forgive me?"

If possible, she looked even more confused.

A redirect was necessary. Time was a'wastin'. Jesse gestured to the bucket. "We need to cool down that leg of yours. Will you let me do at least that much?"

Her lower lip wobbled. "Why should I trust you? I mean, besides the fact that I really don't have a choice?"

Jesse stared at her for a moment. Perhaps if she remembered him from the grand opening of the saloon, it might ease her mind. "Because I'm trying to do now what I failed to do before." And in doing so, maybe he could assuage a little of the guilt he felt over his wife as well.

Miss Gillbard's forehead knit into a V. "What do you mean?" She tilted her head as she studied him. "We *have* met, haven't we? You're...you're that man who saved me from that lathered miner." Astonishment freed her fair brows, and they winged their way upward.

"As I recall it, you saved me right back." A hint of admiration stirred at the memory of the way she'd launched that vase at the sot's head, and with right good aim, too, and a corner of his mouth quirked.

A small breath escaped her. "So I did. I couldn't let him hurt you. Not after you stood up for me like that..."

The transformation in her expression caved his chest in. The unmerited admiration in her eyes forced Jesse's gaze away.

"But you did save me from him. So what did you mean, you want to do what you failed to before?"

Jesse swallowed, glancing at her. "Unless I miss my guess, you needed more help than that."

Miss Gillbard's eyelashes fluttered, and she lowered her gaze. "What do you know about him? My...*guardian*?" The hesitation, the slight emphasis on the word, confirmed his fears.

A noose tightened around Jesse's midsection. Why hadn't he tried harder to check on her prior to leaving town last year? He might have spared this woman a year of suffering. "I know enough." He turned and dipped the cloth in the water, then wrung it out and draped it over the edge of the bucket. "Now, what about that boot?"

When she caught her lower lip between her teeth, then nodded, his uncertainty battled relief. Jesse fixed what was hopefully a calm, confident expression on his face as he slid the hem of her skirt up a few inches and unlaced her shoe as carefully as he could. But he had no idea what to do for a broken leg. If they couldn't send for a doctor, then what?

Jesse prayed Wade arrived soon—with some good ideas.

~

Genny's face must be redder than her leg. And not just from the effort of holding in a cry as Mr. Holden eased her boot off. He'd also started to reach for the garter that nestled just beneath her knee to remove her stocking when she put her hand out. "I'll do it."

That he turned without protest to again dip the cloth in the bucket and kept his eyes averted eased her embarrassment to some small degree. She might trust him more now that she possessed a reference point for his level of integrity, but that only multiplied her shyness. She didn't need to recall the etiquette classes from Mt. Olivet to know the situation she found herself in was highly improper.

Holding her breath and reaching as far as she could without bending her leg more, she managed to get the stocking down about her ankle. Sight of its bluish hue and bloated circumference overshadowed her tender sensibilities, and she fell back on the pillow with a groan. "I can't get it any farther." Tears eased from her eyes.

"It's all right." A cool cloth draped gently over her shin as Mr. Holden spoke. "Just rest a bit."

Genny closed her eyes, surrendering to a moment of self-pity. Why did this have to happen? Here she lay, immobilized, with as much dignity as a possum on its back. Didn't God want her to get away from Charles? Didn't He care anything for her future?

A moment later, she jerked as the rough, cool edge of the cloth touched her cheekbone. She opened her eyes to find Mr. Holden offering her the rag, a look of consternation on his face. He didn't want her here any more than she wanted to be here. That meant that for the moment, at least, she was safe. She relaxed a bit and dabbed her face.

"I'm going to slide that stocking off now," he said. "All right?"

A man who asked before he did something to her...what a strange notion. And he was gentle too. He'd just accomplished the task and returned a freshly dampened cloth to her leg when horse hooves sounded in the yard.

Genny braced her hands on either side of her, her back stiffening. "Who's that?"

Mr. Holden slid off the chair and grabbed the rifle he'd propped next to the entrance. After a quick glance out the window, he threw open the door and strode onto the porch. Toby hopped up and scampered after him, giving a joyful bark of greeting from the threshold. His owner's voice carried back to her. "Wade! I'm glad you came."

"Of course I came." Irritation edged the submerged concern in the unfamiliar man's voice that responded. "You stood me up. Then I found this horse in the woods on my way to check on you. What's going on, Jesse?"

"Thanks for bringing the mare. Saves me from going back for her." Boot steps thumped as Jesse walked to the edge of the porch. "I'm afraid we've got trouble."

His voice faded as he moved into the yard, presumably to tether Belinda. Genny squeezed her eyes shut. Trouble. That was what she was. A pawn to be shifted from one man to another—only, this one didn't know what to do with her. Why had this happened when she was so close to finally making her own way?

A moment later, Toby ran back inside, and a figure, taller and more muscular than her host's, darkened the doorway. The man swiped his hat from coal-black hair, uncovering a classically handsome face—though a scowl currently marred it. "Lord preserve us. It *is* her."

Under his scrutiny, Genny did her best to sit upright and ease her hem down.

Mr. Holden edged his friend out of the way. "Well, don't just stand there gawping at her. Where are your manners?"

"Sorry. I...uh..." Clasping his hat to his torso, the newcomer approached Genny's bedside. "Sheriff Wade Coulter, miss."

Apparently, Mr. Holden had already told his friend her name. "Sheriff?" Genny didn't try to keep the disbelief from her question. She knew the lawman in Auraria, and this wasn't him.

"Hall County. I know the sheriff in Lumpkin, but if what Jesse tells me is true, we won't be fetching him."

Because he was in Charles's pocket. This man was a quick study. Her guard lowered just a bit. "That's right, Sheriff Coulter. Nor the doctors." There might be more than one, but her guardian—and his former henchman—had eyes and ears everywhere and persuasive methods of extracting information.

Mr. Holden stepped closer. "But she's got to have a physician, Wade. I've no idea how bad the break is or what to do for it."

Sheriff Coulter gave a brief nod. "I'll take your word for it." No request to see her leg himself? Amazing. He scratched his head, then replaced his hat. "So I ride back to Gainesville?"

"If I may..." Genny cleared her throat and attempted to slide the pillow behind her back. Mr. Holden moved closer to assist her. She offered him a tentative smile and then turned her focus back to the lawman. "Agnes Paschal, the new owner of the Nuckolls Hotel, is said to be a natural healer. She'll know what to do. And...she won't tell anyone where I am."

Sheriff Coulter didn't hesitate. "Then it's her I will fetch." His unwavering calm boosted her confidence in him.

But something steely that flashed behind his eyes as he turned made Mr. Holden step in front of him. "I'll go."

The bigger man stiffened. "I'm the sheriff. I should handle this."

"That's exactly why you shouldn't." Somehow, Mr. Holden's stance was equally imposing. "Martin and anyone who works for him will recognize you. We don't want trouble. We want help for Miss Gillbard, and fast. Besides, I got a glimpse of at least the build of one of the men who followed Miss Gillbard. I'll know who to look out for." He waited a beat while his friend blew out a breath and rubbed the back of his neck. "You know I'm right, Wade. We can't go charging into town with guns half-cocked."

Why was Mr. Holden speaking with such firmness? And about guns? His regard for her care warmed her, but...

Genny came to attention like a student saying the pledge as Miss Mattie's words returned to her. The sheriff in Gainesville... it was his sister who had been shot. By Charles. And judging by the men's reactions, it hadn't been a former sheriff Miss Mattie was referring to.

Her stomach shrank like an apple laid out to dry in the sun. Of all the people to come to her aid, why did it have to be one whose life Charles's evil had already poisoned? Pity for his loss overrode her learned wariness of men.

"Please..." She held out her hand. "Sheriff Coulter? There's more I should tell you." She ignored the astonished, faintly indignant look Mr. Holden flashed her way as his friend came over and took the chair beside her.

She must entrust her story to someone. And who better than a lawman with a personal stake in Charles Martin receiving justice?

CHAPTER 7

The golden light and trilling birdsong of midday poured through the open windows as the healer examined Miss Gillbard. Jesse sat with Wade at the table across the room, focusing extra hard on their squirrel stew as Agnes Paschal tenderly fingered her patient's shin. The woman had come with him willingly enough when he'd mentioned Miss Gillbard. He'd needed to explain why he was seeking her instead of a doctor—that the young lady had been fleeing her guardian when injury befell her.

"Say no more," Mrs. Paschal had declared with a blaze of determination igniting her dark eyes. She'd plunked a bonnet over her silver-shot black hair and grabbed a brown leather bag, and then, on the ride out, she'd displayed equal zeal in quizzing him the ride long about matters of faith, extending her invitation to the new Baptist church she was organizing in town. When she'd learned his father and brother were both Methodist ministers, she'd dismissed denominational differences with a small wave. "Hardly matters, so long as we all listen to the still, small voice of God."

Jesse refrained from telling her that God's voice long ago

fell silent in his heart. She wasn't the sort of woman one wanted the disapproval of.

But from the time she'd entered the cabin and no doubt confirmed her suspicions he was a bachelor, her thick dark brows weighted down. As though it was his fault the songbird had fallen from her horse on his land.

Or rather, Wade's, though his best friend's perpetual aw-shucks expression had somehow kept him above reproach ever since they were kids in Athens. Even on the day Wade tied a firecracker to a stray dog's tail, Jesse got blamed. He'd felt the same frustration when Miss Gillbard beckoned Wade to her side and sent Jesse to town. And again when he'd returned to find them in close conversation, the young lady using Wade's handkerchief to wipe tears from her eyes but strangely unable to meet Jesse's.

No matter. The thing was to get her well and able to travel. Perhaps he was wrong and this was merely a sprain.

"Seventeen inches." Mrs. Paschal lifted her head and rewrapped a paper measuring tape as she made her sudden pronouncement. Then she helped Miss Gillbard cover her leg.

Jesse sat upright. "Ma'am?" He rested his spoon on the edge of his bowl.

"That's how long you need to make the splints." The healer rose and bustled to the sideboard carrying her leather bag, where she began to unpack containers and bags of all sizes and shapes.

Jesse's heart sank. "It's a break, then."

"A fracture of the fibula...the smaller outer bone in the lower leg. We can thank the Good Lord we don't have to set it." As she spoke, Mrs. Paschal peeked into the water pitcher.

"It's not that serious?" Wade rose and stepped around their guest for a creamware bowl. To serve stew to Miss Gillbard? She must be starving. Why hadn't Jesse thought of that?

"Serious enough that she needs to keep a splint on for

fifteen days." The woman swiveled and looked between them. "One of you, go find a young poplar tree and get to whittling. "The other can stir up the fire, seeing as you don't have a stove. I need some cold water for a poultice and some hot water to make a tea."

Jesse stood and tugged the bowl out of Wade's hands. He blinked wide as Jesse turned for the pot and ladle on the table. He wasn't getting sent on errands again. "I'll help with whatever's needed here in the house, Mrs. Paschal. Would you care for some stew?"

She didn't spare him a glance, instead opening and sniffing ingredients. "No, thank you. I ate before we set out."

He ignored Wade's cocked brow as he swung the kettle over the remains of the fire they'd used to heat the leftovers, then delivered dinner to Miss Gillbard while Wade tromped outside, Toby pattering at his heels.

Miss Gillbard thanked Jesse and accepted the bowl, but the spoon slid off and fell in the folds of her skirt. They both reached for it at the same time, and their fingers curled around each other's. For a split second, Miss Gillbard's wide eyes locked with his. Her face went red. Jesse retracted his fingers and Miss Gillbard her gaze.

"Once the splint is on, will I be able to sit a horse?" She asked the healer the question uppermost in Jesse's mind.

Mrs. Paschal whirled as indignantly as if she'd caught them sparking. "Absolutely not. You're to stay put, Miss Gillbard, and keep weight completely off that leg for the next five days. Only on the fifth day can you take the splint off, and then but for a short rest."

Five days. Jesse did his best to keep his face impassive, though the panic in the glance his unwilling guest shot his way sliced into him. Was the idea of his company so repellent? Or was it simply because he was a man? And yet he'd be willing to bet she wouldn't be half so anxious if it was Wade who was staying rather than Jesse. He had half a mind to tell her his perfect-specimen-of-manhood best friend was not only happily married but the father of a three-month-old baby girl.

"And after that?" Miss Gillbard's thick voice sounded as if she was drowning in a vat of tears.

Jesse didn't dare look at her. He returned to the hearth and used the poker to coax the tongues of orange flames.

"As I said, the splint should stay on for fifteen days." Mrs. Paschal clunked a mortar and pestle onto the sideboard and emptied some dried herbs into the vessel. Then she added what appeared to be wheat bran. "The bone may knit sometime earlier if you follow my instructions, but you should take no chances."

"Fifteen days." This time, without meaning to, Jesse spoke aloud. He straightened and narrowly avoided grimacing. Hopefully, Miss Gillbard hadn't noticed. She was picking a thread on the quilt over her lap.

"That's right." Mrs. Paschal fixed Jesse with a piercing stare. "You can help her to a chair in here or on the front porch after the fifth day, but no farther."

"Yes, ma'am." He half feared she'd return to check on him with a switch behind her back. He slid the fire poker back into its rack. "What can I do to help now?" Anything to keep his hands busy and his back to Miss Gillbard.

Mrs. Paschal selected a couple of pouches and moved them to the table. "I've presorted a blend to help with pain and swelling—willow bark, ginger, and the like. Use a tablespoon in a strainer as she needs it this first week. Sweeten it with honey."

Fifteen days of tea and honey and what else? True, Jesse had chafed under the imposed solitude of these forty acres these past two months, but at least he'd not been forced to measure every expression or word—the few he'd spoken to his dog. Now he was to play nursemaid to a woman who would be privy to his every thought and emotion? The very thing he'd vowed to avoid. There must be an alternative to sharing lodgings they hadn't thought of yet.

"Alternate that tea with one brewed from the contents of this bag." Mrs. Paschal tapped the other small canvas sack.

He blinked and refocused. At the very least, he'd have to care for Miss Gillbard for a day or two. "What is that?"

She opened the drawstring and whisked the pouch under Jesse's nose for him to catch a whiff.

He inhaled and coughed. Spicy.

"My special red pepper tea. Helps promote blood flow and general healing. Saved my life when those doctors back in Bowling Green nearly killed me with their Peruvian bark and brandy. Three summers, our family fought that terrible fever. After that, I swore—no tonics. No quack medicine. No bleeding or blistering. Just fresh air and cleanliness and the plants God gave us. Although I did learn a good bit back in the day from the doctors who used to board with my husband and me in Lexington."

At least she seemed to know what she was doing. She turned back to mixing her poultice, and Jesse followed her directions in measuring and steeping the tea.

Miss Gillbard's quavery voice broke the silence. "I don't expect you could get a wagon to the cabin."

"You saw the trail." Jesse lifted the kettle from the fire with a rag wrapped around the handle and sent her a glance aimed to convey his sympathy. "Just wide enough for a horse."

Miss Gillbard set aside her bowl of stew as if she'd lost all appetite.

Mrs. Paschal paused in pouring water into the mortar to look at him. "I can't stay myself—we're about to start construction on a nicer, newer hotel than that old Nuckolls rat trap— but I might be able to persuade another woman from town to come out and tend Miss Gillbard. Given the impropriety of the circumstances, I think that best."

'Twas all Jesse could do not to drop the hot kettle. "So I'm to have *two* women here?"

"I meant that you would leave."

Curtailing any reaction to the censure in her tone, Jesse took a breath as he poured hot water into the mug he'd prepared with the herbal tea. He waited until he'd rehung the kettle to answer. "I explained to you that Miss Gillbard was fleeing Mr. Martin. What I didn't tell you..." He glanced at the younger woman, seeking permission to continue. She gave it with a small nod.

Quick steps on the porch and a darkening in the doorway announced the return of Wade and Toby. Wade entered holding two lengths of green wood but paused when he took in their expressions. "Everything all right?"

Toby trotted to Miss Gillbard's side, and she cupped his head with her palm.

Jesse lifted his chin toward the healer. "Mrs. Paschal just suggested I vacate the cabin and allow a woman from town to tend Miss Gillbard. I was about to explain to her why that won't work."

Wade set the wood on the table, a muscle ticking in his jaw. "I'm afraid there's more than either of you know. Miss Gillbard shared some things with me while you were gone that bear investigation. She'd be best off here with you keeping a close eye on her and no one else getting involved. In fact, we're counting on your silence, Mrs. Paschal."

Jesse didn't wait for her to answer. His questioning glance at Miss Gillbard met with such a pained expression, he couldn't keep silent. Being trapped here with a woman would be taxing. Being trapped with an unwilling woman would be unbearable. "We can hardly keep her captive here, not if she wants to leave. If we do, we're no better than Martin." He didn't miss the way her brows elevated at his words.

"And if we let her go, she may very well become a real

captive. Or worse." Wade snapped out the statement, then clamped his bear paw-sized hand on Jesse's arm. "Take a walk with me while Mrs. Paschal tends Miss Gillbard's leg. We should talk. Then you can make an informed decision, all right?"

The young woman avoided Jesse's gaze by ducking her forehead to Toby's while Mrs. Paschal looked on with obvious concern. No doubt, Miss Gillbard felt twice as helpless as he did. He'd do well to remember her background and say nothing else to add to her distress. Didn't he know firsthand how another's cruelty could diminish a body?

Jesse handed the mug of tea to the healer. Then, with his boots as heavy as if they were filled with creek sediment, he followed Wade outside.

What else hadn't Miss Gillbard told him? What other circumstances would force their paths to align against both of their wishes?

~

Genny swallowed the words that would've called the men back. Sheriff Coulter—Wade, as he'd asked her to call him—would tell Mr. Holden about Larry Jones and Rupert Hanks's gold, including his threat to kidnap her and his possible connection to Charles. Wade hadn't said anything about the loss of his sister, so neither had she, but she didn't need words to confirm the steely determination in the sheriff's eyes. There was no way he was letting this go. He'd sworn his protection with a fervor that went beyond a lawman's calling. This was personal.

But something gnawed in her gut—worry that this could turn out for her much as it did for Miss Coulter.

There was another reason she hesitated to drag Mr. Holden into this. Wade had hinted that his friend had also suffered a loss recently—that he was here to heal. How could the man do that if Genny was foisted upon him, along with all the trouble that came with her? As much as he'd tried to disguise his dismay, she'd noticed his sidelong glances, the way he'd stiffened when Mrs. Paschal confirmed Genny couldn't be moved. And while his reaction might make her feel safe from any unwanted advances, it certainly didn't make her feel welcome.

She rolled her lower lip between her teeth as Mrs. Paschal patted her poultice over Genny's leg.

The woman paused her ministrations. "Am I hurting you?"

"No, ma'am." It was a partial truth. She'd already cried and whimpered too many times.

Mrs. Paschal's dark gaze missed nothing. "Drink your tea." She gestured to the mug on the bedside table, then scooped another dollop of what she'd called sprain weed compound from her mortar.

Genny held her breath until the healer smoothed the mixture up to her knee before reaching for the brew Mr. Holden had prepared, wrinkling her nose and taking a tentative sip. Still bitter despite the honey. "Thank you for coming, Mrs. Paschal. I don't know what I would have done without you."

"Don't think twice of it, Miss Gillbard. The hotel is just a way to make a living. This is my purpose in life." She paused and wiped her hands on her apron, then met Genny's eyes. "Especially when a body's truly in need—which I believe you are. You don't have to tell me what Mr. Holden started to earlier, mind. I hear what kind of man that Mr. Martin is. I see the way he squires you about town—eyes hungry for you like no guardian ought to have. It's a brave thing you did, leaving him. The right thing. God will take care of you."

Would He? Had He thus far?

"Thank you." Genny swept her gaze down. In truth, wasn't she at least partly to blame for her circumstances? She hadn't discouraged Charles—not when she thought he might marry her. Father used to laugh at her girlish ideals and tell her she ought to be grateful a wealthy man set his sights on her. Had she in some way misled Larry too? Just by being nice to him? "It wasn't only Charles I was fleeing, though. Larry Jones, who works—worked—for him is in on some kind of dangerous mining scheme...and threatened to involve me as well."

"I see." Mrs. Paschal firmed her mouth as she unwound a length of linen bandage. She fixed one end behind Genny's knee and started wrapping it over the poultice. "It sounds to me like you're a woman who needs to stay hidden."

Genny sat forward. "Yes, but not here. I was to go to Gainesville and catch the stage." She clamped her lips together lest she say more. Trusting people—that's what got her in trouble. Mrs. Paschal didn't need to know her full plan. But Genny desperately needed her help. "Can you think of some way to get me there? I can't stay here, alone with Mr. Holden."

The older woman tied off the bandage at Genny's ankle and sat back with a sigh. "Miss Gillbard, I share your concern. Not because I think him a bad sort. I don't. I talked with him on the way here, and I believe he's a Christian man."

"He is?" In Genny's experience, the designation held little weight. Her father and Charles both claimed to be Christian men. But if Mrs. Paschal thought so, perhaps that meant something different.

"Yes, though he's carrying a heavy burden, if I don't miss my guess." The healer frowned and tapped her lips with her finger, her gaze fixed somewhere past Genny's shoulder.

"Sheriff Coulter hinted as much. The last thing I want to do is add to it."

Mrs. Paschal's eyes locked in hers with obsidian intensity. "Miss Gillbard, do you reckon God knows what He's doing?"

"Um, well...yes." Genny hid her uncertainty behind a hesitant sip of tea.

"Seems to me, He's put you right where you need to be. Do

you think it's by chance that you ended up in a cabin owned by the sheriff of Hall County, probably the one man who can deal with Charles Martin?"

Genny startled. In fact, she had thought of that very thing—and quickly shoved the notion from her mind. Why would God bother with her? "But it's not him who lives here. It's Mr. Holden."

"Better yet—a trusted friend to guard you while the sheriff settles matters. If you'd traipsed off to Gainesville and then who knows where, do you think Charles Martin or Larry Jones would leave you be?" Mrs. Paschal pulled a basin that smelled of vinegar from the side table onto her lap. She stirred it with a spoon.

Was Genny going to have to drink that? Might go down easier than the healer's farfetched assumptions about God.

"Do you?" Mrs. Paschal's question brought Genny back to the conversation.

Slowly, she shook her head.

"No. Best to let them deal with the matter, then you'll be truly free to go about your life. 'If the Son therefore shall make you free, ye shall be free indeed.'" Mrs. Paschal dribbled a spoonful of the vinegar over the front of Genny's bandage. "Now, I'm going to leave this by your bed so you can keep your wrappings and poultice damp for the first day or so. That way, you won't have to ask Mr. Holden to do it."

Genny nodded and sat quietly as the woman continued until the linen was wet all the way around, but inside, she was thinking of all the things she wouldn't be able to do without help. Mrs. Paschal offered her no magical solution. Somehow, she would have to tolerate this, at least for a while. "So you think I should trust him...Mr. Holden?"

Mrs. Paschal sat back with a frown, putting her basin aside. "What I think doesn't matter. It's what God thinks that counts.

All I'll say is, the preacher's set to arrive in Auraria tomorrow. You need him, you send me word."

"Wh-what?" Genny clunked her tea onto the table, narrowly missing the edge. The woman couldn't be suggesting what Genny thought she was. "But you said I could leave after the splint is removed. Surely, no one has to know I was here for a couple of weeks. Besides, d'reckly, I'll be living elsewhere." What the busybody housewives on Gold Digger's Row might say about her would hardly matter then.

"Oh, Miss Gillbard...Genny." Mrs. Paschal looked at her with such sympathy that Genny's chest seized. "I'm sorry if I didn't make it clear. You won't be able to travel when the splint comes off. You'll need four to six weeks for the bone to knit securely enough that you won't risk long-term damage."

"Oh, no." Genny's hands fluttered to her mouth. "No." She was well and truly trapped. She'd merely exchanged a lavish room for a log cabin and the devil she knew for one she didn't.

Mrs. Paschal eased onto the edge of the bed beside her, sliding an arm around Genny's shoulders. "I understand. This situation seems impossible. But if we believe God is in charge, we can rest assured that He has a plan. A good plan. "'For I know the thoughts that I think toward you,' saith the Lord, "thoughts of peace, and not of evil, to give you an expected end.'" That's Jeremiah 29:11."

Genny recoiled from the woman's touch and her suffocating Bible verses. She wanted nothing to do with a God that would entrap her here. Nothing to do with a man who would agree to imprison her like this. She might be stuck here for now, but she would not be forced into a marriage of convenience.

CHAPTER 8

A rooster crowed in the cabin yard. Morning. Genny struggled to unseal her puffy, crusted eyes, then blinked against the silvery light slanting in through the cracks in the shutter near her bed. ...Mr. Holden's bed.

Dread weighted her stomach with the force of a falling millstone about the same time searing pain ignited in her leg. It was true...all true. She was incapacitated in this cabin. All she could do was await the return of Sheriff Coulter, who had escorted Mrs. Paschal back to town yesterday. While there, he promised to glean some information about what was happening at the Boom or Bust in Genny's absence. Ever since the sheriff left, Mr. Holden's silence made Charles's sulks—or mutts, as her mother would've said—resemble a spring zephyr.

But where was the man? Was he watching her, even now, as she'd often caught Charles doing? Her heartbeat sped. Genny pressed her hands to the mattress and pushed herself up with a gasp and a crinkle of straw. The cabin was empty, so he must still be in the barn, where he'd gone after supper last night. When he'd explained that his sleeping out there should make

69

her more comfortable, she hadn't argued. Unease overpowered guilt. Until the man took his Bible but left his dog.

Now, not only was Toby gone, but the whale oil lamp on the table burned low, and small flames crackled on the hearth. Mr. Holden must have entered during the few pre-dawn hours when Genny succumbed to exhaustion. The idea of the man moving about the cabin, able to observe her as she slept, ran a hard shudder down her spine. She could do no more about it than she could Charles's bursting into her room. This was Mr. Holden's cabin, after all. For all she knew, he'd offered to sleep in the barn merely to gain her trust. Who knew what went on in that head of his? Though she'd worn herself out guessing as he'd heated beans, ham, and cornbread last night, eaten, and cleaned up, all in silence but for the most necessary exchanges. Genny's attempts to ask basic questions and make small talk had been met with the barest of responses. How was she to bear another day...another week...another month of this?

She blinked back tears. When her sight cleared, she examined the bedside for a chamber pot. She ought to do her business before the man returned. Following a sprinkling of gasps and grunts and plenty of teeth clenching as her movement made her leg throb, as well as other muscles in her body which now decided to protest her fall from the day prior, she finished and managed to slide the lidded vessel slightly beneath the bedframe. How humiliating.

As she straightened, she blinked again. For there on the bedside table, atop a linen cloth laid next to a basin of water and a chunk of lye soap, sat an object that had not been there the night before. The morning light shone on the smooth wood of a carved bird. When she picked it up, it fit perfectly in the palm of her hand. The details of its wings and its little face were amazing. Its tiny eyes seemed to gaze into hers as if the bird wanted to be friends but was afraid to. Her heart lurched as she stroked its head. Mr. Holden had carved this...for her?

What did it mean? And why was she almost crying over it?

Because it didn't take much to loose her tears in her current circumstances. Perhaps he meant the bird by way of apology. A little surge of hope had her setting the carving down and reaching for the buttons of her bodice. She'd best make herself presentable before Mr. Holden reappeared. Perhaps they could start anew today. Come to some sort of plan or understanding.

Genny had completed most of her hurried sponge bath when booted steps on the porch made her almost drop the soap. She plunked it back on the table and scrambled to arrange the folds of her dress. Her heart raced. She couldn't do up her bodice before he opened the door. She—

A light knock sounded on the wood.

She sucked in a breath. "J-just a minute." Genny's fingers fumbled with her buttons. Then a new fear seized her. What man knocked on the door of his own cabin? "Mr. Holden?"

"It's me." Lighter feet pattered, toenails clicking on floorboards, after the man's deep voice spoke, followed by a short bark. Mr. Holden gave a slight laugh. "And Toby."

That hint of mirth gave her courage. He sounded almost... cheery. She smoothed her hair back as best she could without a brush. "You may come in."

But when he entered and his gaze swept over her, a slight frown marred his features, which were offset by the sprinkling of beard on his cheeks and strong jaw. Genny snuck a quick examination of herself. What was wrong with her? Perhaps the sight of her in his bed reminded him of his night on the hard ground.

"How did you sleep?" His question seemed to verify the direction of her thoughts.

Toby darted over to her. Stroking his silky head provided the opportunity to cover her confusion.

"Um...well enough." Saying otherwise would be complaining—a fault of hers, according to Charles. "You?" That was the wrong thing to ask. She hastened to soothe any ill feelings. "Thank you again for giving up your bed. And for the privacy. I feel awful to keep you outside your own home. Just now, I was—"

The wave of his hand cut short her rushed explanation. He lifted the basket of eggs he held. "Do you need anything? Otherwise, I'll start breakfast."

If she did, she would never tell. She already owed this stranger so much. Genny shook her head. But as Mr. Holden cracked the eggs into a bowl and started beating them with a fork, her gaze strayed from the strange sight of a man cooking to the pitcher on the sideboard. She should've sipped some of her wash water prior to using it. A sigh escaped before she realized her lapse.

Mr. Holden glanced up, intercepted her yearning look, and set down the bowl. With a few oh-so-effortless motions, he brought her a glass of water. "I'll have coffee in a minute."

"Thank you." Genny flushed as she accepted the water. "Can I grind some beans for you?"

His lips twitched in the suggestion of a smile, and his eyes —they were such a rich brown, with amber tints. As she fumbled her grip on the glass and brought it quickly to her lips, he tipped his head toward the fireplace, where a blue-speckled coffeepot sat in the coals. "Already brewing."

Genny's stomach bottomed out. This emotional whiplash felt all too familiar. She lowered the glass and blurted out the question on her mind. "Why are you being so nice to me?"

Mr. Holden's face went slack. "I...brought you a glass of water."

"And you slept in the barn, and left the dog to guard me, and knocked and waited before you entered, and you weren't mad—"

"Why would I be mad?"

"And there's this water I didn't even ask for, and now break-fast, and—"

"Miss Gillbard." Mr. Holden grabbed the ladder back of the chair next to the bed and turned the seat around to face him. "Miss Genny. May I call you that?"

"Um…I suppose." What was he working up to?

He plunked down on the chair backward, encircled the back with his lanky arms, and hung his thumbs on the rungs. "I figure we're both going to have to get a few things straight. You're stuck here whether you want to be or not, and you're going to need some help. And I'm going to need to give it."

She swallowed. Was that it—he'd resigned himself to the inevitable? Her gaze strayed to the carving on the bedside table. "Y-you made me a bird." It looked back at her entreatingly, a reminder of his kindness. "Why did you do that?"

"I carve when I can't sleep." He shrugged, but was that a blush staining his cheeks? "Seemed fitting…for the Songbird of Auraria."

"Thank you." Somehow, her voice got lost in the emotion clogging her throat. "I can't remember when anyone made anything for me." However casually he attempted to play it off, his evasion of her gaze verified the gift was a gesture of good-will. Maybe he regretted making her feel bad yesterday. Genny straightened her shoulders. She could work with a man with a conscience. "Very well, Mr. Holden—"

"Jesse."

"Jesse…" Now it was she who couldn't meet his eyes. "I'm willing to throw myself on your good graces, but only on the condition that you allow me to help as much as I can." She swept her hand around the cabin. "Surely, you have some mending that needs doing. And I can chop vegetables or churn butter, things like that. When I'm allowed up in a few days, maybe you can help me sit at the hearth or on the porch to do tasks. I refuse to be nothing but a burden. Agreed?"

"If you insist." He gave a brief nod, then added under his breath, "Though you could never be a burden."

His parents had raised a gentleman, maybe the first true one she'd met, but she'd glimpsed his real feelings yesterday. A person didn't change overnight. Today, he'd somehow managed to secure a polite mask over his annoyance.

"Nevertheless, I'll leave the first day I can sit a horse. Until then, you don't need to go out of your way for me. I won't have you inconvenienced in your own home. Or..." She glanced at the songbird, and the steady tempo of her declaration faltered. "Barn."

Why did her attempt to reassure him make him look so pained? He stood and turned the chair around. "Understood, Miss Gillbard."

"Genny." She spoke to his back as he went to make breakfast.

~

God, I'm not sure I can do this.

Jesse paused in sowing tiny wheat seeds to send the prayer up to the cloud-laden, late-afternoon sky. Had he even heard the Almighty as he thought he had last night? He was so out of practice in praying and listening, maybe he'd imagined the moment the words leapt off the page. After all, it was the first time he'd sensed God during the nightly Bible reading he'd forced himself back into since coming here. But surely, it was no coincidence that he'd resumed his reading in Hebrews at just the spot to come across that verse. *Be not forgetful to entertain strangers: for thereby some have entertained angels unawares.*

Not that he thought Miss Gillbard was an angel. Indeed, the minute he'd offered an olive branch, she'd slapped it back in his face. Even after she'd let him know she didn't require any unnecessary kindness from him, Jesse made himself sit beside her rather than at the table to eat breakfast. She'd told him he didn't have to join her. He'd kept his seat, letting her know he harbored no intentions of treating his guest rudely. Then, rather than ask about him, she'd asked about *Wade*. Asked about the shooting.

In all fairness, she had a right to know what motivated the man's willingness to help her. So Jesse answered her questions as briefly as possible, confirming that yes, in Gainesville last December, Charles Martin accused Rupert Hanks of deceiving him in order to obtain Martin's gold lot. Wade's sister had been accidentally shot while Wade attempted to de-escalate the situation. At that point in the tale, Jesse's appetite withered, and he'd risen rather abruptly, no doubt leaving Genny brimming with curiosity. But why would he speak of his own connection to the tragedy, baring his emotions, when her only interest was to learn more about Wade? And—again, to be fair—her guardian's guilt.

She'd fallen silent while he cleaned up breakfast, only saying faintly when he headed for the door, "Maybe Sheriff Coulter will learn no one has missed me in town, and I'll be able to leave sooner rather than later."

Jesse had paused without speaking, then plunked his hat on his head and departed. This time, he took Toby with him. Clearly, Genny looked to Wade as some sort of savior, when Jesse had been the one to find her and bring her to safety. What did he care, anyway?

Only because something told him she was his responsibility, and sheltering her was his part to play in a bigger production. Something that felt an awful lot like the Spirit of God used to. After all, he could hardly say he was willing to take on Charles but not be willing to shelter the man's victim.

Why did he get the feeling that the latter assignment would be the harder one?

At the edge of the field cleared for wheat, Toby barked. Two —no, three—riders were coming up the path. Jesse tensed. He'd left his rifle on the porch. But Wade's bulky form on his stallion led the procession, and Jesse relaxed. Behind him rode Mrs. Paschal on her mare, saddlebags bulging on each side. What was she doing back here? An unfamiliar older man in a dark suit brought up the rear.

Jesse brushed off his hands and went to greet them. "Wade." He acknowledged his best friend with a tone suited to the seriousness of the occasion, while Toby ran jubilant circles around the man's stallion. Jesse turned to Mrs. Paschal as she reined her mount up near the hitching post. He offered her a hand down. "Mrs. Paschal, come to check on our patient again already?"

"Something like that." Clutching her brown leather bag at her side, she sent Wade a glance that tightened Jesse's stomach. As the men dismounted, the healer gestured to the newcomer. "Mr. Holden, this is Reverend Billingsly, newly arrived in Auraria."

The man with sandy, gray-streaked hair and a paunch under his waistcoat rubbed his leg as if it was gouty and nodded to Jesse. "A pleasure to make your acquaintance."

"Ah. The Baptist minister Mrs. Paschal mentioned. Not wasting any time in making visitation rounds, are you?" Jesse offered a grin, but surely, the man knew neither he nor Genny would be leaving this cabin any time soon.

Rev. Billingsly chuckled. "I'd be mighty pleased for you to join us, for sure. We'll be meeting in Mrs. Paschal's dining room until they get the log church up."

Finished tethering his horse, Wade stepped closer and put his hand on Jesse's arm. "Jesse, why don't we go inside and talk things over while Mrs. Paschal checks on Miss Gillbard?" The lack of sparkle in his eyes warned Jesse the news would not be good.

"Sure. Come on in." He gestured to the porch and allowed Mrs. Paschal to lead the way.

Upon their entrance, Genny set aside the book he'd lent her and studied each face with her brows raised. "Oh my. I did not expect so many callers." She fluttered her hand over her hair, which she'd secured in a loose braid. The style made her look like a schoolgirl. How old *was* she? Young enough to need a guardian.

While Mrs. Paschal made the introductions and set about checking the splint Jesse had finished last night, the men settled at the table, and Jesse warmed some coffee. Only the reverend accepted any. Jesse's roiling gut told him he'd best forgo the bitter brew.

He sat down across from his friend and met his eyes squarely. "What did you learn in town? Any word of Larry Jones absconding with gold?"

Wade shifted and bent the brim of his hat as it lay on the table. "Not so far. Mrs. Paschal suggested she send one of her lodgers over to the Boom or Bust last night to avoid the possibility of anyone recognizing me." He spoke loudly enough that the women could hear as the healer uncorked a brown bottle and carefully dampened Genny's bandages with the contents. "The man reported that Miss Gillbard's absence was the talk of the town. Folks were saying Mr. Martin would be fit to be tied when he got word."

Jesse held his gaze. "Is someone planning to tell him?"

Genny sat unmoving, her white face turned their way.

"Walter did. He's already dispatched a message to Atlanta."

Genny released a soft gasp. "I thought he might let me go." The disappointment in her statement hinted at her sense of betrayal.

"I reckon he didn't have much choice, ma'am." Wade sent her an apologetic glance. "I'm sure both him and Miss Mattie knew their jobs would be on the line, at the very least, if they did not alert him."

Mrs. Paschal corked her bottle. "And Mr. Martin will claim he's searching for you out of concern as your guardian. The fact that he holds that role gives him authority. How close are you to turning twenty-one, child?"

Genny twisted the fold of her skirt in her hand. "October."

The healer gave a firm nod and sought Wade's gaze. "That's not so long."

Jesse could take no more of their coded glances and double meanings. "What exactly is going on here? What plan have you all concocted?"

Wade's face turned a dusky hue as he played with his hat brim. "On the way to Auraria yesterday, Mrs. Paschal voiced her concerns about how improper it is, the two of you staying here together. Not to mention, the need to protect Miss Gillbard. She reminded me Rev. Billingsly was due to arrive today."

"No..." With a strangled cry, Genny raised her hand to her chest. Her face resembled an animal's caught in a trap.

Did Wade mean what Jesse thought he meant? With the preacher and the innuendo... He couldn't. His friend could always be trusted to be the most practical, the most logical, of men. And of all people, he knew the reason Jesse could not do as he suggested.

Wade seemed to follow the frantic darting of Jesse's thoughts. His friend reached across the table, letting his hand fall just short of Jesse's arm. "I'm not suggesting anything that has to be permanent, Jesse. You just heard Miss Gillbard say she'll be twenty-one this fall. But with her being stuck here for some weeks, and Charles certain to send men searching for her...only a legal change in her status might protect her."

Jesse shook his head, then dragged his hand over his face. "This is crazy, Wade. Crazy."

"Look at me." Wade gripped Jesse's forearm, his fingers hot

and pinching through Jesse's linen shirtsleeve. "You know what I vowed when Martin took Emma. I can't have peace until he's dealt with. Can you?"

The pain in Wade's eyes seared Jesse's heart—because another emotion clawed its way to the surface of his psyche. Guilt. And Wade knew it. "How can you ask this of me?" At his whispered words, the good reverend averted his face, his mouth firming into a sympathetic line.

"Because I need time to investigate. I owe it to Emma. And both Miss Gillbard and I need your help."

In the months since Emma's death, Wade never once blamed Jesse, when what happened had so clearly been Jesse's fault. The fact that Wade assumed the burden of finding justice with the anguish of a guilty man made it impossible to deny his request. Jesse blew out an uneven breath.

Pushing his coffee mug aside, Rev. Billingsly cleared his throat. "May I make a suggestion? The marriage could be in name only. If you both so choose, it could then be annulled when Miss Gillbard reaches her majority or when the danger passes, whichever comes first." He glanced between them, his busy brows hovering low. "This is certainly not something I would normally recommend. It goes against everything that marriage should be. But under the circumstances, I think the Lord would understand the need to protect the young lady."

"Is no one going to ask what the young lady thinks?" Miss Genny's strangled voice tugged at Jesse's heart.

Wade was right. This was Jesse's chance to do the right thing. He couldn't allow Charles Martin to destroy a second woman's life. He straightened, still looking at Wade. "Could everyone allow me a few minutes to speak with Miss Gillbard alone?"

After exchanging uncertain glances, they all agreed, rose, and shuffled to the porch. Toby took the opportunity to avail himself of the call of the wild. Though Wade closed the door after them, their murmured voices carried through the open window along with the peeping of spring frogs. Jesse sucked in a breath and crossed to the chair at Genny's side.

She wrung her hands in her lap, her delicate features twisted in distress and panic as she clamped eyes on him. "Surely, you can't be considering this outlandish suggestion."

"Is it so outlandish? It provides the answer to everything."

"It complicates everything!" She threw her hands up. "We're perfect strangers."

"Strangers whose lives have been entwined whether we are married or not. But marriage can protect you from the men who would do you harm. And do you not want Charles Martin stopped? Wade can do that. You trust him, don't you?"

"Yes, I…" She chewed her lower lip, her gaze seeking the floorboards.

Jesse crossed his arms. "You just don't trust me."

Her green eyes found his. "I don't know you. And I'm not being asked to marry Sheriff Coulter."

He relaxed a little. "Fair enough. And by the way, he's already married." He flashed her what might be an inappropriately timed smile that seemed to register, strangely enough, no more than his words did.

She went right on with that unwavering focus of hers. "I know you don't want me here. I heard what you said to Mrs. Paschal. And you wouldn't even speak to me last night." Though she raised her head as if offended, her tone hinted at hurt.

Had he come across that gruff? He'd thought he'd concealed his feelings and avoided awkward topics by keeping the conversation basic. "Guess I figured we both needed space to get our heads around what happened."

"Well, that's not how it came across." She looked away, but her chin wobbled.

Jesse let out a breath. This woman tugged his heart like a

trout taking under a dry fly. "I didn't mean to make you feel so unwelcome. Forgive me?" The look she turned on him, eyes wide and lips parted, made him draw back. He really must've been an ogre. Now it was his job to convince this woman he was trustworthy. Jesse uncrossed his arms and sat forward. "What if I promise to do nothing that goes against your wishes?"

Her fair brows winged upward. "That's a tall order for anybody to keep, Mr. Holden."

"And yet I vow I'll do my utmost to keep it, with God's help." He leaned on his legs, speaking softly, his voice raspy but sure. "We'll go on as we have been. As Reverend Billingsly said, a marriage in name only. I'll continue to sleep in the barn. We'll keep the agreement we made earlier today to help each other. I'll guard you from danger while Wade gathers evidence against Martin. And when it's safe and you're healed, you can go wherever you wish. No one need know what happened here. But you'll be free. Truly free."

His words sparked a hunger in her eyes as she stared out the open window. Like a bird yearning to flee her cage. Didn't Jesse understand that desire? This was why he was here. It all made sense now. Not just to heal...to bring closure to the gaping wound in both his and Wade's lives and to grant Genny the freedom he'd failed to a year ago. And when he'd done that, he could return to surveying in Mississippi with a clear conscience and live a life as unshackled as the one he'd promised Genny.

"Why are you doing this?" Genny's tortured whisper drew his attention. She shook her head, her golden braid sliding across her shoulder.

Her plea carried a desperation he couldn't ignore. She needed more than promises from him in order to trust him. He sat upright and released a heavy breath. "Because Wade's sister, who Charles Martin killed, was my wife."

CHAPTER 9

$\mathcal{E}$mma Coulter had been Emma Holden, Jesse's wife. His *first* wife.

Genny was his wife now.

Not one of those thoughts made a lick of sense. And yet here she sat, still in the white lawn dress Mrs. Paschal had produced from her saddlebag for Genny to be married in. She untangled the wilted dogwood blossoms from her hair and watched the man she'd alternately feared and admired clean up the remnants of their simple wedding supper. Mrs. Paschal truly had thought of everything. She'd packed fried chicken, biscuits, boiled potatoes, pickles—even a spice cake. Not that Genny had done more than nibble at the food. She'd been too overwhelmed by the words she'd just spoken, the vows said, linking her to this man, if not for life, for an untold amount of time.

A man whose motivations and intentions she had doubted. Now everything made so much more sense. Of course, he'd been upset to find himself saddled with an injured woman. He'd only been a widower for...what? Four months?

And here she'd pitied Wade. Guilt twisted her stomach.

"

"Is there anything I can do?" She had to ask even though she already knew the answer. "I hate that everyone hurried off and left you with the cleanup. A man shouldn't have to wash dishes on his wedding night." The implication behind her words hit her the moment they left her mouth, but it was too late to take them back.

Jesse didn't seem to notice. He merely shot her a quick glance while he raked crumbs from the table into his hand. "A woman shouldn't have to be confined to bed on her wedding night."

Soon as he said it, he froze. His expression of chagrin was so obvious, the double meaning of his words so much more blatant than hers, there was no point in trying to cover it. His eyes met hers, and he so resembled a guilty schoolboy that Genny burst out laughing. When he joined her, she relaxed. At least the man possessed a sense of humor. That alone was more than she could say for any of the previous males in her life.

Jesse dumped the crumbs in the fireplace. "In any case, I can hardly complain when Mrs. Paschal brought the whole buffet. I wonder what she woulda done if we naysayed her fine plan."

Genny chuckled and sipped the medicinal tea the healer pressed into her hands before departing. "I doubt she would have left without us giving our vows in front of the preacher. Never have I seen a more single-minded woman." She touched the delicate embroidery that trimmed the collar of the dress she wore. "Although it sure was nice of her to bring this gown."

She would need his help getting out of it before she slept, given the fact that it closed in the back. The thought made her mouth go dry. She'd put that off until later.

Jesse paused to gaze at her. "I agree." Two seconds, then three passed while still he gazed. "You look...awful nice in it." He stumbled over the compliment like a root in a trail and grabbed a dishcloth to give the table a vigorous wiping down right after, but Genny's heart warmed.

What must the compliment have cost him? And yet somehow he'd known a woman needed to hear such on her wedding day, even one as unconventional as theirs.

"Thank you." She murmured her response.

Until recently, she'd thought she would be planning a summer wedding to Charles. Somehow, she'd believed that gaining the status of being his wife would solve everything. After all, his role as her guardian placed him in an impossible position, needing to protect her while at the same time developing feelings for her. Or so he had said. And it did seem that everything was perfect when they could get away, just the two of them. But hadn't he shown her his true self? She must remember that. Back in Cornwall, they would call him a *janjansy*—a man with two faces.

What would he do when he learned she had married someone else?

Jesse went on as if she hadn't spoken, hadn't fallen down a rabbit hole with her thoughts. "Yep. Having Mrs. P camp out here would ensure I got hitched in short order." He waved the cloth toward the open door. "Good thing they didn't linger, if for no other reason than there's a real thunder-boomer coming."

As a breeze with the hint of rain blew into the cabin, Toby lifted his muzzle from the rug, and he sniffed as if to test his master's theory. Indeed, the frogs down by the creek had gone silent, perhaps battening down for the coming storm.

"Weren't you sowing wheat earlier today?" Genny cocked her head. "Will a gulley-washer carry all your seeds to the creek?"

"Very well might. Shoulda seen that one coming, but it blew up fast." Jesse stacked their dishes, then carried them to the front porch where he left a bucket of water for washing. He paused on the threshold. "Guess it's a good thing our company's arrival interrupted me."

Toby hopped up and streaked out, Jesse following in his wake. While he was out on the porch, splashing around in the water bucket, talking to Toby, Genny finished her tea and smiled at the first patter of raindrops on the roof. How vividly green the new leaves looked outside, gleaming in the twilight. She held her hand out toward the window, seeking the cool dampness that misted her fingers, and breathed in the refreshing scent of loam and new life.

Could Mrs. Paschal be right? Could this be a fresh start for her? But what about Jesse? There was no way he was ready for a new chapter, not so soon after burying his dreams with Emma. What kind of woman had she been? Anything like Genny at all?

When Jesse and Toby returned, he secured the door behind him. The rain was picking up, the sky and interior of the cabin darkening. He made quick work of drying the dishes and returning them to their places on the sideboard. He collected the candle from her bedside and set it beside the whale oil lamp on the table. Then he took a long piece of twisted wood from the spill holder by the fireplace. After he held it in the embers a moment, the tip ignited, and he carried the flame over to light the candle and lamp.

Genny was reaching her mug to her bedside table when pain shot down her leg, and she cried out.

"Easy." Jesse was beside her in an instant, putting down the candleholder he'd brought back, taking the cup from her, and helping her ease back against the pillows. "I think you maybe overdid it today."

"How can I have overdone it?" Tears sprang to her eyes as she rubbed her thigh in an effort to relieve the tension in her lower leg. "I haven't even left the bed."

"Be patient with yourself. Your body needs time to heal."

Her watery gaze must've made him pity her, for he leaned over and gently removed a limp dogwood blossom from above the curl over her left ear. A hint of the outdoors, of smoke and pine, along with a musky male scent uniquely his, made her catch her breath. His brown eyes sought hers, and an awareness hummed between them that he must've surely felt, for he froze a moment. And then quickly stepped back. He let the blossom flutter to the bedside table and moved toward the open window.

As he pulled in and latched the shutters, Genny chided herself. She must do nothing to give the impression that she expected aught from him but the kindness of a friend. The rush of energy she'd felt—surely, it had only been due to the change of atmosphere the building storm created. And maybe the tension of two strangers who found themselves in close quarters made unexpectedly cozy by the flickering of candlelight. She cast about for a safe subject, for even the silence was fraught with...something.

"You said you should have known the storm was coming. Have you been a farmer long?" Ah, that was a good choice. She knew so little about his background.

"Two months." He turned back to her and flashed a grin. So much for defusing the atmosphere. The mere sight of his laugh lines ignited her senses faster than striking flint to kindling. Most ladies might consider Wade Coulter more handsome, with his stunning blue eyes and firm muscles, but Jesse's boyish charm set whatever remained of her girlish heart aflutter.

"Two months?" Her mouth dropped open as his answer finally penetrated the cobwebs in her mental attic. "But I saw you almost a year ago in the Boom or Bust. What were you doing then, just *fossicking*?"

"'Fossicking'? What's that?"

She waved her hand. "Just the Cornish way of saying 'prospecting.'"

"Oh." His face brightened. "I was doing this…" He stepped over to the trunk on the wall side of the bed, opened it, and drew out a polished wooden case which he laid on the mattress beside her with as much care as he might show a baby.

When he lifted the lid, she stared at a large, glass-covered dial with two needles, set in what appeared to be a bronze mount. The directional markings on the face told her what the instrument was, although other metal parts she did not recognize nestled in the velvet-covered interior. "It's a compass."

His expression contained the most enthusiasm she'd seen from him as he nodded. "The Improved Compass by William Young, to be exact. Vernier style, but see here?" He pointed to a spot on the dial. "It has this graduated circle for reading horizontal angles independently of the needle." At her slight frown, he waved his hand as if to excuse the disinterest he'd anticipated and reached for the lid.

"Wait." Genny stopped him with a touch to the edge of the case. His obvious passion for the instrument compelled her to learn more. "What's a Vernier?"

Jesse tipped his head to one side. "You really want to know?"

"Of course. You're…a surveyor, right? That's what you were doing in Auraria last summer, laying out the lottery plots."

"With my pack man, two axe men, and a cook—my team from Hall County, yes."

"That's how you know Wade."

"Actually, we grew up together in Athens." Jesse's smile contained a treasure trove of boyhood secrets that Genny dearly wished to explore. "His family attended the church my father pastored."

A pastor's son? No wonder he'd taken his Bible to the barn last night. Doubtless, he knew the book cover to cover, whereas Genny only clung to the faded memories of her mother's instruction. What would he think of how little she knew of

God? "Mrs. Paschal said she believed you to be a Christian man. It's one reason I went through with this." Before the gravity of their commitment could alter his mood, Genny tapped the case again. "But you were telling me about this."

He hesitated a moment, then settled on the far edge of the bed. "The earliest compasses, made by clockmakers after the Revolution, were fancy—etched and expensive—but didn't always point to true north."

"Why not?" Genny spoke a little louder above the increasing tattoo of the rain. "Goodness, 'tis *henting* out there."

"The direction of the North Pole is always shifting. The Vernier compasses account for that. The needle still points to the magnetic north, but the true bearing is to the object you're trying to sight."

She stared at him, close enough in the cool shadows that their elbows brushed. "I have no idea what that means, except the bit about true north is kind of like our circumstances in life."

"How so?"

"They're always changing. We have to keep our goals in sight, or we might get lost."

Jesse closed the case. "And what are your goals, Genny Gillbard?"

"I want to prove my father wrong. I want to show that I can make my own way in life using my singing...and not in a saloon." She smoothed the folds of Mrs. Paschal's loaned dress, the very color of it reminding her that she was as far off course as if she'd read her life compass upside down. "I secured a position teaching, you know, at Mt. Olivet in Gainesville, where I went to school. Father let Charles pay for my education as part of his wages."

"I know..." Jesse's soft reply almost got lost in the rain. "That you went there, I mean."

She snapped her gaze up. "How do you know?"

"I saw you on the grounds, a time or two." When she widened her eyes and blinked at him, he hastened to explain. "I was there for some social occasions, visiting Emma. She was a couple of years ahead of you."

Genny's lips parted. "What did she look like?" She would've been a Coulter then. Maybe the familiarity of the name was part of why she'd trusted Wade so quickly.

Jesse shifted as if he would get up, turning his face away from her. "Tall, willowy. Dark hair…" His Adam's apple bobbed. Instead of the eagerness that infused his tone when he spoke of surveying, reluctance slowed every syllable.

"I'm sorry." She touched his arm, and he flinched slightly. "You don't have to speak of her. I only wanted to see if I might have known her."

"And did you?" He cut her a sideways glance.

Genny frowned. "I'm not sure. I might have known *of* her." Tall and dark-haired described a lot of girls, but if she was the one Genny thought she remembered, Emma had been every-thing Genny aspired to be—poised, innocent, a well-bred young lady. Everything Genny was not. Before she could ask more, Jesse nudged her shoulder with his.

"What happened? Why did you leave?"

She released a sigh. "A hoity-toity parent recognized me as the Songbird of Auraria."

His quiet chuckle drew her gaze. "Did you ever think how that happened?"

"Oh." Genny giggled. "I see what you mean." More than one naughty husband was known to slink up to the hills to pan for gold and sample the boomtown's guilty pleasures.

"There's better than Mt. Olivet out there for you, then." He pulled his case toward him and eased off the bed. His care not to jostle her made Genny's heart squeeze.

"What makes you so sure of that?"

"Well, who gave you that voice of yours?" Jesse moved some things around in the trunk.

She shifted to better see what he was doing. "God, I suppose."

"Right, and His Word tells us that He has a good plan for those who follow Him. That means something better in store." Jesse glanced up, holding a small stack of books with what appeared to be a framed picture on top.

Genny gave a soft laugh of disbelief. "That's what Mrs. Paschal said. She quoted that very verse to me." But *did* Genny follow God?

"Well, there you go." He shrugged. "God is our true north, Genny. Long as we keep our bearing on Him, we can't go astray."

A faint memory lingered of her saying a prayer trusting her Heavenly Father with her life. Perhaps her faith then had been lacking since it seemed to prevent damage about as well as a cabin without chinking.

Quicker than she could sort that out, Jesse bent to resettle his armload of items in the trunk. His other hand shot out to right the picture on top, and the emotion that transformed his face startled Genny more than the loud crack of thunder the next second. What was it she spied there? Something sharper than mere sorrow...

"Is that...Emma?" The question wended its way out of her with as much subtlety as a strumpet sallying down the street.

Soon as she spoke the name, a shutter came down over Jesse's face. He shut the lid and straightened. "You need anything before I go out to the barn?"

His dismissal stung, right when she'd let her guard down. "Will you tell me what happened?" She leaned forward as he walked around the bed. "You said earlier, when we talked prior to the ceremony, that Wade has been looking for a chance to bring Charles to justice. That this would be our chance to stop him from hurting others."

"That's right, and for now, that's all you need to know."

Stonewalled—exactly as she'd been with her father and then Charles when her requests or needs weren't convenient. Did this not intimately involve her, his story intertwining with hers? She had shared her own tragic circumstances—well, at least the basics. Why couldn't he?

As Jesse pulled a coat off a hook near the door and shrugged into it, Genny held her hands open. "I'd just like to know what else Charles is guilty of."

"Stay," he said to Toby, who was watching with ears perked. Jesse put his hat on, tipped his head to her, and turned for the door. Thankfully, it closed with a latch instead of the plank that required bolting from the inside like most cabins.

Was he not even going to tell her goodnight? Because she'd dared to ask a question? "Wait." Genny pushed herself upright on the bed. "Please don't go out there. It's storming. You shouldn't have to spend the night in the barn." *Our wedding night*—though she couldn't bring herself to say it. Doing so seemed absurd given the current mood.

Not looking back, Jesse let himself out with a rush of wind.

After the door closed behind him, Genny sat unmoving in the wedding dress she'd now have to sleep in. Tears of regret filled her eyes. How had they so quickly gone from a pleasant getting-to-know-you conversation—even an underlying awareness of each other, if she hadn't misread him—to the dreadful silence she seemed to earn from all the men in her life?

CHAPTER 10

*J*esse hadn't gotten out of Hebrews 13 again last night. There was too much there to think about which applied to his current circumstances—and the verses smote his conscience for his abrupt exit when Genny questioned him about Charles and Emma.

> Let brotherly love continue.
> Be not forgetful to entertain strangers: for
>   thereby some have entertained angels
>   unawares.
> Remember them that are in bonds, as bound
>   with them; and them which suffer adversity,
>   as being yourselves also in the body.
> Marriage is honourable in all...

Everything there told him he had done the right thing in marrying Genny, but he chafed at the forced proximity. Just as he had with Emma.

He washed in the frigid mountain runoff of the stream as the sun bled its oath to gift them with a fair day over the horizon, and then he drew a bucket of water to start breakfast. He'd make porridge today. It was really no trouble to double whatever he cooked. In fact, having to provide for someone else pushed him to prepare it better. Maybe while they ate, he and Genny could get back to that comfortable sort of exchange they'd enjoyed before she'd brought up Emma. No...he had done that, hadn't he? So whatever followed was on him.

As he trod the leaf-strewn path to the cabin, Jesse navigated the branches last night's storm had hurled to the ground. He mounted the steps quietly so as not to wake Genny in case she'd managed to achieve a restful slumber. He knocked softly. When there was no reply, he worked the latch and pushed open the door. As he did, there was a scrape and a crash, followed by a small cry. Jesse let the bucket thud to the floorboards and hurried inside.

Toby met him halfway across the floor, running a circle around his legs.

Genny sprawled on the bed, which sat slightly crooked. Her splinted leg lay atop the rumpled quilt, while the other dangled over the far side. As his gaze traveled beyond her, he froze.

The lid of his trunk stood open.

Some angel.

By the look on her face, even before he rounded the bed, he knew what he'd find—Emma's portrait, painted for their wedding, lying on the floor. Trying not to look at it, he bent and picked it up and replaced it in the trunk. "Satisfy your curiosity?" he asked as he shut the lid. He turned to face her, cold all over.

"I-I'm sorry, Jesse. I shouldn't have pried. I just wanted to know if she was who I thought she was." Balancing in a semi-upright position, Genny held out an entreating hand.

He should've taken it. Should have helped her settle back on the mattress. But he didn't. He just glared at her. "How could you have gone into my personal things?"

As if apologizing for his master's accusing tone, Toby darted over and licked Genny's fingers. She gave him a reassuring pat, then tucked her hand in her lap.

"I said I'm sorry, and I am." Genny's hair frizzed about her face, disheveled from her braid. Innocent-looking in her white dress as a girl, but he refused to allow her show of vulnerability to soften him, even when she blinked back tears. "Can you blame me for wanting to know more about the man I married? About his life?"

"If I recall, it wasn't me you wanted to know about last night. It was Charles." Jesse crossed the floor to the sideboard. He tossed Toby a strip of bacon left over from the previous morning. The Irish setter chomped down on the treat and settled back on the rug beside the bed to devour it.

Genny looked over Toby, seeking Jesse's gaze. "Of course, I want to know about you, but how can I if you won't tell me?"

Did he have to spell it out? He wasn't ready to bare his soul. Might never be. He collected the water pitcher and one of Mrs. Paschal's biscuits wrapped in a napkin and brought both to her bedside table. Disgusted with her as he was, he could hardly leave her without food and water. "Here. I'll be at the creek closer to the road this morning. I'll leave the door cracked so Toby can nose his way out. Send him if you need me." He turned for the exit.

"You're leaving? But I need your help with…"

Jesse whipped back around to face her. "With what?"

She stared at him a moment with huge eyes. Had he snapped that much? Well, she couldn't go through a man's things and expect him to thank her.

She sagged against the headboard. "Nothing."

He grabbed a biscuit for himself, his canteen, and his rifle on the way out. He'd planned to sow the rest of the wheat—the damp soil would be perfect—but now all he wanted was to be as far from the cabin as possible. He'd placer test that bend in the creek with the deep banks, where it curved near the trail. Best place to check for a gold-bearing layer, according to what he'd picked up from local miners. Whatever flakes erosion might wash into the stream that didn't sink to the bottom would be caught at the turn with other rock and mineral particles, forming a gravel layer. If he found good color, he could move his sluice box over there.

He swung by the barn for his forearm-length shovel and tin pan prior to setting out down the lane. A mourning dove hooted its lonely call from an overhanging pine branch as dawn's gentle golden fingers pushed back night's shadows. His boots tromping the red Georgia clay, Jesse washed down bites of biscuit with metallic water from his canteen.

A quarter mile or so before reaching the road, he turned left toward the creek. He skirted a mini-forest of low-growing mayapple plants—innocuous-looking with their white flowers peeking out but poisonous even to touch—sheltered by a stand of ash and sycamore trees. The Dutchman's breeches that flourished near maples and earthen ledges were also putting out this time of year, their snowy flowers resembling upside-down women's pantaloons. Both plants put Jesse in mind of the woman he'd come here to avoid.

But upon reaching Baggs Branch, he soon settled into the rhythm of scraping up creek-bed samples, plunking the contents of his shovel into the pan with a wet slurp, and swirling water over the sediment. The process mercifully blocked out all other thoughts as he studied each panful for the bright flakes that would make Wade a wealthy man. If Jesse found anything of note, his former brother-in-law could direct his resources to a more serious mining endeavor. It was the least Jesse could do to help him out, much as he owed the man. Although...Jesse himself would be long gone to Mississippi by the time serious money started rolling in. Jesse's gold was adventure, freedom.

And here he'd gone and sacrificed both. And for a woman he knew so little of. Well, he knew she'd lived a hard life. She'd said she was merely curious about Emma, but could she have been after more in his trunk than information about his personal life? She talked like she was a godly woman, but what sins might lurk in her past?

Let brotherly love continue.

Jesse paused to wipe a splash of creek water from his cheek. Had he shown brotherly love by stalking out on her—not just this morning, but also last night? He'd been set to make things right between them, and then he'd gotten steamed and gone and done the same thing all over again. He'd almost made her cry, for Pete's sake. Maybe she had after he'd left. That was no way to treat a sister—much less, a wife. Even a wife in name only. His father would say he ought to treat Genny as his sister in Christ. His mother...well, his mother would ask if he'd lost his ever-loving mind. His own opinion tottered somewhere between the two.

Jesse leaned his shovel on the creek bank and lifted his hat to swipe his hair back. Genny had been wrong to pry, but he'd been doubly so to turn his back on her when she was an invalid in his house. He'd probably made her feel worse than Charles ever did. His stomach sickened so fast at that, Mrs. Paschal's biscuit practically went rancid in his stomach.

He couldn't leave this unsettled until dinner. By Jove, he was going to have to march back to the cabin and talk to her right now. He left the pan and shovel sheltered under an overhanging root and with rifle and canteen set off through the forest, making no effort at stealth—until a flash of movement ahead on the trail halted his steps. A man on a horse.

Jesse leveled his rifle and crept through some pines the full limbs of which swooshed in the breeze. The lanky stranger possessed a long red beard and rode a dapple-gray stallion. Jesse hadn't gotten a look at the intruder on the ridge the day

Genny showed up, but hadn't the horse been that color? Could be coincidence.

Not likely.

He cut down an embankment and across onto the path ahead of the rider. Might be less than mannerly to greet callers at gunpoint, though plenty of suspicious miners did so these days. Some shot first and asked questions later. But he was more concerned about the young woman he was sheltering in his cabin—the one he'd just treated poorly himself.

Jesse spoke as the man pulled up reins. "Howdy. Can I help you?"

The man's brows disappeared beneath the brim of his holey black hat. "Well, now. Good mornin' to you too. I'm guessin' by your warm welcome, you ain't William Bradshaw."

"What business you got with Bradshaw?" Jesse knew the man. He'd be willing to bet this unwelcome visitor didn't.

"Got a delivery from town for 'im." Redbeard patted his bulging saddlebag. "New screen for his sluice box."

Jesse lowered his rifle a few inches. "His lot is on Lily Creek, a few miles south." He jerked his head to the right. "But I reckon you knew that."

Redbeard drew back his shoulders. "No need to be unfriendly, now. Been mining up near Headquarters, or Licklog, as some calls it, but my luck's been more akin to Reverend O'Barr's than Benny Parks's."

Jesse grunted in acknowledgment. Much like Martin and Hanks, the two men had gotten into an altercation after the preacher allowed Parks to lease the land and mine west of the Chestatee where he'd found the nugget that started the mad scramble for gold—and then gotten mad when Parks struck it rich and refused to sell the land rights back. "So now you're helping Bradshaw?"

"Nope. Making deliveries for Mr. McLaughlin." A merchant in Auraria. "But I'd be open to prospectin' down this way, should the occasion arise. Your plot backs up to the Etowah, right? You seen any color?"

Jesse flipped his rifle to ride his shoulders but maintained his stance in the middle of the lane, feet planted wide. "Nothing to mention."

"Shame. Seems prime gold land." Redbeard shifted in the saddle with a creak of leather. "Been here long?"

"Since February." This man sure was curious. Jesse eased the rifle back down to his side, not liking to feel exposed. "Why do you ask?"

"Oh, just wonderin' if you needed a partner. Takes a man a while to test out stretches of creek and river both." He cocked one russet eyebrow. "Unless you got some boys helpin' you already. Brothers, mebbe?"

Jesse's uneasy gut prompted his reply. "I got a partner. He's often here with me and the missus."

"A missus, huh?" One side of the man's mouth split in a smile that was more of a leer. "Sounds like you got you a sweet spot."

More like a rock and a hard place. "That's right. So I'm not looking to take on any help." He gestured up the trail. "Best be on your way. Save Bradshaw a day of work if you get that screen to him this morning."

"I reckon that's so." Redbeard tipped his hat. "Sorry for the intrusion, Mr....?" He let his apology trail off with the lilt of a question on the title.

Jesse responded to the part that was not a query. "No problem." He stared the man down until he flashed an ugly grin and pulled on his left lead, circling his dapple gray to head back the way he'd come. Jesse remained in place, watching until he rode out of sight.

He'd best make up with Genny...because he wouldn't be sleeping in the barn again. Tonight or any other night.

~

"*F*orgot to make the coffee."

Those were the words Jesse uttered after he knocked and banged back into the cabin an hour after he'd left Genny with a dry biscuit and some water.

"Y-you came back...for coffee?" She hesitated to ask, the way he still avoided her gaze while he set about starting a blaze on the hearth. She arranged herself in bed as neatly as she could, given her desperate need for a bath and the rumpled state of her borrowed dress.

"And porridge. I think I want porridge." He turned from adding kindling, finally meeting her gaze. "I shouldn't have left you without feeding you proper."

Was that his way of apologizing? She'd work with it. For now. "And I shouldn't have gone into your trunk."

A brief nod, and he reached for the bellows. "Changed my mind about panning too. I'll be working in the garden today."

Something in his tone made her frown, but questions didn't seem to work so well with this man. Instead, she let misgiving color her agreement. "Very well..."

After a minute of coaxing the fire, he hung the bellows up and stood, brushing off his brown wool trousers. "I met a man on the trail who said he was looking for a miner who lives down on Lily Creek. Only, I don't think that's what he was really about."

Genny blinked, then widened her eyes. "You think he was looking for me?"

"I didn't like his mannerism."

Whatever that meant exactly, Genny was not to know, for Jesse bustled about the hearth like an industrious housewife, fixing their porridge and brewing their coffee, then sweetening both with cinnamon and honey. As delicious as it was, and as much as he finally talked, the sense of security Genny craved continued to elude her. For he said little of consequence. He detailed everything he planned to plant that year and how he'd go about planting it. Perhaps he thought she might help with some of the gardening when she got better—assuming she was still here. But the way he prattled on, he seemed almost... nervous. As though he was avoiding the real topic.

It wasn't until he went outside that the reason for the swirling in Genny's stomach became clear. Jesse was acting like Charles did after a disagreement—as though nothing of importance had occurred. True, Jesse had acknowledged he shouldn't have abandoned her, but he still hadn't apologized. Not really.

She couldn't decide which was worse, his silence or his manufactured cheer. Both discounted her feelings. Neither provided any resolution.

And why was she more worried about Jesse's responses to her than the fact that a man had probably come today hunting her?

So...she devoted the afternoon to that concern. Toby wasn't even there to distract her, for Jesse had called him outside while Jesse planted wheat. Presumably, Toby was to survey the perimeter and sound any necessary alarm, since the friendly setter was clearly not a guard dog.

By the time Jesse came in for supper, her stomach was in a knot, her leg ached, and the rest of her body protested two days of sitting in bed. She declined any of the leftovers Mrs. Paschal had packed for them.

"Will you at least have some tea and cake?" His hair darkened by his wash in the creek and spiking on the ends, Jesse peered at her with what appeared to be genuine concern. That earnestness was hard to deny. Reluctantly, she agreed, and he sat with her while they ate. "Tell me about your childhood. Where are you from? You say things differently at times."

Genny managed a slight smile. She didn't want to talk about herself, not after a day of such *whimmy* emotions. Whimmy—

changeable—now that was a Cornish term. But had she not wanted to get to know this new husband of hers? The least she could do was reciprocate. She told him about growing up in Cornwall, her mother's death on the voyage to the North Carolina mines, and then her father being hired by Charles.

"I'm sorry." He stared at her, leaving the bones and some scraps of chicken on his plate.

"For what?" Had something in her story prompted the apology she'd sought earlier?

"The loss of your mother. Were you close?"

"Very close. She's the one who taught me about God." Genny fought the tears rising in her eyes.

Surely, Jesse would understand her sense of loss, but it felt cheap to share it with him after his insensitivity today. If only her mother were here now. She would know how to advise Genny. If she were here, Genny wouldn't lack words for the sad decline of her life after her mother's shroud-wrapped form was thrown to the sea. Had she a mother's guidance, Genny might even compare to the perfect Georgia belle Emma Coulter Holden's portrait verified she had been.

Genny blinked rapidly and set her mug atop her plate on the table. "I'm sorry. I'm very tired. I think I want to rest if that's all right." Even as she said it, she felt guilty for not answering his questions. She always tried to do what was expected of her because she always seemed to have a lot to make up for. In this case, being thrust upon a grieving widower.

But Jesse rose immediately and raised the quilt over her legs. "Of course. Is there anything you need?"

Yes. She needed out of this dress of Mrs. Paschal's that she was ruining, its seams pulling at her back and arms as she lay down. But she couldn't bring herself to ask him. Genny merely shook her head. When he hovered a moment, she closed her eyes until he went away.

Small bumps and scrapes attested to his setting the hearth

area to rights. When would he finally go to the barn? Suddenly, he moved toward her, and her heartbeat kicked into a mazurka. Genny squeezed her eyes shut. But he crossed behind the bed and got something out of his trunk. She peeked as he walked with it to the door, Toby following. Was that...a fiddle case?

She struggled upright, but the door swung shut behind him. She sat in the purpling twilight, breathing shallowly and listening, until a long note resonated from the porch. Middle C. It vibrated through her being with a richness and purity that anchored her, as grounding as the firm earth and the whisper of grass under her feet. Then a string of several notes formed a chord. A few moments of tuning, and then he started to play the song she'd performed the night she met him, "Highland Mary."

Her hand went to her mouth. Not only was this man a surveyor and a farmer...he was a musician. And a gifted one, at that. He played with precision, but what's more—he played with soul. The mournful and wistful tunes he spun so drew her that it was all she could do to stay abed. Had he chosen this moment to reveal his talent because he wanted her to know they shared more in common than she realized?

CHAPTER 11

*J*esse closed his eyes and gave himself to the melody and the soft breeze caressing his face. The music always said what he could not. Tonight the melodies he chose were plaintive rather than joyful. The weight on his chest called for introspection.

Despite his best efforts to smooth things over with Genny, she'd withdrawn, lying down and closing her eyes, though he'd felt her watching him as if waiting for him to be gone. He hadn't known how to tell her she'd have to endure his presence from this night forward. The sting of her rejection tripped a deeper hurt that he didn't want to examine. So he put it to music. But while the old ballads and laments might give voice to the ache, they failed to ease it.

At last, he turned to the hymn his father often had them sing at the close of his services. *Rock of Ages, cleft for me, let me hide myself in thee...*

Near the end of the first stanza, his fingers almost slipped from the bow, for a sweet soprano drifted from the cabin. *Save from wrath and make me pure.* Toby even picked up his head.

The Songbird of Auraria completed Jesse's tune in a way he hadn't even realized had been lacking.

Somehow, he made it through three verses, but his mind and spirit were no longer floating over the mountains with the music. Everything in him was keenly attuned to the woman in the cabin behind him. She ought to be on the bench beside him, breathing the clean, sweet air and blessing God's creation with her voice. Surely, that was the only arena deserving.

When he finished, he lowered the instrument and swallowed past the thickness in his throat. The notes seemed to linger in the darkening dusk. With reverence, he replaced the fiddle in its case. The bench scraped as he rose and went inside and closed the door behind Toby. In the faint light from the windows, Genny's pale face glowed. She sat upright, her posture as straight as she could make it, watching him expectantly.

Jesse cleared his throat. "That was beautiful."

"So was your playing. I had no idea you were a musician."

"Oh, I'd hardly call myself that. It was just a way to channel my restlessness when I was a boy. My father's idea, since my mother didn't like me always wandering off and getting into trouble." Why he shared that, he wasn't sure. Jesse secured the fiddle case in the trunk and went to light the lamp.

Genny shifted to follow his movements. "I'd say, you're too humble."

"Can a man be too humble?" He shot her a look as he adjusted the wick.

Her eyebrows rose at that. "'Rock of Ages' was my mother's favorite song." She brushed her hand across her cheek.

Jesse would give his eye teeth to have a mother who provoked such sweet memories. "My father's too." It would seem both of them had one good parent—another thing in common.

"Tell me about..." Genny seemed to catch herself, and her gaze dropped to her lap as he lit the candle at her bedside.

He had done that—made her afraid to ask anything about him. His chest squeezed. He pulled the chair close to the bed and leaned forward, arms on his legs. "I reacted too strongly earlier when you looked in the trunk."

"No, you didn't." She shook her head with quick movements, her gaze lifting to his. "It was terribly invasive of me. I know better...because I've never been allowed to keep anything to myself. So the last thing I should have done was take that privacy from another person..." Her sentence caught on a quavery breath.

"I told you I forgave you." Without forethought, Jesse reached for her hand. How small and smooth it was.

"It wasn't that." She squeezed his fingers, but her throat worked, and she averted her eyes.

"What, then?" He fought to keep the frustration from his tone. He didn't know how to do this, didn't understand women.

Genny pulled back and settled the quilt over her lap. The silence stretched between them, long as a full skein of thread through a spinning wheel.

Awareness pricked Jesse. Something more than his awkwardness or abruptness made her afraid to speak her mind. A compassion flowed over him that was not his own, and words came from somewhere—he knew not where. "Tell me. I won't be angry." Was that his voice, so gentle?

Her gaze flashed up to him. "It was the way you left, and then...how quiet you were." Her hand rose and flittered about her throat. "I could abide railing better than silence. My father...and Charles...that was their way when I displeased them."

Remember them that are in bonds, as bound with them; and them which suffer adversity, as being yourselves also in the body. Surely, such behavior bound and controlled. He hung his head a moment, then looked back up. Honesty was what was needed here.

"I didn't mean to hurt you. I'm just not good with women. With talking. With emotions." Jesse ran a hand through his hair. In seeking to allay Genny's discomfort, he stirred his own agitation. "And when I'm upset, I need time to think. That way, I can come back and be normal again."

She sucked in a soft breath and eased forward. "But don't you see? Ignoring something hurtful should not be normal. You can't act like nothing happened. Not when there's no resolution, no real apology."

He stared at her a minute. The pleading in her face—so earnest it was almost fearful—diluted the urge that rose up to defend himself. "And that's what I did." Which was why she hadn't wanted to talk to him tonight. Jesse let out a heavy breath. "I told you I'm not good at this."

"You were married before." Genny surveyed him with a gentle but expectant expression.

"And I was bad at it before." He puffed out a laugh, which she possessed the grace to join with a chuckle of her own. Some of the tension eased.

"Why do you think that is?"

Jesse blinked at her as that query stabbed somewhere below the breastbone. She was asking questions he should have long ago asked himself. But he'd reached a wall, just as he had when he'd found her with Emma's portrait—the limit of his reserves. Because that wall held back a wave ready to swamp him.

Genny shook herself as if in sudden awareness. "I'm sorry. I usually don't ask so many questions. You just seem to pull them out of me."

He threw her question back at her with a grin. "Why do you think that is?"

She held her hand to her mouth and giggled—such a

girlish sound, his tense shoulders relaxed. "Touché. I will answer. I think it's because you are so different from the men I've known. Quite opposite, in fact. I'm simply trying to understand you."

Was that good or bad? Jesse settled for a half smile. "I didn't realize I was such a mystery."

"Oh, you are. But..." Genny's lashes fluttered. "We did just meet. And we both have mysteries, I think. Things we may not be ready to talk about yet. So I will make you a deal..."

"Another deal?" He cocked up one eyebrow and sat back, crossing his ankle over his knee.

"I will try not to pester you with questions if you will try not to go silent or disappear when you're frustrated."

Jesse curled his fingers under his chin and laid his thumb over his lips for a moment. Then he lowered his hand and held it out toward her. "Sounds like a fair exchange."

The broad smile that lit her face made his heart leap. "Good, then." She slipped her hand into his, and tingles shot all the way to his elbow. He forced himself to pump her hand rather than letting go like it was a lit fuse.

"Very well. Um..." He stood with a little clatter of the chair that made Toby jump. "I've got to go to the barn to—"

"Oh!" Her sudden exclamation stopped him from turning away. "Before you go, would you...do something for me?"

If his eyes weren't deceiving him, her face flushed in the candlelight. "What is it?"

She angled away from him and pointed to her neck. "I'm afraid Mrs. Paschal didn't think about the fact that this dress buttoned in the back." She peeked over her shoulder beneath down-swept lashes. "If you could just get those tiny buttons between my shoulder blades that I can't reach..."

"Of course." What a dunderhead that he hadn't thought of it himself. He'd just let her loll about for a night and a day in the restricting dress she'd been married in. He moved back to her side.

"I'm sorry. I hate to ask." She grimaced as though she'd cave into the mattress. He'd need to tighten the ropes with the key soon, or she might do just that.

"Now this is a case where there's no need to apologize." He reached for the long braid that hung down her back and slid it over her far shoulder. He could almost imagine tugging his fingers along the silky lengths, setting those strawberry-blond tresses free. He swallowed hard. That wasn't where his mind needed to go. Keeping her at arm's length had its benefits.

"I suppose." She kept talking as he worked the tiny buttons that resisted his clumsy fingers. "I don't mean to make you uncomfortable. It's just that the dress is rather tight...hard to sleep in. And I'm afraid in doing so, I'm ruining it."

"There's also no reason to explain."

Her head swiveled around, and she flashed him a wide-eyed look. What had he said to earn that reaction? His fingers stilled as she clamped her mouth shut. "You all right?"

Genny faced the other way again. "Yes. Just realizing I have some things to work on too."

Had she felt the need to justify everything she needed up to this point? Pondering that helped keep his mind off the soft, bare skin that appeared down to the top of her cotton chemise...where he stopped unbuttoning. "That far enough?" He hoped so.

"Yes. Thank you." She faced him with a tentative smile, holding the dress closed at her neck.

Jesse took a step back. "You need your things?" They'd left her belongings in the saddlebags rather than him unpacking them in a drawer so she could access them more easily while she was bedridden.

"Please." She waited until he laid the leather bags beside

her on the mattress to thank him and add, "Now I can finally change into something comfortable."

Guilt smote him. The first night, she'd been so exhausted, she'd slept in her dress, and last night, he'd left her in Mrs. Paschal's. Some gentleman he'd been. But that raised another concern. "About that..." He shuffled his feet and hung his thumbs on his suspender hooks.

"Yes?" Her query hitched up a bit with alarm.

"I'm going to fetch my bedroll and Bible from the barn, but I'm not going to stay there."

"Y-you're not?" This question trailed off in volume.

Jesse shook his head. "Not after that stranger came a-callin' today." When her eyes went wide, he splayed his fingers in her direction. "Don't worry. I'll sleep by the hearth. But I think it's wise if I'm in the cabin...from now on out."

She didn't speak. Her eyebrows didn't settle.

Then it hit him. He'd told her, not asked her. His shoulders drooped as he released a breath. "That is...if that's all right with you. I realize it alters the terms of our original agreement."

Finally, she nodded, still holding her dress in place.

Jesse turned and hurried from the cabin, but her agreement left him far from relieved. If he couldn't leave...if he couldn't wall her out with silence...how was he going to keep the distance he needed to avoid eventually hurting her? Or himself.

~

The fifth day after Genny's fall, she didn't know which she yearned for more—the splint and bandages to come off or a good hair-washing. She settled for the one Jesse already knew she'd need him to provide. And what heaven it was to sit for an hour without her leg bound up. She used modesty to hide the fact that it was still swollen and bruised, and after she rewrapped it, she managed to persuade him to help her to the front porch. She sat on the bench against the cabin with her foot on an upside-down bucket.

There, her mood soared with the birdsong. In a brilliant welcome to May, the colors and smells outside the cabin burst upon her senses with overwhelming vividness. Beyond the patch where Jesse set out cabbages, flame azaleas and white rhododendrons brightened the greening tree line. And she could make out the music of the creek above the sounds of his hoeing. She sang a little ditty about an English maid that made Jesse stop and grin at her as he leaned on his hoe. And that made her forget the next line.

But by the time he half carried her back inside, the ache in her leg had her clenching her teeth. She managed to keep a moan from escaping as he eased her onto the bed, but there wasn't much she could do about the perspiration that sprang to her brow.

He surveyed her with a flash of concern. "I'll brew your tea."

"Don't bother. I used the last of it this morning."

Jesse removed his hat and swiped his forehead with his sleeve. "Didn't Mrs. Paschal say she was going to call again?"

Genny settled against the pillow. "In three days."

"Three days, and this is five. Where is she?" He gestured with his hat in his hand.

"I suppose something detained her." She arranged her skirt over her legs. "Before I left, I heard there was cholera north of town. She could've gotten called away."

"And Wade said he'd check on us at the end of the week. So what are we going to do?"

Was that concern on his face...or frustration? She could read him better every day, but there were still times his restlessness bled through his polite resolve. They'd eased into a routine, him spending most of his time working outside the cabin or panning within earshot, them sharing safe conversation about music and mining and childhood adventures over meals. He'd read the Bible before bed while she mended something. Then he'd say good night, extinguish the lamps, and wrap in his blanket next to the hearth's glowing embers. The first night, she'd barely slept a wink, so unsettling did she find a man's presence in the room. But soon enough, his deep, even breathing lulled her to sleep, his presence a defense against whatever creatures made the sounds in the forest.

Concern or frustration—she dismissed either with a wave. "It's not that bad. I'm sure once I rest, it will be fine."

Jesse stared at her as if unconvinced, and then he went to hang his hat by the door. "Very well, but if it's not, I'll ride into town in the morning."

Genny's spine went stiff as cold fear washed her. "No!"

"I could be there and back in half a day." He turned back from unwrapping a pone of cornbread. "Even if Mrs. Paschal is away, I should be able to get something from Linton & Bacon. Their sign said *drugs, medicines, and dyes.*"

"You can't leave me here alone!"

His jaw firmed. "I'm not leaving you to suffer either."

"What if that man comes back?" She clutched the edge of her quilt.

"I'd leave you my pistol, loaded. And the dog, of course."

"I've never shot a gun. And what if there were more than one man?"

"Genny." His gravelly tone silenced her—not because it was rough, but because of the emotion behind the roughness.

She went still. What was that? Protectiveness? Or control? How did one tell the difference?

Jesse dumped lima beans from a glass jar into a pot and shot her a level look. "I promised to take care of you, and I will. We'll see how you are tomorrow. No need to worry about it now."

She nodded, but her stomach was so queasy at the thought of him leaving her here, injured and unable to fend for herself, that she could barely choke down the ham and cornbread. She ate a few spoonfuls of beans and lowered her plate on the rug. Toby streaked over with his long tail flopping back and forth and gobbled down her leftovers.

When Jesse lit the lamp and opened his Bible an hour later, Genny bit her tongue to keep from asking him to read aloud. He was so private, he'd surely consider his faith a personal thing. But maybe the words in the thick book would comfort her like the hymns did—for despite her brave words about her leg improving, it didn't. It throbbed with a vengeance.

And despite her best attempts, she kept knotting and breaking her thread as she attempted to stitch together a small tear in one of Jesse's shirts. Finally, she gave up and put the mending aside. She rested her head on the wall and closed her eyes, determined not to let out a whimper.

When Jesse laid his hand on her right knee, she jumped a country mile. Her eyes shot wide, but he stood over her with his gaze trained on the Bible he held in his other hand, as if oblivious to the impropriety of his touch.

"I'm reading in Hebrews. Listen to this." His voice deepened. "'Wherefore lift up the hands which hang down, and the feeble knees; and make straight paths for your feet, lest that which is lame be turned out of the way; but let it rather be healed.'"

A tingle of amazement traveled through Genny. The way he read it, the authority that rang through his words, he might as well have been the preacher rather than his father. Or was it the words themselves that held the authority?

His fingertips still resting on her skirt, Jesse raised his chin and closed his eyes. "Lord, this we ask in Jesus's name. Amen." He opened his eyes and stared at her a moment, then he abruptly turned and strode across the cabin.

Genny looked after him with her mouth ajar. So many questions bubbled up, they almost choked her. But she didn't dare to ask them any more than she dared to let on that the bone in her leg throbbed like a rotten molar.

When night descended and Jesse and Toby found their repose, she eased with inheld breath from her back to one side and then the other, but sleep eluded her. With naught else to focus on in the dark, the pain seemed to magnify. The man had just prayed for her healing. Why wouldn't God answer? No, not *the man*. Her husband. And the way that gesture made her feel was more confusing than the reason she was here in the first place.

At last, Genny started to drift off. But just as she was about to sink into sleep, a soft creak from above her made her eyes fly open. As she watched, held fast in the grip of terror, the shutter slowly swung inward. Moonlight filtered in, and framed in the opening were a pair of glowing eyes...over Charles's leering grin.

Genny shot upright. "Jesus!" She had meant to say *Jesse*. How had the other come out?

But somehow, Jesse was by her side. "What is it?" He fumbled for her in the darkness, his hand landing on her arm.

She grasped onto him. "At the window! He's at the window!"

Fast breathing. Footsteps. But the window was shut...until Jesse cracked open the shutter. He closed it again the next moment. "There's nothing out there."

"He was there..." She panted in the darkness.

"Who?" Jesse sat beside her and reached for her hand, while Toby huffed and whined and licked her other one.

Genny covered her face. She couldn't say it. Was she losing her mind, the isolation and confinement doing her in? "It was just a dream." She said it aloud to convince him as well as herself.

Jesse's fingers brushed hers, urging them away. Then he pressed his fingers to her forehead. "You're hot. Do you feel fevered?"

She shivered in the damp chill of the evening, in the aftermath of her fright. "I'm freezing."

He drew the quilt up over her. For propriety's sake, she wore her chemise and pantalets under her gown, but the layers weren't enough. She burrowed against his shoulder. For a moment, he froze. Then his arms slid around her with that scent of pine and smoke and man, and her tears wet his soft cotton shirt. Her forehead rested perfectly in the curve of his neck. Awkwardly, he patted her shoulder.

"I'm sorry." She sniffled. "I don't know what's wrong with me."

"You've had quite a time of it. I'd say you have every right to cry." He squeezed her forearms, then rubbed them briskly, warming her. "Your leg is hurting, isn't it? I heard you stirring through the night."

And here she'd thought he'd been sleeping. "I…" After that prayer, in his arms which made her feel secure for the first time since her mother died, she found she couldn't lie to him. "Maybe a little."

He drew in an unsteady breath and began to unwind his arm from behind her.

Genny snagged at his shirt before she could stop herself. "Don't go."

"I don't want to bump you if I fall asleep, but I'll be right here. I'll move my pallet to the rug beside you."

She couldn't bring herself to protest. But what a weakling he must think her. And what a thing to expect of him, sleeping beneath her with the dog. Worst of all, that she had trusted him in her bed. What had she been thinking?

That his mere presence by her side was enough. Enough to quiet her fears, her pain, so she could drift back to sleep.

But when she woke to a sliver of sunlight streaking past the shutter onto her forehead, he was gone. A pistol with a note sat beside her bed.

CHAPTER 12

Genny's prediction about Agnes Pascal being called out of town had proven true—though for scarlet fever, not typhoid. After learning of her absence, Jesse pushed through the crowd that gathered on the porch of the Nuckolls Hotel around former Vice President John C. Calhoun anytime he was in residence. The man visited Auraria periodically to oversee the progress at his mine—progress that was quite good, if the more than nine-pound chunk of gold recently uncovered there served as any indication. Jesse didn't pause to determine whether the nugget or states' rights was the subject of conversation before he headed to the drugstore. Shameful, how both Calhoun and his opponent, Andrew Jackson, were determined to expel the Cherokees from the state despite the Supreme Court's decree that they were entitled to federal protection.

At the moment, Jesse was more interested in protecting the woman struggling to heal back at his cabin. And protecting her looked like leaving her for half a day, despite her protestations. Yes, leaving made him nervous. But her suffering and the possible onset of fever last night made him more so. He wouldn't fail her as he had Emma.

He was low on supplies, so he made a quick stop for the basics at the cash grocery owned by Major John C. Powell, who also operated an assaying and refining lab with his partner.

As Jesse tucked his purchases in his saddlebags, the confectionary down the street drew his eye. Perhaps something special from the shop would soothe Genny's ire upon his return. It was not yet noon. There should be time for one more quick stop. Jesse buckled the pouches and hurried in that direction.

As he stepped into the street, he bumped shoulders with a passing man—young, stout, and wearing a scowl.

"Watch where you're going," the stranger practically growled.

"Sorry." Sight of the rifle the man held had Jesse raising his hands.

With a huff, the young man crossed the street toward Towns & Riley, where the postmaster, Robert Ligon, sat visiting with another man on a bench out front. Jesse paused on the boardwalk in front of the confectionary to glance back. The angry man leaned one foot on the bench, though his manner was anything but casual. The nature of his harsh demand to the postmaster got lost in the rattle of wheels and plodding of hooves from the street.

"Looks like trouble brewing." A middle-aged woman in mourning clothes stopped beside Jesse, following his gaze.

He gave a nod. "Any idea what about?"

"No telling." Her double chin wagged as she shook her head. "There have been two horses stolen from town inside a week, and folks are on edge about the announcement that the new courthouse will be built north of here, where Parks found his nugget, rather than in Auraria."

"Are you serious?" Jesse gaped at the woman, woefully behind on the news. "But why?"

She shrugged. "'Twould seem the land Auraria sits on was fraudulently chosen for a man who posed as married to get an extra draw. His deed will be voided."

Jesse threw out his hand. "Is there no end to the shenanigans that go on here?"

"Apparently not. I suppose it's the center of the county, and there's a good spring, though the roads are so bad, how will anyone be able to get there?" She gestured down the street to where the recently arrived stagecoach from Athens unloaded.

They turned as the postmaster's voice carried across the street. "You never paid the postage for your lottery sheets, so how can I give them to you?"

The younger man with his back to the street held his rifle in both hands. "I'm not bound to pay as I did not get them."

A few more heated exchanges from the men across the way and Jesse rolled his eyes. "Are you headed into the confectionery?" He touched his companion's elbow. "Now might be a good time if so."

"I couldn't agree more, sir. My niece loves the rock candy, and she's coming to visit this week."

Jesse tilted his head. "In that case, might you advise me what a young woman might like best?" He'd never been inside the fancy shop himself, but if the tantalizing smells coming from the interior as he held the door were any indication, he'd be taking home more than just treats for Genny.

"Why, of cour—" Profanity from across the street stopped her agreement. The widow slanted an imperious glance over her shoulder. "Well, I'll be. Such language with ladies and children around."

Ligon was on his feet, hands in his vest pockets.

"Don't you call me that ever again." The stranger who had bumped Jesse stood as stiff as a poker.

The postmaster lowered his arms to his sides and answered.

Quick as a snake striking, the younger man's rifle popped up and hit Ligon on the left temple. A crack. Gasps. The postmaster crumpled to the porch with blood gushing from his ears and nose. The widow beside Jesse covered her mouth as the young man strode away with his rifle over his shoulder.

"Get him!" The cry from an unknown man who vaulted onto the porch to check on the postmaster sent several others into motion, sprinting after the culprit. Another went for the sheriff.

"Oh my. Oh dear. Have we just witnessed a murder?" Jesse's companion dug in her reticule until she came out with a lacy bag of smelling salts. "I fear I must sit."

Jesse guided her toward a bench in front of the shop, sweet treats forgotten in the ensuing hubbub. Indeed, the woman had gone quite pale even as she pressed her bag of herbs to her nose. No doubt, the tightness of the corset that restrained her ample girth curtailed normal breathing. He knelt beside her. "Can I get you anything?"

"A sip of water would not go amiss." Before Jesse could rise, her hand shot out and clasped his arm. Her blue eyes bore into his with entirely too much admiration. "Thank you, young man."

"Um...of course." The faster Jesse could get away from this unprincipled town and its colorful inhabitants, the better. Wade's little parcel of land was feeling more like a haven and Genny's care like a simple assignment every minute. "I'll see if Mr. Ware can spare us any."

The widow whipped out a black fan and applied it with the force of a blacksmith's bellows, her gaze glued on the arrival of Dr. Ira Foster to the porch of the mercantile opposite while Jesse slipped into the confectionery. He found the proprietor in want of an account of what was transpiring outside, which Jesse was obliged to give while the man poured a glass of water.

"Thank you." Jesse took the drink from him and glanced at some chocolates in a nearby display case. "I'll take two of those." He pointed to the closest choices.

Mr. Ware wrapped the treats, placed them in a tiny box, and handed them to Jesse. He tucked the box in his vest pocket and returned to the woman with her drink. She accepted it as she offered an update on the drama unfolding across the street. "They're taking him to the doctor's office, soon as they can best figure how to transport him. Won't you sit with me a moment while I recover?" She patted the bench next to her as though they were watching a play at the theatre.

"Thanks, but I'd best get home." What had made him think adding a stop for candy was a good idea? Just went to show that he'd best stick to business. "Ma'am..." Jesse lifted his hat and turned to go—right into a man with piercing eyes and a badge on his chest. Sheriff Samuel Jones.

The lawman steadied Jesse by the arms. "Sorry, son, but I'm afraid I'm going to have to ask you to hold that thought. We're looking at assault here. Maybe murder. I'll need to collect statements from all witnesses before they leave town."

Jesse's heart melted about as fast as the chocolate in his pocket. How long would that take? Why had he ever left Genny alone?

~

That Jesse had left food on her bedside table along with the pistol, beside the carved songbird, as well as two buckets of water on the floor did little to alleviate Genny's sense of betrayal. Hadn't she begged him not to leave? Told him she'd never shot a gun? But he'd gone, anyway, and with just a note to say he'd left prior to sunup so he could be back well before dark.

And yet daylight was seeping through the trees like whey through cheesecloth and still no Jesse.

Why did he not wait to see if his prayer had any effect or how she was when she woke? She was much better, thank you very much. Her leg hurt less after her rest, and the chills had abated with her fears. Some faith he showed.

Her anger burned off after the first hour or so, but shame scampered in on its heels. She argued with herself while she sat in the bedside chair doing the mending. Clearly, he didn't care how she felt or what she wanted—even after she'd thrown herself into his arms. And cried like a frightened child. She'd displayed such embarrassing neediness, no wonder he'd fled. She knew better than to require anything from a man.

She must do something to distract herself. She eyed the buckets of water. If she maneuvered just right, she could immerse her scalp and finally wash her hair.

In her convolutions in doing so, she splashed out half the contents on the floorboards and was forced to leave half the soap in her locks, but at least she got rid of some of the grease. Genny couldn't recall the time her hair had ever been so filthy. And she'd thought Jesse might somehow find her pleas appealing?

There she went again, self-recriminating. An idle mind was the devil's workshop—that's what her mother used to say. Jesse had left his Bible lying on the table after his reading last night, only a few steps away. Surely, Genny could hop that far without incident, couldn't she?

She made it and puffed as she eased herself onto the bench, extending her leg so that it barely touched the floor. She couldn't maintain this position for long, not without elevating her foot soon, but the little bit Jesse read aloud the night prior had whet her curiosity.

Where to start? He seemed to be at the end of Hebrews, so

she marked his place and flipped the thin pages gently. There, in the middle...the book of Psalms had stanzas of what looked like poetry...or songs. Short and easy to read. Their descriptions of anguish of the soul, of fleeing a relentless enemy quickly absorbed Genny's attention. How closely this psalmist's experience mirrored hers! And yet he seemed to have found a refuge in God, whom he described as his shield and strong tower.

It was the dog that finally drove her to open the door. Poor Toby, locked up inside all day with her. She didn't stop him from doing his first order of business in the fireplace ashes, but by the time the second order came due, it was clear some intervention would be necessary. The frantic creature whined and repeatedly circled from the door to her and back again. Toby always returned when Jesse called him. But would he do so for her?

Genny sighed and glanced at the bedside table. Should she take the pistol with her, perhaps in her pocket? No. With her luck, she'd stumble and shoot herself.

Her leg beginning to ache, she made it to the threshold without a spill and stood with her hand upon the frame, panting worse than Toby. He scampered up behind her and stuck his nose on the door.

"Now, Toby, soon as you're done, you must come back." She frowned at him and emphasized each word with a pointing finger. "Come when I call you. You hear me? Come." On the last command, she tried to firm her voice like Jesse's.

With a twitch of one doggie brow, Toby rolled his eyes sideways at her and let out an ear-piercing whine.

Genny worked the latch and cracked the door. The dog nearly toppled her in his haste to exit. She peeked out just long enough to watch him streak for a line of blueberry bushes near the cornfield. The sun rode low on the swayback of the mountains, its golden fingers reaching up in a final adieu. Genny shut the door with a small sigh. What would she do if Jesse didn't return tonight? Had something happened to him?

She sucked in breath as a new fear punctured her chest. What if he'd had enough of her and left for good?

His trunk—she could check it. He wouldn't have gone far without his compass.

But first, she had to get the dog—

A flurry of barking and snarling outside the cabin made Genny stiffen. A wild animal? Jesse said he often saw bears, coyotes, bobcats, and panthers, any of which the Irish setter would be no match for. Too late for the pistol. She snatched open the door as a blaze of fur scampered into the tree line.

A shot rang out.

Toby yelped. Last year's carpet of leaves scattered as he skidded.

"No!" Genny's hand flew to her mouth. Someone was out there. And they had shot Jesse's dog! "Toby!" Terror made her voice shriller than usual.

He looked her way.

"Come!" Maybe she could get him inside before the person fired again.

It took a second for her to hear what Toby doubtless already had—hooves pounding up the trail. But rather than dashing for the cabin or accosting the rider, the dog bounded into the forest. Was he crazed by his wound?

Or were there two men? Just as she had feared and said to Jesse. With a sob, Genny slammed and locked the door. It wrenched her heart to leave the dog out there, but she must make herself as secure as possible. And fetch the pistol. If the intruders broke in, maybe she could at least take out one of them.

She whirled and stumble-hopped across the floor. Another

shot exploded outside. Oh! She barely caught herself from putting down her right foot. Had they killed the dog, the better to come for her now?

Genny hopped twice more and fell against the bed with both hands, bracing her leg. Breaths wheezing in and out, she sat and fumbled for the pistol. Nowhere to hide. Best to stay put and ready her aim. The way her hands were shaking, her shot would fly out the window.

She closed her eyes briefly. *God, please. Protect me.*

Hooves galloped all around the house—once, then twice. Yelling and more hooves in the distance. Were they gone? Or was it a trick to get her to open the door?

She waited, breathing fast.

Booted steps pounded up to the porch.

Genny jolted and let out a cry.

The latch rattled. "Genny, are you there? Genny! It's me. Jesse!"

Genny's hands went limp, and the pistol thudded on the floor. By the grace of God, it didn't go off. A moan left her lips.

"Are you all right?" How frantic he sounded. "Can you open the door? If not, stand back. I'll kick it in."

"I'm coming!" Genny skip-stepped through the cabin, skimming, practically floating in the euphoria of relief. She turned the latch and fell into Jesse's arms.

He moved them beyond the doorframe, and then his hands and arms were everywhere, touching and turning and supporting her as he inspected her for injury. "Are you unhurt?"

"I'm fine, but Toby—" She gasped as the Irish setter scuttled up the steps and wrapped his body around Jesse's legs. "I thought he was dead!"

"He was grazed, I think, but we'll tend him. He'll be all right." As the dog ran by them into the cabin, Jesse cupped her face between his hands. "But you...I could have lost you. If I had been a few minutes later..."

"Are they gone?" Genny clung to his shoulders, peering past him into the darkening yard.

He stroked her cheeks. "I think so. I ran off two of them. I'll stand guard tonight, and Wade comes tomorrow. We'll make this right, Genny. I got delayed in town. I'm so sorry." His harried words finally ceased as he laid his forehead against hers.

A rush of thankfulness left her weak. He had come back. He had apologized. Her whole body went limp, and Jesse barely caught her before she crumpled.

He bolted the door behind them and carried her to the bed. After he tenderly deposited her on the mattress, he straightened. Then his brows flew up and he reached into his vest pocket and extracted a small box. "Oh, and I brought you chocolate..."

She lifted her head off the pillow to peer at the contents as he opened the lid. "Creams?"

His face puckered as he surveyed the melted mess inside. "Puddles."

"My favorite." She started to reach for them but then withdrew her hand.

What was she doing? Settling, as she always did. She had allowed gifts or flattery or even fake apologies to salve a hurt or betrayal too many times. She might be injured and stranded, but she didn't have to be that same weak girl so easily bent to the will of a man again.

Jesse's brow furrowed as he pulled the box back. "What's wrong?"

"You left me when I begged you not to, and your dog and I both could have died—that's what's wrong. A couple of melted chocolates won't make me forget that. Neither will a simple 'I'm sorry.'" She crossed her arms, willing herself not to falter when his one brow quirked low. "If you truly want to set things right, I think you owe me an explanation."

Genny braced herself for the onslaught of defensiveness and anger certain to come. By not going along with him, had she just made her situation immeasurably more unbearable?

CHAPTER 13

$\mathcal{A}$n explanation? Jesse gaped at her. She had no idea what she asked of him. He didn't talk about that part of his life...not with anyone.

A whine from Toby broke their locked gazes apart.

Genny sighed and settled with her back against the pillows. "You'd best see to your dog."

"Emma's dog." Jesse wasn't sure what made him say that, except perhaps the way her disappointment already worked to wheedle an explanation from him.

The setter circled on the carpet, trying to lick a nick where blood darkened his fur to a walnut color, far too close to his spine. The sight twisted Jesse's gut. She was right. He could easily have arrived home to find Toby dead and Genny abducted. Or worse. He'd realized it the same the instant he'd heard the shot when he was but a minute from the cabin, which explained the blind panic that seized him.

I could have lost you. Had she heard what he'd let slip out in that moment? Apparently not, and it was just as well.

"Looks like he might need a stitch or two." Setting the box

of chocolates on the bedside table, Jesse knelt and hugged Toby's neck. "You were a good boy. A good boy, huh?"

"I'll take care of him if you can lift him up here." Genny patted the mattress beside her.

Jesse shot her an uncertain glance, then ruffled Toby's fur. "You'd best not get used to this, bud." A lick on the face served as his agreement. As gently as possible, he placed the injured canine next to the woman he'd guarded despite not being a guard dog. Jesse blinked away a sheen of moisture, refusing to look up and display his weakness. Instead, he stroked Toby's side. Emma's dog, indeed. "I've got some dried plantain you could use for a poultice."

Genny nodded. "Just pour some water on that cloth there first and hand it to me, please."

He did as she asked, then brought her the container of the herb he'd learned to collect while surveying near creek banks, dry, and crush for such emergencies.

She caught her lower lip between her teeth as she inspected the dog. "I've never made a poultice."

Jesse looked up from lighting the lamp. "I can do it when I get back, but I need to see to the horse." Another survey of the perimeter would be wise also.

"I'll do it." She spoke in a firm voice.

She was changing. Growing stronger. That was a good thing, even if she sometimes challenged him. Soon, she'd face the world alone. Jesse caught her eye. "Thank you."

Fifteen minutes later, with Perseus tended and the peaceful chirp of crickets and the soft hoot of an owl assuring him all was settled around the house, he returned with his saddlebags over his shoulder to find Toby snuggled up to Genny. Genny had closed and covered the dog's wound with the herbal remedy. The dog lay with her hand on his back, his muzzle on her skirts, and his brown eyes blinking at Jesse, almost as if to say, *look where I am.*

Jesse couldn't refrain from a quick smile as he deposited his load on the table. "I can see we're starting a bad habit here."

"He just needs a little extra care tonight." The wobble in Genny's voice suggested she might too.

Jesse paused the unloading of supplies he'd started. That could wait. Even making her willow bark tea could wait. What couldn't wait was the plea in her voice. She needed to feel safe again. He walked over to the bedside chair and sat down, leaning forward to capture her hand. "Can you forgive me for leaving you today? I was afraid you were worsening. It was a mistake, but one I made with the best intentions."

She blinked, for it was her eyes now that were suddenly swimming with tears. "What intentions?"

Jesse blew out a breath and drew his hand back. She was going to make him spell it out. "To protect you, of course. The way I didn't protect Emma."

Her eyes widened. "You were there when it happened?"

"No." He hesitated. If he didn't share more now, any rapport they'd established would surely be lost. Too much time together lay ahead to allow that to happen. "That was the problem. She wouldn't have even been in town to walk up on the altercation between Charles and Rupert if I *had* been home. I went to survey the new Mississippi Territory. Left her with her brother. Wade."

"But wasn't surveying your job?"

A sudden longing for the shadows of the porch had Jesse scrubbing his hand over his face. It was all he could do not to blow out the candle. "It used to be, but not since I married her last summer. I was working as a bookkeeper for Emma's father in Gainesville. That was where they all wanted me—Emma, my parents, her family—but I couldn't sustain it. So I left."

Her slightly furrowed brow betrayed her curiosity, but she refrained from asking the questions he almost wished she would. He needed someone to guide him through this unchartered territory. Instead, she gave a slight nod and said, "I'm listening."

Jesse rocked slightly back on the rear legs of the chair, crossing his arms. "I was never one to sit at home. I was forever getting into trouble and scrapes, bringing home wild animals, and getting lost in the woods—unlike my brother, Oliver."

Genny's brows rose. "I didn't know you had a brother."

"Six years older, studious, neat—the perfect son, according to our mother. I tried to be like him. I did. I followed him everywhere, him and his friends. One day, when I was supposed to be playing in my room, I snuck out to follow Oliver to his buddy's house." He paused and set the chair down, but her murmur of misgiving prompted him to go on. "I lost sight of them. I tried to take a shortcut and ended up falling down a creek bank and hurting my foot. I managed to limp back home...just as the bishop was arriving." Jesse grimaced and would have left off his story but for Genny's prodding.

"What happened?"

"My mother caught an eyeful of me covered in mud—"

"*Dappered*, we'd call it." She pressed her lips together, flattening a smile.

"Right. Dappered...and told me such a disobedient boy could stay outside until the company left."

Genny gasped. "Didn't you tell her about your foot?"

"I tried, but she didn't believe me. That was, until Oliver came home. He found me outside with my foot twice its normal size." Jesse flinched at the memory.

"Oh no!" She covered her mouth.

"The doctor was sent for, and the bishop witnessed it all." A chuckle that held no mirth escaped him. "To this day, Mother thinks that was the cause of my father losing the appointment to a large church in South Carolina. That's where we lived then. Instead, we had to move to Athens. Oliver is still there. He took over my father's church when our parents relocated to Gainesville."

"Surely, she can't really believe that." Genny's chiding tone brought heat to Jesse's face.

"You don't know my mother." If she did, she would understand how the incident related to his wanderlust. "Let's just say I found the outdoors a lot more pleasant, and I picked an occupation that would allow me to spend most of my time there."

"So you chose to leave rather than being asked to."

The discernment in Genny's quiet statement momentarily knocked the wind from him. How had she instantly put into a succinct sentence what he'd struggled for years to grasp? "I guess that's about right."

"Until your wedding." She pressed her mouth flat and stroked Toby's head.

"Yes. And I should have known I couldn't trade in my compass for a ledger, the fresh air for office walls. Trying to be someone I wasn't was a mistake. One that cost Emma her life."

"But if she loved you—"

"Some things are incompatible." He couldn't let her finish her line of thought. Despite his reluctance to speak of his background, maybe it had been for the best. His story reminded both of them of the temporary nature of their arrangement. He rose. "As long as you're here, though, I have no intention of letting history repeat itself. I can promise you, I'll make better decisions in the future."

~

*W*ade came two days after Genny's scare and a day too late for both Genny and Jesse. That Jesse chafed with the sole burden of guarding her so closely, his veneer of politeness failed to disguise. Resentment also stirred in Genny. Jesse thought he had it hard? Try being confined to the cabin of a stoic bachelor! Any flashes of humor he'd shown her—much less, any affection—he'd subdued since telling her about Emma. About his mother.

Now she knew the nature of the burden Mrs. Paschal had mentioned, but at what cost? He either regretted telling her or regretted the need to, which was worse. For all Genny might admire about the man, his guilt and grief had clearly made him determined not to form attachments. Or maybe Genny just wasn't the sort of woman he was attracted to.

Wade explained the delay in his arrival by relating that the young man who'd assaulted the postmaster had been taken to his jail. A doctor from Gainesville visited Robert Ligon to trephine his skull. He was not expected to survive. "You may be called upon to testify," he told Jesse with a frown.

"I hope not to be here by the time the case goes to trial." Jesse spoke under his breath, but Genny heard him just the same from her chair by the bed.

Very well. Two could play that game. Genny set aside *the man*'s sock she'd been darning. "We understand you have other duties, but we so need your assistance, Wade." She put some honey and some drawl into her voice, drawing his eye. "I'm afraid Jesse's been stretched too thin of late, watchin' out for me by himself."

"What's this?" Wade swiveled to his friend, who bristled at Genny's implication. "Has something happened?"

While cracking peanuts he'd boiled earlier, Jesse related what transpired two nights ago. He concluded by saying, "Genny's right in that they could come back any time. We're both prisoners here, for all intents and purposes."

Did his friend take note of the thinly veiled resentment in his voice?

Wade leaned one elbow on the table and stroked his bristled chin with his other hand. "I believe those two were sent by Larry."

"Why do you say that?" Genny reached down to pet Toby.

"Well, my duties haven't given me freedom to return to Auraria, but I've had someone gathering information for me. Far as I can tell, Charles hasn't left Atlanta. Not that he couldn't have sent men to look for you, Miss Genny, but given how quickly the first pair followed you, as though they set an ambush that day, I think it was Larry. And then maybe they returned to search near where they lost your trail."

"And you're sure Larry is still in the area?" Jesse popped a boiled peanut into his mouth.

Wade gave a nod. "Turns out, he's one of the scarlet fever victims. He's recovering, but slowly. Charles is getting married and leaving for his honeymoon. Both situations buy us time, but clearly, either man can send their lackeys." He sat up straight. "Let me see who I can rustle up when I get home. I'll send a couple of guards who can pretend they're here to help do some mining." When Genny's brows flew up, he held his hand out. "Don't worry. They can camp down by the creek. But it ought to take some pressure off Jesse while I seek some answers."

Jesse sighed and reached out to grip Wade's hand in a shake. "Thanks, my brother."

"Welcome."

"That should help us sleep better at night, but..." Genny hesitated. It went against everything ingrained in her to make demands, but she needed some hope...hope that she might get away from here before her heart was trussed up tight as a salted ham. "What's being done to stop Charles and Larry? They need to be brought to justice as much as the man who attacked Mr. Ligon."

"I understand, Miss Genny." Wade's face twisted with regret —and concern. "I'm working on getting a man under cover at Rupert Hanks's gold mine. Beyond that, well...in all honesty, your marriage might or might not make you safe from Charles, but Larry...that's a different story. And if Charles is involved in the plan to steal the gold from Hanks, you could still be in danger from both of them. I've thought it best to refrain from investigating too actively until you're better enough to travel, should needs be."

Silence fell over the cabin. Genny released a sigh. The dog sighed louder.

Wade rumbled a chuckle. "Tell you what. Give yourself a couple of weeks, and before my next visit, I'll talk to the saloon manager who helped you. What was her name...Miss Mattie?"

Genny nodded.

"You think she can be trusted?" Jesse's low-pitched question drew her chin up.

"Yes, of course. Why do you ask?"

"Wade's right. Hiding's best for now. We can't have her figuring out my association with Wade and telling anyone you might be here." The firmness in Jesse's tone and his willingness to continue to shelter her salved a raw place in her heart. If nothing else, the man possessed honor.

"You can trust her." Miss Mattie had resented the interest of both Charles and Larry in Genny and would be happier with her gone.

"That's good." Wade drew his hat from the table and knocked it on his knee. "We could use an ally in town. So we have a deal?"

Genny looked to Jesse, who gave his friend a somber nod. Accepting, if not approving. Perhaps having the guards on the property would take some of the burden from his shoulders.

While she waited for physical healing, though, who would protect her emotions? For, despite her knowing better, she kept being drawn back to the man who had twice saved her. And if a third time came, would she be as lucky?

CHAPTER 14

JULY 4, 1833

Jesse had been dreading this trip to town as much as Genny had been looking forward to it. His hands easily spanned her small waist as he lifted her with the utmost care onto Perseus. She tucked her weaker limb around the front of the saddle, allowing the still-healing lower right leg to dangle on the same side as her left. He frowned as he stuck his boot into the stirrup and swung onto the stallion behind her, easing down with the utmost care.

He might not mind a break from plowing corn and sweet potatoes. Even less would he mind a letup of the tension of sharing an increasingly intimate space, despite his best attempts to keep their relationship platonic. But this trip would bring even bigger challenges—of which riding to Lumpkin Courthouse double mounted could be just the start.

A red sunrise burning off the haze promised a fair but hot midday. Hopefully, they'd reach their destination before the sun reached its zenith.

Genny giggled. "I don't know why you look like such a

thundercloud. Mrs. Paschal said I was cleared to travel. And it took her long enough to get here."

He took both reins in hand. "I imagine she was busy moving into the new hotel they built."

"And tending to all the cases of fever she mentioned."

Jesse nodded. The healer had lamented both the extreme heat and the foolish preference of the townsfolk for cutting all trees in range. She'd also confirmed that the postmaster died after being moved to his home. The impending trial for Jesse Brown, his killer, was just another reason Jesse himself needed to move things along with the Martin investigation.

"You're not going to hurt me." Genny's wry comment brought the realization that he hadn't moved.

"Right." He nudged Perseus back from the cabin with his heels. Did he really need to remind her they couldn't risk a setback? "Would you tell me if I did?"

"Maybe not." She pressed her lips together as if to subdue her mirth, but it shone from her face, irrepressible and annoyingly captivating. "It's been six weeks in that cabin. Can you blame me?"

He couldn't, but would she blame him if things worked out like he thought they might and he didn't bring her back? He'd allowed her to believe they'd packed simply for their overnight. He didn't mean to be deceptive, but too much remained uncertain to distress her for no reason. He clicked to Perseus, and when the horse turned away from the cabin, Toby started down the porch steps. Jesse spoke sternly over his shoulder. "Stay."

Genny's face twisted under her bonnet as she looked behind them. "Oh, poor thing. He wants to come too."

A pang of guilt hit Jesse. Genny loved that dog, and Toby loved her. But that couldn't be a factor in his decision.

"A Fourth of July celebration is no place for a dog. Besides, the men will look after him." He'd given the men Wade hired leave to use the cabin while they were gone. So far, they'd proven themselves noninvasive and resourceful.

He could have wished they'd been a bit *more* invasive. The more mobile Genny became, the harder it was to escape her. He'd fashioned her a crutch when Mrs. Paschal said it was time, though he still carried her longer distances such as when she'd wanted to sit and weed the garden or watch him pan at the creek. She had become adept at getting around the house, even taking over the cooking with surprising skill.

"Why do you look so blowed?" she'd asked when he'd tasted the first meal she prepared. *Blowed* being her word for *surprised*, as she'd explained. "I cooked for my father before he passed."

Her cooking was about as hard to resist as her voice, which she'd taken to serenading him with on the evenings Jesse brought out his fiddle. She knew most all the sprightly English and Scottish tunes he did, even the off-color ones—though she possessed such a knack for rhyming her own more appropriate verses off the cuff that Jesse's laughter often brought an abrupt halt to his fiddling.

He couldn't remember the last time he'd laughed out loud. As the sound rang through the hazy summer twilight, it was as foreign to his ears as her singing was magical.

But perhaps the most effective bonding between them was the nightly Bible reading she'd requested after his return from town. She'd made a point to tell him how his prayer worked wonders on her leg. Personally, Jesse could hardly believe it was that. He didn't even know what possessed him to lay hands on her in prayer. But he could hardly deny slaking her spiritual thirst. So every night since, he'd read from the Good Book aloud, Genny gazing at him intently as though she was trying to lap up every word lest they fall to the floor.

As the days passed, like a wilted flower taking in water and sunlight, she'd grown more serene. Stronger. Reviving before his eyes, and the change was compelling. Somehow, instead of arguing more, they argued less. Not at all, really. Which was very disconcerting.

"Even though we're going to Lumpkin Courthouse rather than Auraria, I can't believe you agreed to take me to the celebration." One forearm locked over his on her waist, she smoothed the skirt of the white lawn dress Mrs. Paschal had insisted she keep. She wore her blue bonnet and had added a blue sash at her waist—a memento of Emma he'd remembered when Genny lamented her need for patriotic attire. No sense letting it gather dust in the trunk, was there?

Jesse grunted. He did his best to focus on the conversation rather than the gentle swaying of her body against his. "Still not sure it's a good idea." Resettling Genny elsewhere might prove a necessary one, though. "Besides, I could hardly leave you at the cabin with the men on the property."

She swiveled to look at him. "Don't you trust them?"

Her face was in such close proximity, Jesse didn't dare breathe, much less answer.

Thankfully, she turned back around. "Well, anyway, I'm glad. I wanted to go ever since Mrs. Paschal told us about the rival celebrations. She was awfully sore about Lumpkin Courthouse stealing the orator when Auraria already had their barbeque and toastmasters lined up."

"Sounds like they'll be lucky if that's all Licklog steals." Or Lumpkin Courthouse or Headquarters or whatever the new town would be called. He continued speaking above the droning of crickets and morning birdsong. "I'm expecting a big crowd since they're selling town lots during the oration and the dinner to follow. Which is partly why I'm not sure this is a good idea."

Genny turned her head to admire some orange daylilies as they made the turn onto the road. "Everyone we know should be in Auraria. Mrs. Paschal said Mr. Calhoun is in residence, and there were a lot of people visiting already to see the Burmese natives the missionary brought to speak at the Baptist Church. I'm sure we've not to worry. The faithful Aurarians will never be enticed away by whatever pleasures Misters Bracken and Bugg might offer up the hill."

He'd told her he'd sent ahead to secure a room for them at Anslem Bugg's new house of entertainment where dinner for the festivities was also being held. Genny had been so transported at the notion of travel that she hadn't even questioned his rather simple explanation that he needed to meet a contact of Wade's.

The day Wade escorted Mrs. Paschal to visit, he'd shared a general update with everyone. He had spoken with Miss Mattie as he promised, although he'd declined to tell her where Genny was staying. She confirmed that Larry had been siphoning money from the Hanks mine—money she believed both Larry and Walter planned to abscond with. Only now, following his recovery from scarlet fever, Larry had been installed as manager over the two mines Hanks owned. No doubt, the roughneck took the promotion as an opportunity to set aside more gold while Charles was in New Orleans, including a steamboat cruise that was part of his honeymoon.

The second part of his report, Wade imparted to Jesse privately. They'd walked by the creek while the healer assessed Genny's leg. It seemed the man Wade placed in the Hanks mine on the Chestatee had gotten in a fight and been dismissed before he could learn anything of note. Wade needed someone to replace him undercover, someone he could trust to stay on task—Jesse. And he'd set up a meeting for tonight in Lumpkin Courthouse with Hanks's foreman, David Taylor, for that purpose.

Jesse's saddlebag also carried the letter Wade had brought him. The need for a timely response to it was the final nudge Jesse needed to risk bringing Genny to town. He would tell her about it after he met with Taylor...though he dreaded wiping the joy from her face almost as much as he dreaded parting with her.

~

The narrow rope bed in the tiny Lumpkin Courthouse room squeaked beneath Genny's recumbent form as she stirred the redolent air with her fan. The space's confines proved stifling even as darkness descended over the mountain town. She'd not protested when Jesse went downstairs after they'd brought supper up to their room earlier. After over a month spent mainly indoors and in solitude, she'd found the crowds, the noise, the hours of orating and toast-making that followed the reading of the Declaration of Independence more than a bit overwhelming. Not to mention the bright sunlight that beat down on the rostrum outside the tiny log courthouse, its door so low a tall man would have to stoop to enter through it. Hardly an impressive start to this village of multiple names.

But she'd not expected Jesse to be gone this long. What was he doing? Why hadn't she asked more about this meeting of his?

Because she'd been so excited at the thought of going somewhere with him that all other considerations—even those that affected her safety—had gone straight out of her mind. As she'd ridden the dusty miles cradled so close to his chest, his voice and laugh rumbling against her back, she'd allowed herself to entertain fanciful notions of him escorting her about town on his arm. Not dumping her in this coffin of a room and disappearing for two hours...to do what? Surely, his meeting couldn't have taken this long. Was he downstairs playing cards? Fiddle music penetrated the uninsulated boards of Bugg's inn. She couldn't help but imagine Jesse dancing on the square with one of the sun-browned mountain maidens.

The sprightly notes of "Jump Jim Crow" made her throw her fan on the bed and sit up, easing her legs over the side. Of course, she couldn't dance. And she did so want to dance with Jesse, despite the warning the wiser part of her nature whispered in her head. At the least, she could perhaps glimpse him in the crowd milling around the bonfire on the square.

As she approached the window and peered out the wavy glass, flames illuminated the partially built buildings around the square, including Harrison Riley's new store, where she'd purchased some much-needed personal items earlier that day. Couples formed a reel line in front of it, too far away to discern faces. Men stood on porches talking and smoking, the butts of their cigars glowing with faint orange lights, or staggered about clutching jugs and flasks. A couple of boys with a cluster of bonneted girls watching shoved each other, then fell to the dirt, grappling and punching while onlookers gathered to cheer them on.

Maybe it was just as well she wasn't down there.

Genny backed away from the window, and her foot hit the cane-woven stool where Jesse had deposited his saddlebags. They toppled to the floor, allowing a few items to spill out. She reached down to repack the bag, but her fingers closed over a folded missive. A long, scrawled word caught her eye. *Mississippi*. Hadn't Jesse said that was where he'd last done survey work?

Her fingers shook a little as she bent to retrieve the note. She should put it back in his bag. It was none of her business. But...wasn't it?

She shuffled over to the bed and sat down in the circle of light from the lamp, her pulse racing in time to the ever-increasing tempo of the minstrel tune. Genny unfolded the letter. Block letters were printed across the top—*Public Land Survey System*. She released a gasp as she read the contents. *Your application to resume survey work on the recently acquired*

Chickasaw lands has been approved. You may start immediately upon your return to the Mississippi Territory.

Her heart pounded as she balled her fist at her lips. Never once had Jesse mentioned a desire to return to Mississippi. What else hadn't he shared with her? Was this what his meeting was about? He was leaving, and he didn't even think it important enough to tell her?

How foolish she'd been to believe they had established a connection—a friendship, at the very least. One based on mutual trust...something she'd always craved from a man but never received. Now it seemed their connection had been an illusion as well.

Genny refolded the letter—smaller this time—and unbuttoned her frock to slide the paper between it and her corset. With the letter secured, she rose and reached for the crutch Jesse had insisted she bring. Well, she'd use it now to find him. She wouldn't sit in this room like a discarded bobbin another minute. She'd confront him and demand to know the truth of his plans—and how they affected her.

She took a halting breath. She must brace herself. Most likely, he aimed to get shed of her before they even knew if she was safe.

And thinking of safety...it was best if she kept a low profile, even in the dark. She donned her bonnet. Then, after turning the lamp down low, Genny locked the room behind her and slid the key into her pocket. Smoking oil lamps in fixtures on the walls cast eerie shadows along the narrow hall leading to the stairs.

She dreaded exposing herself to the common room below where boisterous prospectors and slimy businessmen filled tables covered with barbeque and whiskey. But she must ascertain if Jesse was among them before venturing outside...to even greater potential danger. Surely, she'd lost her mind. No. She'd just had enough of being stuffed in a corner until a man told her his pleasure.

Her descent on the stairs brought a hush to the foyer, but none of the upturned faces were Jesse's. Genny was all too accustomed to the expressions on the faces of the grizzled men present—ranging from admiration to outright lust. Oh, there were plenty of women around. But most of them either sported the low-cut gowns of ladies of the night or the sunburned visages of one too many days laboring in the hot sun.

She managed to find a place to scour the dining room from the shadows. Her heart sank when she didn't see him, but she forced herself to continue on to the porch. She stood there a minute overlooking the square, trying to suck air into her lungs but feeling as if she only drank in the heavy humidity. Perhaps the music had drawn Jesse as it would have her.

Genny leaned lightly on her crutch as she stumped her way off the porch and set across the dirt clearing. She'd only gone a quarter of the way when a hand gripped her arm, turning her to face the last man on earth she ever wanted to see again.

"It *is* you." Charles's declaration shuddered with obsessive amazement as his green gaze swept her from beneath his gambler hat. "My Songbird of Auraria."

CHAPTER 15

The man who introduced himself to Jesse in the inn's dining room had not been David Taylor. Rather, the dark-bearded, blue-eyed miner gave his name as Miles Prescott and told him Taylor would join them any minute. That had been over an hour ago. He had insisted Jesse sit down with him and a few others in a private room to an unfamiliar game of cards which required a lot of bluffing and raising. Thank heavens the stakes involved chips rather than gold or cash because Jesse would surely have lost his shirt otherwise. Needless to say, neither of his parents approved of gambling.

Miles's jovial countenance, surprisingly boyish beneath all the hair, grew more flushed and more jolly the more whiskey he consumed. While the others at the table maintained straight faces, Miles's grin never faltered. Still, his cheer seemed to be working for him, for he raked more and more chips toward himself. Judging by the tension in the room, Jesse had to wonder if more lucrative stakes were arranged earlier in the evening.

By the time Jesse could drop out, his patience had expired. He couldn't keep his mind off Genny, alone upstairs. He was about to push his chair back when Miles banged his hand on the table. The chips rattled. "There he is!"

David Taylor? Jesse looked up to find a lanky frame filling the doorway of the back room. His heart nearly stopped. The man he'd deemed Red stared back at him.

~

"Charles!" The name croaked from Genny's throat and nearly withered on her lips. She took a step back. Everything in her clamored for her to run, but that was impossible on her newly mended and still-weak leg. She'd have to rely on her wits—and something else. Something new to her...God's wisdom. "I...I thought you were in New Orleans."

Still cupping her arm, he removed his hat with the other. His gaze never left hers. "I was...until I heard about the town lots being sold off here. I couldn't let such a ripe opportunity pass me by, so I cut my trip short."

Of course. He would have people closely monitoring anything of interest to him here. Genny eased her arm from his grasp. "What opportunity?"

"Why, to build a hotel and saloon that will make the Boom or Bust look like a frontier tavern, of course." His eyes glittered. "And I need my songbird to make it a success."

"I'm not your songbird anymore." She lifted her chin. The proprietary way his gaze devoured her may have once made her feel desirable, but now it sat with her about as well as Mrs. Paschal's willow bark tea.

"I understand." Charles's voice dropped as he moved closer. "I hurt you when I gave in to my father's demands that I marry. But you must know, it was never my intention to mislead you. I...wanted you."

The rough edge to his tone scraped her like a broken medicine bottle, bristling the hair on her arms. "Oh, I have no doubt you did."

"No, I mean...as my wife." He brushed the back of his knuckles against her cheek.

Genny swatted his hand away. Never before would she have dared such a thing, but Jesse had lived with her in the same cabin for almost two months and never dishonored her in any way. If he could do it, any man could. "Well, that's impossible because not only are you married now—I am too."

"What?" The horror that twisted Charles's features might have been humorous if it wasn't so foreboding.

"That's right." She tossed her head. "I'm here with my husband." If only she knew where he was. She started to ease toward the inn, her instincts crying for her to gain shelter, but she made herself stop even as Charles seized her arm again. She couldn't have him follow her there. Couldn't risk him running into Jesse.

His fingers bit into her flesh. "Who is he?"

Neither could she tell him who Jesse was—not if Jesse still aimed to aid Wade in his investigation. Even if he wasn't telling her the details now. "It's no longer any of your concern." She managed to infuse bravado into her response. "With my marriage, your guardianship has ended."

"I want proof." He loomed over her, brandy on his breath. "I demand proof!"

"Let go of me." *God, help me.*

"Never. Your father entrusted you to me. What happened when you ran away?" He eyed her crutch. "My people couldn't find you. You were injured, alone. What did this man force upon you?"

"He forced me into nothing!" Genny shouted the answer in his face, half taunt, half wretched admission. If Jesse had made their marriage genuine rather than keeping her at arm's length so he could escape to Mississippi, she would not be in danger now. As it was, should Charles discover her marriage went unconsummated, he would find some way to challenge its legitimacy.

Some boys in suspenders, linen breeches too short for them, and checked shirts darted through the crowd. One of them threw something on the ground with a cry of exultation. Firecrackers exploded inches from Charles's feet. He whirled with a curse on his lips.

Genny seized her opening. She slid behind a line of young women walking arm in arm and darted toward a partially erected building catty-corner to the inn.

"Hey!" Charles's cry rang in her ears.

She dropped the crutch and ran.

~

Jesse made his way from the private room of the inn with cotton in his brain. What just happened? Redbeard—David Taylor—had asked how Jesse's mining efforts went on the Etowah. If he had been sent to ferret out whether Jesse sheltered Genny that day, he gave no indication. They'd talked about Rupert Hanks's mining plans for a quarter hour. When David said Hanks switched over to deposit mining, Jesse had been sure he'd lost his opportunity. He possessed no experience tunneling. But David had assured him if he knew how to dig and push a wheelbarrow, the miners could show him the rest. What was important, he'd said with a gleam in his eye, was to find trustworthy men.

Had Jesse stumbled into the most fortuitous assignment ever...or a trap?

He needed to talk this over with Genny. The back stairs offered the quickest route up to their room, but before he could take them, the rear door banged into him, and he stumbled into a woman with her bonneted head down. When he grabbed her arms to keep himself from falling and possibly taking her with him, she let out a shriek. It didn't lower the volume of the house's occupants for a second. But a look at the woman's face dried the protest that sprang to his own lips.

"Genny?"

"Jesse!" Her frantic exclamation of his name lashed panic around his heart like the tendrils of an invasive vine.

"What's wrong?" He curled his fingers around her forearms, steadying her more than him now.

"Charles!" She hissed the name with a tortured glance over her shoulder. "He's here. We must get inside."

Charles? Hadn't Wade said the man was steaming his way up the Mississippi River? But there was no doubt of the terror on Genny's pale features. Jesse slammed the door, took her hand, and pulled her up the stairs. Only at the top did he remember her leg. He whisked her around the corner with an arm about her waist and practically carried her into their room.

With the door closed, Genny pulled the key from her pocket and attempted to insert it in the lock, but her hand shook, and the piece of metal clattered to the floor. She let out a strangled cry, and he leapt forward and locked the door for her. Then he dragged the only chair in the room over and wedged it under the doorknob. And finally, he laid the loaded pistol he'd been wearing on the bureau.

He turned to find Genny shaking in the middle of the room like the last autumn leaf clinging to an oak. In two strides, he crossed the rug and reached for her. But rather than melt into his embrace, she knocked his hands away. Then flew at him, pummeling his arms and chest.

"You traitor! How dare you?"

A heavy draught of air rushed from his lungs. "How dare I what?" He attempted to stay her fists. "How dare *you*? Didn't I tell you to stay put? Was that really too much to ask?"

She pulled back even though he locked his arms around

her waist, afraid she'd topple to the floor. "Just because you told me to? When you didn't tell me about this?" She unbuttoned a spot in the middle of her bodice and pulled out a folded paper. Before he could determine what it was, she smacked him across the face with it. "*Mississippi*?"

Oh, no. No, no. Jesse let out a groan as the letter of employment fluttered to the rug. "I was going to tell you...tonight. After I met with David Taylor and found out if I got a job with him or not."

"*Who?*" Genny's face twisted as she spit the word out.

He dropped his arms. "The foreman for Rupert Hanks's mine on the Chestatee. Only, he wasn't who I expected. But that can wait. What was Charles doing in Lumpkin?"

"Purchasing a lot to build a new hotel."

That possibility should have occurred to him. He never should've brought her here. When she swayed, he gestured toward the bed. "Please, Genny, won't you sit?"

Her back firmed, and her chin lifted. "Not until you tell me your plan. What's this about a job working for Rupert Hanks? I thought Wade said he had a man there already."

"He did but it didn't work out."

"But why you? And what do you intend to do with me?" She rolled her shoulders back. "Should I go find Charles and tell him I need a job, after all?"

"No!" He wrapped his fingers around those stiff shoulders of hers. "You wouldn't dare."

"Like you wouldn't dare to marry me and then leave me?" She flung the question at him as an accusation, but the waver in her voice gave her away.

Jesse's chest squeezed. She relied on him. Had grown attached to him. And he'd let that happen. He'd failed to walk the line between being kind and misleading her.

"Ohhhh..." The word rushed out of her on a breath, half

whisper, half moan, as her face and shoulders crumpled and she drew her hands into a ball beneath her chin.

"What?" He was mystified.

"The way you're looking at me...don't ever..." Her expression was so grieved as she turned her head to one side, as if to avoid his eyes, that it left a caring man no choice.

He drew her into his arms. "Genny, I didn't mean to hurt you...or deceive you. I sent my application to the land service long before I found you on my land. And who better to investigate at the Hanks Mine? Rest assured, I'm not going to ride off into the sunset and leave things unresolved with Charles Martin." He stroked her back and laid his cheek against her hair. A mistake. She'd washed it for the outing, and it smelt of lavender.

"You're not?" The question was so small, it almost got lost in the raucous noise rising through the floorboards at their feet.

"Of course not. I made a promise. I'm good for my promises."

She lifted her face, her nose bumping his chin, and he adjusted to gaze into her shimmering eyes. "Because you want to avenge Emma."

He could lie and say that was all it was. But that was Wade's quest, not his. At least, somewhere along the way, Emma ceased to be all there was to it. Now there was a living, breathing woman he held in his arms who stirred him in ways Emma never had. That he had feared no woman would. It would be disingenuous to allow Genny to think he cared nothing about her.

"Because I want to protect you."

Soon as the admission left his lips, a soft breath left Genny's, and her hand slipped up behind his neck. Did he move, or did she pull him down? Either way, their mouths met, his firm lips pressing into her soft ones with a need that ripped a low moan from his chest. A man couldn't sleep feet away from such a woman for over a month and not burn to make her his. His self-control shriveled like a leaf in the fire.

Her soft hands massaged his shoulders, the tight knots of muscles there, and his slid to her waist, pulling her taut against him. She pressed closer, her lips yielding to the exploration of his with a hum of pleasure that ignited his senses.

"Genny…" When he got her name out, he meant it as a warning, but it vibrated with need.

Her finger traced the curve of his jaw to his lower lip. Her lashes brushed his cheek. "I'm your wife. Make me your wife. Charles…"

When Jesse stiffened, she didn't finish her sentence. This was about Charles?

She hesitated, drawing back a fraction as if to gauge his reaction. "I would never have to worry about him again." This spoken in a whisper.

Cold reality washed Jesse, and he dropped his arms. *That* was her motivation? "I can keep you safe from Charles. You don't have to sacrifice your virtue."

"I-it's not…" She spluttered. "We're married." Entreatingly, she held her hands out—hands that were shaking. That was fear, not desire.

He narrowed his gaze on her. "What did he do to you, Genny?" He'd never dared to ask directly, though her areas of sensitivity offered clues.

A sob bubbled from her throat. "N-not that. At least, he hadn't…yet."

"But you never felt safe from it." Jesse spoke with clear conviction. When Genny gave a bob of a nod, something black and vile stirred within his gut. Only the lowest worm of a man would make those in his care afraid of him. A soft growl clawed its way up his throat. "He will be dealt with. And until then…"

Until then, he must set aside his feelings for Genny. Only after the threat was removed could he dare to assay those feelings, test their purity. And Genny needed that chance even more than he did. Her desperation tonight showed she was far from healed. But he could hardly verbalize that—not without hurting her worse.

"Until then, I'll do what I must to keep you safe."

A shuddering breath left her visibly spent, and she fumbled behind her, then sank onto the bed. Her eyes entreated him. "So you *are* leaving me?"

"Tomorrow morning, we ride out ahead of dawn. I'm taking you to Gainesville to stay with my parents while I hire on with David Taylor."

"What?" Her hand fluttered to her chest. "No!"

Was she more afraid for her...or him? "You'll be safe there." Surely, his mother would welcome the chance to help bring her daughter-in-law's killer to justice. Taking Genny into her home would be her part in that. "Wade will help protect you while I find evidence against Larry...and hopefully, Charles." He pulled the extra quilt from the bottom of the bed. "I'll sleep against the door tonight."

"Jesse, please don't do this." Her fingers dug into the fabric of her bodice, twisting it. "It's too dangerous. What if someone recognizes you as being associated with Wade...or me?"

Someone may already have, but he didn't need to tell her that. He couldn't risk *comforting* her again. "It will be fine." He spoke matter-of-factly as he worked his boots off and let them clunk to the floor. "Soon, God willing, we'll have the culprits in Wade's jail. You'll be free to choose what to do with your future." He gave her a meaningful look, one that reminded her that if she gave herself to him, she no longer would be.

He couldn't bear to make a commitment again, only to have it torn asunder by the destructive force of his own nature.

CHAPTER 16

"*Y*our *what*?"

If the perfect whitewashed house with window boxes of daisies and surrounding white picket fence just off the Gainesville square was not enough to intimidate Genny...

If the woman who came to the door with nary a tawny curl out of place or wrinkle in her tucked linen dress was not sufficiently austere...

The horrified screech of a question from Jesse's mother when he introduced Genny was surely the thing to make her sink beneath the floorboards of the porch. It was all she could do to keep her head held high.

Jesse wrapped his arm around her waist. "My wife. Mrs. Genevieve Holden of Auraria."

Memory of his rejection from the prior night still brought as much heat to Genny's face as his mother's current shocked perusal of Genny's person—which presently included a sunburned countenance and her sweat-and-dirt-stained brown calico frock. But when the spires and roofs of Gainesville came into view, Jesse had spoken of the importance of allowing his parents to believe their union was genuine...permanent. She had thought that was for the benefit of public opinion. Now she knew the real reason. She didn't dare pull away.

"Auraria? What type of wife does one meet in such a place? I thought you were going there to tend Wade's land, to get yourself together. And you come home with a *wife*?" Her brows rode so high, her forehead bore more lines than Auraria Road did ruts.

"Well, if you let the poor couple in, Dorothy, I'm sure they'll explain." A mellow male voice came from behind Mrs. Holden. Long fingers wrapped around the edge of the door and pulled it open to reveal a tall man with silvering golden hair, a dark suit, and a hopeful expression. "Jesse!"

With a huff, Mrs. Holden moved out of the way to allow her husband and son to embrace. The step she took back was marked enough to suffuse Genny with guilt for merely entering the foyer. When Jesse placed his hands on his mother's shoulders and bent toward her in a tentative embrace, she remained so stiff, she looked like she might break in his arms. Surely, she wasn't always thus. But was she truly so upset over Genny's presence?

Mr. Holden's reaching for and bowing over her hand brought a fleeting smile to Genny's face. "Welcome," he said. "I am Jesse's father, Reverend Peter Holden."

"A pleasure, sir." She dipped a curtsy.

Mrs. Holden sniffed.

Genny cast a quick glance at her boots. Had she tracked dirt on the painted floor?

His brows bunching, Jesse's father released Genny's hand. "You must forgive my wife's surprise. You can imagine, since this is the first we've heard of this marriage..."

"Of course. The circumstances were rather sudden for all of us."

"Although, I made the acquaintance of Miss Gillbard when

I was previously in Auraria." Jesse bent his arm and threaded her hand through, patting her fingers as though she were a debutante on promenade.

His mother blinked at him. "Before you married Emma?"

"Yes. In fact, Genny was a schoolmate of hers."

In the silence that fell, Genny stared at Jesse. If he expected to thrust her on his parents' hospitality, he would have to tell them of the dire circumstances she found herself in. But first, he was doing all he could to cloak her in respectability. How quickly would that fig leaf be yanked away once they learned she'd been Charles Martin's ward—and a singer in his saloon?

Finally, as a maid came forward to take their hats, Reverend Holden cleared his throat. "Forgive us. I fear we are rather stunned. You see, we never thought Jesse would marry again."

And certainly not so soon. Although they went unsaid, the words reverberated in Genny's head as clearly as if they had been spoken aloud.

She failed to meet the earnest reverend's eyes. How close they were to the truth. So close that even her throwing herself at Jesse last night failed to bind her to him. And today, his polite reserve while he rode so close to her on Perseus, as though he determined not to repeat the mistake of showing her any affection, revealed exactly how much he esteemed her—when his question about the nature of her relationship with Charles should have already done so. All these weeks, she'd thought his self-control sprang from honor, but perhaps he'd merely viewed her as an unworthy candidate to call his wife. As his parents clearly did.

"There is much I should tell you, but..." Jesse squeezed her hand, perhaps noting its trembling. "We've been traveling in the heat all day, and my wife is weary. Perhaps it would be best if I explained while she rested in the guest room."

She shot him a thankful glance before she could stop herself.

"A good idea." The older woman gestured to the maid. "Penny can deliver tea to her in the room...and fill the washbasin." Her nose turned up as if Genny stank of the hog pens outside Auraria, the gesture the only indication she realized Genny was in the room. With her thus dismissed, Mrs. Holden turned to her son. "Will you be staying? Naturally, you find us unprepared."

"We'll discuss it, Mother." Jesse's tone firmed and his posture tensed, but his touch to Genny's waist when he dropped her hand was tender. His voice rumbled lower, near her ear. "Go with Penny for now. I'll check on you in a bit."

She wanted to fight him. To ask him why he was being nice to her now when he'd made his rejection of her so clear. To demand a reason she should stay with the parents of a man who viewed her as an obligation. Part of a score to settle.

But nothing good could come of causing a scene. Genny lowered her head and followed the servant in her crisp cotton uniform and apron up the stairs, past a ticking Grandfather clock on the landing and portraits of what must be Holden ancestors in Colonial attire. She might have little choice at this moment, but she possessed enough money to take the stage to Pendleton after Jesse left. Maybe Miss Mattie's sister would still help her.

~

*G*enny had barely disappeared from sight when Jesse's mother turned to him, her hazel eyes flashing fire. "What trouble have your reckless ways gotten you into now?" Her tone, words, and expression were exactly the same as they had been when he'd returned home as a boy covered in mud and with his ankle swelling.

"It's not me that's in trouble. It's Genny." Best come to the point as quickly as possible. There was no way to soften the blow, though Jesse had hoped his mother would have at least pretended to be gracious in front of Genny. He should have found some place she could clean up before presenting her to his very proper parents. Maybe the hardships of her life would squeeze some sympathy from them. "And it's the same trouble that killed Emma. Charles Martin is after her."

"What?" His mother's already impeccable posture went rigid.

"Come. Let's sit down." His father held out his arm toward the parlor.

Once they were seated in the familiar room with its walls painted the Federal blue that was all the rage when he was a boy, Jesse related finding Genny wounded on Wade's land and how she overheard Charles's former employee plotting to steal gold from Rupert Hanks and possibly kidnap Genny.

His mother sat unblinking with her hands in her lap. "But why would Charles care if this man took Genny?"

Jesse met her gaze. "Because when his mine manager, her father, died, she became his ward." No way around stating it, but she had no reason to know about Genny's work at the Boom or Bust. Or that Charles coveted Genny for his own.

He didn't need to tell her. Already sufficiently disgusted, Mother turned her head aside and let out a little breath. "That you could marry such a woman, Jesse, when a treasure like Emma was yours, yet you squandered your life with her by taking off for Mississippi..."

Jesse didn't so much as flinch, though the barb stuck straight into his heart. "It's because I want to do right by Emma that Wade and I decided I should take Genny in and give her the protection of marriage." At least, that's how it started. What it came to was him assessing every man they encountered on their way to Gainesville as a potential assailant. And the way his heart hammered with fear for Genny's safety had nothing to do with his former wife. But telling his parents so would not help win their trust. "Don't you see, Mother? This is our way to right the wrongs of the past."

Father sat forward on the damask-upholstered mahogany Cabriole sofa, his arm over his knee. "How is Wade involved?"

Jesse explained how his former brother-in-law had been investigating the possible robbery plot but needed a man undercover at the Hanks Mine. "The foreman has agreed to take me on, but I must return to Lumpkin County immediately." He had yet to tell Genny that. What he said was true—time was of the essence. But neither did he think he could spend another night in her presence without succumbing to temptation. "Larry Jones is likely to make his move soon now that Charles is back in the area. But I need you to take care of Genny. Wade will help, but she needs a secure place to stay."

His mother shook her head. "I don't like it. It sounds reckless, dangerous."

"You love this woman, son?" Father's gaze bored into him with a discernment he never could evade.

Love? That was not part of the plan. Jesse shifted on the splay-legged klismos chair his mother was so proud of. "I... cannot lose her too." That was as much as he could admit.

Mother waved her hand and spoke as though Jesse had not. "Of course he doesn't love her. Haven't you been listening? He was forced into this to protect her reputation."

"To protect her *life*." Jesse crossed his arms over his chest and scowled at her. "And I do care for Genny. I expect you to treat her with respect and regard. Will you do that much? If not for me or Genny, for Emma?" It was the one argument that stood a chance of swaying his mother.

"You don't even have to ask, Jesse. You know we will." Father offered him a gentle if sad smile, then turned his attention on his wife. "Won't we, Dorothy?"

She returned his stare for several moments, then her shoulders relaxed. "For Emma's sake and to see this culprit brought to justice." Her gaze swiveled back to Jesse. "But then what? Will you leave this one the same way you left *her*?"

~

Genny couldn't prevent the soft gasp that escaped her when she overheard Mrs. Holden's harsh words. She'd washed up and partaken tea and biscuits in a green-toned room with gilded mirrors and heavy mahogany furniture, but she couldn't bring herself to lie down on the poster bed with its pristine white counterpane. Besides, a normal wife would rejoin her husband for such an important occasion as a first visit with his parents. She hadn't expected Reverend Holden's words to freeze her boots on the stairs.

You love this woman, son?

How recklessly her heart had beat out of her chest. The hope that ran rampant revealed the truth she'd been fighting for days. Weeks. She'd fallen in love with Jesse.

And he *cared* about her. No wonder his mother expected him to abandon her.

When steps approached and Jesse hurried toward her from the door of the parlor, she saw no reason to pretend she hadn't heard. She gripped the balustrade while Jesse's anguished gaze met hers. "Is she right? Will you even come back before you leave for Mississippi?"

"Of course I will." Swift steps brought him to stand just below her. He reached for her free hand, but she yanked it into the folds of her skirt. "Genny, believe me when I say this is the best way I know to keep you safe."

"But you're leaving today for Auraria. Now."

"I have to." The anguish in his face could almost convince her he loved her—if she didn't know better.

"No, you don't." That he would dump her here when his mother couldn't stand the sight of her hardened her face, her voice, her heart. "There are always choices. But I suppose you *will* come back. You'll want to annul—"

He swung her off the step and against him so fast, she would've cried out if his hand hadn't gone over her mouth. His warning glare ensured her silence prior to the removal of his hand. "Come outside with me."

"I don't see the point—" But his grip on her arm, drawing her toward the porch, brooked no argument. He didn't stop until they'd descended the steps and sought the shade of a dogwood tree in the side yard.

Finally, he turned to her, his hands on his hips. "What choices are there? Tell me, Genny."

How could she, without revealing her heart? She wet her lips. "We could leave. Let Wade deal with Charles. It's his job, after all."

"And do what? What kind of work?" He flung one hand out.

"You could survey somewhere else."

"A survey crew is made up of men, living rough in the wilderness. There's no place for a wife."

She shrugged and crossed her arms. "I could live in a nearby town."

"There is no nearby town. Even if there were, how would you be safe there without me to protect you? What kind of life is that, always looking over your shoulder?"

His questions drilled into her like bullets into firing range targets, shooting down her resistance. "Charles would eventually forget about me."

"You willing to bet your life on that?" He held out his hand to her, palm up. "No, Genny, there's only one way you can be free of him, and Wade needs my help to make sure that happens."

She angled away from him. "You talk like this is about me when we both know it's not. I heard what you said to your parents, and I understand. Emma is the only woman you'll ever love." She did her best to speak without emotion, but her stupid voice wobbled on the last word.

She wasn't prepared for the sigh that rattled out of him, nor the way he slumped like a scarecrow after a storm. "You don't understand." His words were so low, the rumble of a passing wagon almost devoured them. "I didn't love Emma."

Genny's gaze turned to him, widening. "What?"

He took a shaky breath and lifted his stubbled chin. He met her eyes. "I didn't love her."

She sensed it was the first time he'd admitted it, and the truth shook her to the core. Here she'd been thinking desire to avenge his lost love motivated his actions, while she could never compare to Emma's perfection...and yet he'd never loved her? "Why?" The question escaped on a breath.

He shook his head. "I should have. She was everything a man could want. Everything my parents approved of. My best friend's little sister. But the more she needed from me, the less I could give. The more she demanded, the more I withdrew."

Genny went cold. Was this the way he would become with her if their relationship continued? "I...don't understand."

"I didn't either. I fought it with all I had. Maybe because she wanted me to be someone I wasn't." His gaze went past her to the house. Did she imagine it, or did the curtain move in the parlor window? "Or perhaps my mother is right. Something's wrong with me. It's better that I leave before I hurt people."

Genny's lips parted. "Or maybe you leave because they have hurt you."

Jesse's eyes darted back to hers. "How do you do that?"

"Do what?"

"See into my soul?"

Her lips lifted in a shaky smile. "Only God can do that." A warmth filled her. Though God could guide her...when she wasn't too immersed in her own hurts and selfish desires to listen. "But it doesn't take a spiritual revelation to see how hurtfully your mother treats you. Just know one thing before you go. I'm not her, Jesse."

One step closer and his boot tips bumped hers. He cradled her face in his large, rough hands and stared intently into her eyes. "You almost make me believe it's possible."

"What's possible?" She had to whisper it, her throat had gone so dry at his nearness.

"Love."

CHAPTER 17

"This is where we originally got the best color." David Taylor's dapple gray stallion splashed to a halt in the shallows of the creek southwest of Auraria. The Hanks Mine foreman turned to look at Jesse astride Perseus. "You see how close we are to where the branch joins the Chestatee. Much like Baggs Branch and the Etowah. That's why I thought your place would be so rich."

Was Redbeard—*David*—squinting from the noon sun or from suspicion? Did he still suspect Jesse of ulterior motives for being here?

Jesse shifted with a creak of leather. "Told you. It was my friend's land. He brought in extra men to pan."

"And you gotta make more money for that little missus of yourn. Yeah, yeah. Well, by keepin' the operation small—unlike them bigger mining companies with multiple investors—Hanks has his hands bringin' in three dollars a day. You'll soon get your money saved for your own parcel."

His missus. Jesse avoided a grimace. Had he done enough to convince her two days prior to wait out the investigation with his parents, despite his mother's rude welcome? Or would it be his own ambiguity that drove Genny away?

He'd been unable to speak the promises that might have offered her security. How could he think of the future until he'd dealt with the demons of his past? Being around his mother resurrected the crippling sense of inadequacy. He must show his parents, show himself, that he wouldn't run from this.

The most he'd been able to admit was that he cared about Genny—enough to want what was best for her. Had she grasped what he meant by that? That maybe *he* wasn't best for her? Or had any reasoning gone out of her head when he kissed her goodbye despite being pretty sure his mother looked on...partly *because* his mother looked on?

"From here, we worked our way upstream." David resumed his guided tour to the Hanks Mine, kneeing his stallion, and Jesse clicked to Perseus to follow. "Panning until the gold content bottomed out all of a sudden-like. You know what that means, right?" David slanted him an eye.

"There's a vein in the hills nearby. You soil test until you find it." The rushing of water, the trilling of crickets, and the whirring of dragonflies were almost soothing enough to make Jesse forget he rode into danger. Friendly as the foreman seemed, he could already know Jesse was hiding something. And either or both of the men who had hunted Genny could also be on his mining crew. Not to mention Larry Jones. Would he be at the camp? Would he recognize Jesse as the man who defended Genny at the Boom or Bust?

"Right you are. Glad to hear you occasionally got in a little minin' on that friend's lot of yourn. In that there hill up ahead"— he pointed—"we followed a nice pinch o' color that's currently runnin' about six inches wide. We're tunnelin' along it, but Hanks wanted to also sink a shaft farther on. See if he could find a swell."

"How far down are you going?" Last place he'd want to toil

would be at the bottom of a vertical dig, especially if it was as deep as one he'd heard about in White County that ran as much as a hundred-and-thirty feet.

"Oh, we're only at fifteen so far. Most holes hit water level at twenty or thirty."

"So two teams, one for each mine?" Jesse strained to see around trees in full summer leaf as the camp came into view— a smattering of ecru tents, a log shed, and a couple of bark huts.

"Three, actually." David left the creek to make for the encampment. "See over there in that flat area? That's where we set up the stamp mill."

Jesse's eyebrows rose. "Water-powered?" He'd heard some of the larger mining operations used two to ten stamps, operated by a canal, an undershot wheel, a shaft, and a screen that supposedly held back the heavier particles.

David chuckled. "Nothin' so fancy. Just a bent hickory and a log with a metal plate on the bottom. I'll show you. Takes two more men to operate. After grinding the ore, the gold is panned out of the dust."

"Where does Hanks take his gold?" Jesse didn't react when David shot him a glance. It was a fair question. No bank in Auraria yet—only the Pigeon Roost Mining Company which dealt in credit notes. And Lumpkin Courthouse was an even newer boomtown than Auraria, even if talk was that lots of businesses were relocating there. Including the sheriff and the clerk of superior court. When the foreman didn't answer, Jesse grunted as if disinterested. "Gainesville, I reckon."

"I reckon." With that noncommittal reply, David halted next to a picket line where about half a dozen horses browsed among tall grasses in a small meadow.

Best not ask how often the gold went out. He'd keep his mouth shut and watch for a while. While Jesse unsaddled and tethered Perseus, he surveyed the camp at the tree line. "Don't see signs of anyone." But the crack of an ax splitting wood rang through the woods.

"That's because they're cuttin' timbers today. The mine has to be shored up before we go any farther. The cave-in that just happened at Franklin Mine killed a whole crew."

Jesse hefted his saddlebags over his shoulder. "I'm glad you give some thought to safety. My bride would be none too pleased if I never came back to fetch her from my parents'." Sticking as close to the truth as possible might prevent verbal slip-ups.

"We wouldn't want that, would we?" David slapped his shoulder. "Leave that load under yon tree for now. I'll show you where you'll be workin'."

A few minutes later, Jesse stooped to peer into the blackness of a six-foot-square hole in the earth. No track. No carts. Just a wheelbarrow outside. And barely enough room to stand upright. His stomach shrank at the dank, earthy smell that wafted on the hot breath of the mine. This was where he'd be spending his days for the foreseeable future. The question was...with who?

~

Jesse squinted and the already oxygen-starved lantern flickered in the swirling dust as he and Miles Prescott fitted a notched ceiling beam over two support posts, then used mallets to secure it squarely into place. His muscles, fatigued from three days of timbering the mining tunnel, burned in protest at the extended reaching above his head. The shoring-up really ought to be closer than five feet apart, and done with braces and nails rather than notched logs on foot plates, but Hanks was holding off on such details until he saw how profitable this vein proved.

Of all the men in camp, Miles was the one Jesse would have

chosen to work with, so it was his good fortune that the man Wade previously installed on the job, the one who got in a fight with one of the quick-tempered brothers who ran the stamp mill, had been Miles's work partner. One punch with the weight of Shawn Wilkerson's massive arm behind it had been all it had taken to lay the sheriff's spy out cold. Miles's cheery whistling and quick humor almost made the back-breaking work in the dark, entombing environment tolerable.

"Last one for today." Miles clamped Jesse's shoulder, then lifted his canteen from the ground, uncorked it, and guzzled a long drink.

Jesse swiped his slick face with his filthy cotton sleeve. The close air hung heavy with the scents of sweat, dirt, and whale oil. "How's that? It's not quitting time." When last they'd emerged into the blistering July day to drag more timbers into the mine, it had appeared to be midafternoon—a good many hours before they normally stopped work for a late supper around the campfire.

"It's Friday. Payday, remember?"

"Yeah, but I thought you said Verne Marshall would bring the money back with him." Jesse's patience had borne fruit that morning. Verne, the one man in camp he couldn't figure out—a lanky, dark-haired fellow of middling years who rarely spoke and spent his time mending tools, cooking for the camp, or working on ledgers beneath the lean-to of the one small log structure—loaded canvas sacks from the cabin into his saddle-bags and then headed for the main road. David Taylor rode with him, and both carried rifles and wore gun belts with a brace of pistols. Miles told Jesse they were bound for Auraria. "Didn't you say the assayer would give him cash in advance of sending the gold to the bank in Gainesville?"

"That's right. Most of us prefer to go into town and get it from Larry there, though. Pretty much already spent, anyway."

Miles winked, then collected the mallets and plunked them in the wheelbarrow.

"Larry doesn't come out to camp much." In fact, Jesse hadn't seen him at all yet. He sipped from his own canteen.

"Mr. Hanks bought in on another mine, and Larry is busy setting that up, but I'd expect once David tells Larry about you, he'll be eager to meet you. If you make it a full week, that is. Last one didn't." Miles chortled and handed Jesse the lantern.

Jesse straightened. "Any chance of us taking the gold shipment next week?"

"Not us." Miles turned around and drew the wheelbarrow from the tunnel behind him, Jesse following. "David always goes with the gold."

Did that mean he was involved in siphoning off Larry's share? Or was the close-lipped Marshall with constant access to the gold the thief working for the manager? Was it done in town, or was a portion left here? Jesse needed to see inside that log shed.

Miles abandoned the wheelbarrow in the mouth of the tunnel, stretched, and took a deep breath—though the sultry afternoon swelled with cicada song and enough humidity to choke a bullfrog. "I'd say we're well overdue a good dunking. Can't go see the ladies lookin' like this." He ran his hand down the length of his shirt, so red with clay that the white stripes were barely discernable, and his teeth flashed in a grin from his dirt-and-beard-covered face. "You comin'?"

"You go on. I wanna write a short letter first." It was the best excuse he could think of to delay. This might be his only chance to get into the building where the gold was stored—if Verne Marshall left it unlocked after taking the shipment.

"Aw...missin' your woman, are you?" Miles elbowed him.

"Something like that." Jesse avoided his gaze. He wasn't far off target. Strange, to spend the evenings playing cards and push pin, then bed down in a tent and fall asleep to the night sounds of the forest and the snores of the other men rather than the nightly Bible reading by the hearth he'd become accustomed to, then listening for Genny's soft, even breathing until he could relax. The memory of it stirred a pang in his heart. How was she faring with his parents?

Back at the tent he shared with Miles, Jesse pretended to search his bags for writing supplies until Miles headed for the creek, lye soap and a change of clothes in hand. Only when the hollering and splashing convinced him the miners were well occupied did he slip out. He carried his own bar of lye soap and change of clothes, but keeping to the trees as much as possible, he made his way to the shed.

His heart sank as he approached, for the padlock he'd noticed earlier in the week hung on the door. Marshall carried the key. And with no windows, there was no other way to access the interior.

Maybe Wade had been wrong to send someone as inexperienced as Jesse. All he knew how to do well was run. Even when Emma had been his bride of only a few months, he'd succumbed to his frustration, his restlessness...his emptiness... rather than look at the cause for it. Yes, Emma's need of him, her unrealistic expectations, had drowned him, but it went deeper and farther back than that. Genny was right. It went back to his mother.

Jesse raised his face toward the bright blue sky, to where a hawk circled high above. *Help me, God.* He couldn't do this by himself. How long did they have until Larry absconded with the gold meant for Charles...or Charles traced Genny's whereabouts to Gainesville? And how was he to find evidence against the blackguard when Jesse spent every day underground?

Helplessness weighted his shoulders as he headed for the creek, seeking a spot upstream, away from the levity of the men. After leaving his boots on the shore and rolling up his trousers, he waded against a burbling shoal, his toes seeking purchase on small stones and sandy creek bottom in the cold, rushing current. On the opposite side, quiet waters lapped a pool at the base of some jutting, horizontal boulders partially submerged in the hillside. A perfect place to wash.

Sloshing over, he shrugged out of his suspenders and reached down to tug his shirt over his head. Then froze. Just beyond the opening in the rocks, a strange object glinted from the sand—not fool's gold. And not there by accident. Someone would have to squeeze through the boulders to drop something there.

Jesse waded out of the creek, then bent to pluck his find from the sticky sand. A gold coin, one recently minted in North Carolina. What was it doing here?

He slipped the coin into his pocket and looked around. No one in sight. He sucked in his breath and eased between the boulders...right into an overhanging branch of mountain laurel. He shoved it aside, expecting to encounter solid hillside. But instead, he stared into a tunnel opening.

CHAPTER 18

Genny sat upright against her chair in Reverend and Mrs. Holden's dining room on the Friday night after her arrival, *cabobbled* over which fork to use with the brandied peach set before her. She sipped her water, stalling until Mrs. Holden picked up one of hers—ah, that little one with the ivory handle—and then did likewise.

"Did you not like your new gown, my dear?" Mrs. Holden pierced her with a stare from across the snowy white tablecloth gleaming with china and silver and illuminated by an Argand lamp. Jesse had not warned her that his parents enjoyed a formal supper every evening—nor that they dressed for it. "My seamstress stayed up until all hours to alter it for you, you know."

Genny pinched a fold of her white lawn gown in her lap. Had she been expected to wear the new dress tonight? "I do, although as I said, it comes far too dear."

Mrs. Holden had insisted they go shopping the day after her arrival. They found the striped peach-and-gold silk taffeta dress with its puffed sleeves and satin sash ready-made in a modiste's shop, but it required some alteration before Genny could wear it. They had picked it up prior to the shop closing today.

"Pawsh." Jesse's mother waved her hand at her. "We do not speak of such things."

"I...thought it might be *fitty* to save it for church on Sunday." Uncertainty made her statement waver—not only over when to wear the dress but how she was to endure such a public gathering where she would be on conspicuous display as the minister's new daughter-in-law. And Jesse not even there to help her.

But *would* he help her? Or was this all a charade to him, a burden he'd be relieved to get shed of after he dealt with Charles? He'd kissed her goodbye, yes, but it had been nothing like the kisses that fused them together in the inn. There she'd dared to hope he shared her feelings. Now he was already gone and apologizing for it. And then she'd turned to glimpse his mother at the window—the display most likely for her benefit.

Reverend Holden cast Genny a soft smile. "You will look lovely in it, I am sure."

His wife sniffed. "How would you know? You haven't seen it. Well, at least Miss Gillbard will be suitably attired to meet members of our congregation."

"Why do you insist on calling her by her formal title, and her maiden name, at that?" Reverend Holden's brows lowered, as did his tone. Though the gentle man often attempted to take his wife in hand, she clearly resented his interference, displaying a willfulness Genny failed to conceive of. Was there not some moderation to be found between the complete control Genny once suffered under and Mrs. Holden's spurning of even guidance meant for her betterment and kindness to others?

Mrs. Holden blew a little breath out between her pursed lips. "Forgive me, but I find this whole thing rather hard to believe. I know you said you and your father came here from

North Carolina, but surely, we would have crossed paths earlier if you and our Emma ran in the same social circles."

Genny dipped her chin. "I'm afraid I lived rather quietly while I was at Mt. Olivet, Mrs. Holden." There had not been money or invitations to do otherwise. Everyone there knew Genny did not enjoy the same family connections and privileges as her classmates. "My goal was to study and show myself worthy of my benefactor's investment."

"And did you?" Mrs. Holden held Genny's gaze even as her husband gaped at her temerity. "Show yourself worthy? What did you do after you graduated?"

Genny's fingers tightened around the stem of her glass. "Why, I...taught for a bit."

"Taught? What did you teach?" The woman's tone suggested Genny might have prostituted herself. If she learned the truth about Genny's life in Auraria, she'd likely come to that conclusion.

"I was a voice instructor." Genny's description of the accomplishments of her pupils and the Christmas cantata filled the gap until Jesse's parents led the way into the parlor for their nightly Bible reading. It was the only time in their household Genny could relax.

Tonight's passage came from Ephesians 2. Genny frowned as she settled into a tufted chair facing the couple on the sofa. Had they not read from a different book the night prior? As Reverend Holden read aloud, Genny closed her eyes and let the affirming words, so foreign to what she believed about herself, wash over her.

Loved greatly and raised up, seated with Christ in the heavenlies? Created to walk in specific good works rather than being merely a burden? And this gift of God, eternal life—she had believed in Him as a child, but had she ever truly received His grace?

She opened her eyes to find Jesse's father watching her.

Something about his tender expression made tears spring forth. Had he chosen this passage with her in mind?

Genny batted her lashes before her response could invite another interrogation from Jesse's mother. She rose quickly. "Thank you. I...uh, believe I'll retire now." Sudden fear shot through her. Mrs. Holden seemed to expect her availability at all hours. "That is, if it's all right with you."

"Why, it's not even—"

"Of course, Genny." Reverend Holden cut off his wife's protest, closing his Bible and rising in deference to Genny's departure. "We trust you will sleep well."

"Thank you." She hastened from the room, her heart beating rapidly in relief at her escape, but as she mounted the stairs, Mrs. Holden's voice drifted from the parlor.

"Cater to her all you want, Peter. I'm telling you, something is not right about that girl."

Genny curved her shoulders inward and hurried upstairs as fast as her tired leg would allow. At the top, however, the room across from hers drew her gaze. It had done so through the partially open door every time she had passed thus far. The glimpses she obtained of the blue walls and collectibles and books hinted this might have been Jesse's room. Now, with the Holdens ensconced in the parlor, would be a perfect time to take a quick peek.

She pushed the door open and slipped inside. Yes. Everything in here spoke of Jesse's past, from the volumes on mathematics, surveying, and nature, to the simple compass and battered violin case on the desk. Even the frock coats and fine wool trousers she found hanging in the armoire—finer clothing than she'd ever seen him wear, albeit with a whiff of mothballs. And a telescope at the window! Genny hurried over and bent to look through the lens. Past the edge of town, a hazy panorama of blue-green hills loomed up in the distance.

"Jesse was forever gazing through that thing." The voice

behind her brought Genny upright with a gasp. A hand in one pocket, Reverend Holden leaned against the doorframe. "Whether at stars or mountains."

"Oh…I think he might forever be doing that." Genny gave what she hoped was a playful grimace, though her heart was still hammering. "I know he still does, though without the telescope, of course."

"Yes, he's always exhibited a certain…restlessness of spirit. It must be hard to be parted from him under these circumstances, so I can't say I'm surprised to find you in here."

"I-I'm sorry. I should have asked first." Flushing as hotly as if she'd just done the polka in the full sun, she took a step back from the telescope.

"Ask to come into your own husband's room? We should have shown it to you the first day." The reverend straightened, dropping his hand. "No, indeed. I'm the one sorry to disturb *you*."

"Did…did you need something?" She folded her hands behind her back, fighting the urge to scamper out like a naughty schoolgirl despite his polite reassurance.

"Only to check on you. You seemed a bit out of sorts. I hoped it wasn't something we said or did."

Apart from his wife's declaration that there was something *not right* about her? But she wasn't supposed to have heard that.

Jesse's father read her slight hesitation. He gestured toward the chair by the desk, which she reluctantly sank upon, while he perched on the edge of the bed. "You were not in agreement with Jesse about coming here, I take it." His slight smile was understanding rather than accusing, inviting her confidence.

She let out a sigh. "I only knew the day before. I believe Jesse felt he was given no other choice."

His father firmed his mouth. "Yes, I would imagine he would feel that way."

"I fear it has been an imposition."

"To me, not at all." He lowered his voice. "My wife is less—how shall we say?—flexible. But please know, that has nothing to do with you personally."

Didn't it? Genny clamped her lips shut. She had already said too much.

The reverend carried on speaking in his soft, resigned tone. "She and Jesse have always been opposites. It's where that restlessness I mentioned earlier comes from, I believe. But for me, I am glad...relieved...to see that Jesse cares about something again. About you."

"Oh." She placed her hands on the arms of the chair. "I don't know." When his eyebrows winged up, she lowered her gaze. "You maybe can tell we did not know each other all that well. I'm afraid Jesse felt trapped by circumstances into helping me."

An unexpected sound from the minister—a rumble of a chuckle—drew her gaze back up. "It may have started that way, my dear, but the way my son looks at you now...well, I'll just say, it's something I have never seen."

She studied him, fishing for hints of insincerity. Did he mean...

"Never."

Yes. He meant with Emma. Genny let out a little breath and sat back.

Reverend Holden rested his hands on his knees. "He may have gone to help Wade entrap Charles, yes, but mark my words, he did so as much out of concern for your wellbeing as any belated sense of retribution."

How Genny wanted to believe that. Her heart squeezed at the hope that she might get to know the man who had left evidence of his life—a life she found rich and fascinating—in this room. Evidence of the interests that filled the void his mother's lack of love created?

Her...father-in-law drew himself up. "And I'm proud of him.

For the first time, he's not running away. He's confronting his problems head on. Now the question is, will he rush in recklessly in his own strength, driven by a desire to prove he's good enough, or will he allow God to guide him? Yes, we should pray for that." As if coming to a decision that ended his discourse, Reverend Holden gripped his knees and rocked forward to stand.

But Genny could not let the moment pass. Something about this man tugged at the depths of her being, dredging up her deepest doubts and needs. "I understand that...not feeling good enough."

"Oh? How so?" He settled back onto the bed.

Genny swallowed hard and pushed her question out lest her anxiety get the best of her. "What you read this evening...do you truly believe that God has a purpose for each of us...even women?" The last two words escaped so softly, had Jesse's father even heard them?

She didn't have to wonder long. A guffaw burst out of him, making her jump. "'Even women?' My dear, women most of all. For it is through the fairer sex that God leads the stubborn men of this world." She joined halfheartedly in his laugh for a moment. "Whatever would make you think such a thing?"

"I...have never been around men who give the women in their lives the...kindness, the grace that you give your wife...or that Jesse has given me. Almost like a...servant."

"Indeed, Christ Himself was a servant."

Genny shrugged and shook her head. "For my father, it was the opposite. Women were there to serve men. But I failed him. I was the reason he was forced to give up his family farm."

Reverend Holden's brow knit. "But how could that be?"

"Well, he needed sons to work the land." She held her hands up. "My mother...she tried...but after the loss of several baby boys, I heard him one night, telling her they wouldn't keep trying, but he'd have to go to work in the copper mine.

Mother tried to convince him we could help him enough, especially as I got older. Father said..." Genny dropped her gaze. "The only way I could help was to marry well."

"Ah, I see." Was that speculation in his soft observation?

Genny's lashes fluttered. "Not Jesse. Father had other plans for me. It was why he wanted me educated." She hurried on. "Anyway, after he went to the mine, we scarcely saw him. He worked all the time, became a foreman, and when he wasn't at the mine, he was at the pub with his men, drinking. Then we moved to North Carolina, and I lost Mother on the way."

"I'm so sorry to hear that. I'm sure that left you feeling quite alone in the world."

"Yes." She tucked her chin. "After that, no one talked about God anymore. It certainly seemed like He didn't have a good plan for my life."

"Oh, my dear, what a sad tale. I can see why you would feel that way."

This man of the cloth didn't judge her lack of faith? Genny glanced up at him. "That's...only part of it." Though it would be unwise to admit the rest of her sordid tale. Surely, even the good reverend had limits to what he would accept in a wife for his son.

But he didn't ask. Didn't press her. Just leaned forward and took her hand and squeezed it. "I'm so sorry for the pain in your life, Genny, and I'm not here to offer platitudes. But I will say that you have much life yet to live, and if you walk with God, He is perfectly capable of restoring the years the locusts have eaten."

Genny blinked at him. "I'm not sure what that means, but it sounds too good to be true."

Reverend Holden laughed. "It's part of Scripture, so it is true. And what He speaks over His children will come to pass."

"I would like that very much." Her soft admission hung in

the air between them. Genny didn't even know exactly what she was asking for, but Jesse's father seemed to.

He sat forward, bridging the distance between them. "Then let's pray, committing your life, and your life with Jesse, to Him. All right?"

Genny nodded. A life with Jesse. Could that really be a part of God's plan? And what if it wasn't? If she was restarting her life alone, would God be enough?

CHAPTER 19

$\mathcal{S}$unday morning at the appointed hour, Genny descended the stairs with a rustle of silk taffeta and a flutter of butterflies in her stomach. She fully expected Jesse's parents to be waiting in the foyer with hats and gloves on. Instead, as a rich voice boomed forth from the parlor, she nearly lost her footing on the bottom step.

> Come, Thou Almighty King,
> help us Thy name to sing;
> help us to praise:
> Father, all glorious,
> o'er all victorious,
> come and reign over us,
> Ancient of Days.

Goodness. This must be Reverend Holden's tradition of getting in voice for his sermon. He certainly possessed a rich baritone, and it was easy to see where Jesse came by his musical talent.

Genny pressed her reticule against her waist and moved to the door of the parlor.

The minister stood by the window in a fine suit of light worsted wool, a gray swirled tapestry vest, and a black silk cravat. "Ah, there she is. Just in time to help us greet our guests." He placed some papers he'd been holding on the desk.

"Guests?" Genny's eyes sought Mrs. Holden, who was directing the maid in circling the furniture and bringing in extra chairs from the dining room. The minister's wife also wore what must be one of her best dresses, a heavily pleated dove-gray silk gown with black kid slippers and black stockings decorated with blue thread. A lace-trimmed white cotton day cap fluttered above her side curls.

"Congregants." Reverend Holden spread his hands.

Mrs. Holden finally took notice of Genny. "Yes, you can remove that bonnet." She frowned at the faded blue contraption atop Genny's head. Wide-brimmed bonnets hardly fit into saddlebags, so her best headwear had been packed in her trunk, to be sent to Pendleton by Miss Mattie. Had her trunk arrived without her? Perhaps she could prevail upon Mrs. Paschal to receive it and then deliver it to her? "Thank goodness, for that eyesore ruins the dress."

Genny reached up to untie the bow beneath her chin. "But I thought..."

Reverend Holden's smile broke forth. "Oh, you thought we were going to a church. A perfectly reasonable assumption. However, for now, in the manner of the early believers, this is our sanctuary." He approached, gesturing around the room. "I'm afraid we do not have a building quite yet."

"I see." Genny removed her bonnet and let it hang by the ribbons. Truth be told, she was relieved not to have to wear it.

Mrs. Holden made a scoffing sound. "We are only here because the reverend disassociated from the conference when we moved from Athens. We had to, you see. The last Methodist circuit rider to attempt to conduct a service in Gainesville was ridden out of town."

"Oh my!" Genny blinked. "You must be very determined to spread the Gospel, in that case."

"Or to salvage what we sacrificed in South Carolina." Mrs. Holden's muttered comment was not lost on Genny, though her husband did not rise to the bait.

Instead, Reverend Holden's lips turned up. "We have only fifteen to twenty congregants each Sunday, but we do our best to honor our Savior as we follow in the tradition of the Wesley brothers—the great minister and evangelist, John, and the inspired hymn-writer, Charles. After all, God does not reside in a building, but in the hearts of the faithful." He touched Genny's elbow, and she returned his smile.

Fifteen or twenty...that sounded so much less intimidating than a large church full of people. Maybe she could manage this, after all—especially without her old bonnet.

About that time, someone tapped the door knocker. Genny gave the maid her hat and reticule and joined the Holdens in the foyer to greet the first arrivals.

All in all, the churchgoers—who seemed a far humbler sort than the Holdens—welcomed Genny with warmth and no untoward curiosity. They all spoke sincerely of how happy they were that Jesse had found love again. Of course, Genny made no effort to correct them, though she felt Mrs. Holden's sharp gaze upon her.

When the circle in the parlor was almost complete, Reverend Holden consulted his pocket watch and said to his wife, "It is time, my dear."

She pressed her lips together and shot a glance at the door. "But Samuel and our dear Belinda are not here yet. I did so want Genny to meet them."

She did? Warmth washed through Genny. "Who is this?"

"Strong supporters of our congregation." Reverend Holden

leaned closer and lowered his voice. "Likely to be instrumental in helping us acquire a building."

Jesse's mother raised her eyebrows. "More importantly, their daughter attended Mt. Olivet. I was hoping you might know her."

Genny's stomach went as hollow as the diving bell miners submerged to dredge gold from the Chestatee. "What is her name?"

"Shh." With an eye to the congregants, who had fallen silent, Reverend Holden drew them toward the parlor. "It's time to start."

Genny clamped her lips together and settled beside Mrs. Holden as her husband welcomed the worshippers and directed them to a joint reading in their prayer books. She had just fastened her attention on the page when the maid admitted a group of latecomers. Two women swept into the parlor in a rustle of silk, followed by a man in a black frock coat, hound's tooth trousers, and a black top hat.

Genny's heart went cold. The Culpers. The gaze of the younger woman fastened on her with surprise and the older woman's, with something akin to horror. And horrified she might well be, for as far as she was concerned, she was looking at the soiled songbird she'd seen dismissed from Mt. Olivet.

~

*T*he Good Lord might strike him dead for deception— and on the Sabbath, no less—but pretending to leave for church had been the only way Jesse knew to investigate the land across the river. He would've done so Friday night, but as soon as he crawled back out of the tunnel that was about half as narrow and wide as the Hanks Mine, Miles's voice rang across the river, calling him. Jesse let Miles believe him maudlin for

Genny as an excuse to stay in camp. But by the time all the men were ready to set out for town, David Taylor returned. He said at no point did they leave the camp abandoned.

Soon after, Verne Marshall arrived and distributed pay. As he whittled a chess piece that night, Jesse watched him across the fire, smoking his cigar with no expression on his face whatsoever. And silent as the grave. If Jesse was picking thieves, such a stoic man would top his list.

Attending Auraria Baptist offered as good an excuse as any to leave camp Sunday morning. Jesse doubted he'd make it in time for service, though he might eventually get to town...especially if he had a report to send to Wade. He tucked a pencil and paper in his pocket just in case.

Until he figured out what kind of structure the tunnel ended in, all he could tell his buddy was that he'd crawled in the pitch dark through a three-foot-square tunnel about a hundred yards. Then it widened prior to terminating in a wooden door bolted on both sides. Shoddily reinforced and dug from clay and rock that—so far as he could tell merely by striking flint here and again—contained no trace of gold veins, this was no mining tunnel. He could only surmise it was a transport tunnel.

Had he found the way Larry was getting his secret cut of Hanks's gold out?

Heavy gray clouds provided relief from the sweltering sun but trapped in the humidity as Jesse headed for the main road atop Perseus. Only after riding a quarter mile did he cut back through rugged terrain and cross the creek. He followed it downstream until he came out of a stand of black walnut and tulip poplar trees, startling a host of butterflies from the scarlet flowers of several rhododendrons atop the bluff above the mystery tunnel entrance. Jesse dismounted and led his stallion through the dense foliage in the direction he believed the tunnel ran, keeping a close eye out for snakes and an even closer eye for the human variety.

About a hundred yards in, no structure could be seen. Was this the right direction?

Then he rounded a massive chestnut tree, the kind as wide as a man was tall, and there beneath a clump of white pines sat a bark hut, the type swindlers trespassing to prospect tossed up. The pine needles hadn't even been cleared from the circumference of the round hut, and no chimney poked from its roughly thatched roof. In fact, there were no signs of residence at all. The only indication the hut might have been used recently was a picket line, loose and empty, sagging between two trees.

Thank You, God. With any luck, he might find an unlocked door. Or at least one easy to break into.

Jesse chuckled to himself and started forward when a loud snort from a horse froze his steps—coming from the direction opposite the hut. With a hand to Perseus's nose, he backed his stallion behind the chestnut, on the other side of a mountain laurel.

The rider whistled a stanza of "The Hunters of Kentucky" as he rode up and dismounted. Was that some sort of signal?

Jesse peeked around the chestnut and stiffened. He recognized that brown stallion...and its rider. The same pair he'd accosted by Wade's creek. Only, the clean-shaven face was bare today. Not one he'd seen before, except briefly on the day he'd found Genny. But the man's lean build and languid movements left no doubt as to his identity.

The newcomer tethered his horse and took a few minutes pulling bags and parcels from his saddlebags—not the kind that clicked or seemed as weighty as if they held gold, but the kind that bulged as though they might be full of foodstuffs. Was he preparing to stay for a while? To ready the place for visitors? He carried the bags to the entrance, set them down with a grunt, and reached into his waistcoat pocket for a key. Strange...

a bark hut with a proper lock. The man went inside and shut the door behind him.

Jesse led Perseus back toward the creek. He had a message to send to Wade.

~

"What is *she* doing here?" The imperious voice rang out behind Genny before she could make her excuses to Mrs. Holden and escape upstairs, and mere seconds after the benediction of the Sunday service. This, after Genny's nemesis remained angled away with her nose in the air, markedly ignoring her for the duration of the service.

Genny didn't have to turn around to envision the wealthy matron's horrified visage, down to her flushed cheeks and the silk flowers under the brim of her deeply scooped bonnet rim, practically trembling in her indignation.

Mrs. Holden let out a little puff of air. "Why, this is the new Mrs. Jesse Holden." Probably her mother-in-law was more affronted by her favorite's tone than her implication.

"Say it isn't so! Samuel, come here and verify this is the same young woman we had cast out of Mt. Olivet lest she lead our young daughters astray." Mrs. Culper groped behind her until her husband took her hand and came to her side.

"It certainly is," he said.

A full gasp now from Jesse's mother. "Whatever do you mean? Miss Gillbard was a pupil there, then an instructor of voice."

Their daughter, Marianna, edged forward, speaking in a tentative tone. "Mama—"

"More like, an instructor of vice!" Mrs. Culper's backward swatting motion silenced her offspring and made Genny cringe. "What else could be said for Charles Martin's kept woman?"

Whatever other conversations buzzed amongst the little clusters of congregants ceased. Shocked faces turned their way.

Genny might wish to disappear into the pile of the Oriental carpet, uncovered by the drugget for the service, but a snippet of Scripture Reverend Holden had read earlier that week flooded her mind. *We are His workmanship.* She lifted her chin a fraction and met Mrs. Culper's eyes. "I was Mr. Martin's ward, not his woman. And now I am Jesse's wife."

Reverend Holden hurried over. He slipped his hand under her elbow. "That is correct, Mrs. Culper. Perhaps there has been some confusion. I'm certain you did not intend to disparage our new daughter-in-law."

Mrs. Culper's gaze cut to him. "If you have taken in this light-skirt, I fear for the future of this congregation, Reverend Holden. Ask around. You'll find it is common knowledge Miss Gillbard was not only a singer in Mr. Martin's Aurarian saloon, but he also led her a merry dance, letting her think he would wed her, only to cast her aside, her reputation ruined."

"If that is true"—Reverend Holden's tone was gravelly—"then it should be pity offered by good Christian folk, not judgment."

"Pft. If you wish to preach to riffraff rather than establish a real church, who am I to say you nay?" Mrs. Culper turned for the door, her family in tow.

Marianne cast Genny a sorrowful look as she passed. The other churchgoers filed out with murmured goodbyes, their downcast glances indicating they harbored no wish to share in the private moment that would surely follow. Genny managed to remain upright on her trembling legs until the door closed behind the last of them. Then she would have sank to the floor had Reverend Holden not upheld her.

"Come. Sit." He led her to the nearest chair. "That was not to be borne. I am speechless."

"So am I." Mrs. Holden's bosom seemed to swell. "It appears

Miss Gillbard is not the only one to have been led a merry dance."

Genny and Reverend Holden gazed at her, mouths open.

She remained focused on Genny. "Does Jesse know? Or did you lure him with your charms and then conspire together to deceive his parents about what type of woman he had wed?"

Genny swallowed the rock in her throat and pressed Reverend Holden's hand when he would have protested. Only the full truth would do now. "Jesse knows. He...saved me from a raucous miner the first time I sang at the Boom or Bust."

His mother released a strangled moan and lifted her hand to her chest.

"I was too young and naïve to realize how singing there would harm my future. I thought it was a stepping stone to a musical career." She chanced a glance at Reverend Holden's concerned countenance. "My father...left me in the care of Mr. Martin. It was true he led me to believe he would marry me, but I...I didn't..."

"It's all right, my dear." He patted her hand.

"I'm not a light-skirt."

"Of course, you aren't."

In fact, despite all the other ways Charles had compromised her, she was still pure, though she would hardly declare that to her husband's parents. She chose a different tack. "But Charles...Mr. Martin...did treat me poorly. He was a man of... evil character." She dropped her hand to her side, her limbs suddenly limp. "Jesse saved me from that too."

A beat of silence followed, after which Reverend Holden murmured, "No wonder you love him."

"So you are telling me..." Mrs. Holden squared her shoulders, drew a breath, and started over. "You are telling me that our wayward son, who spurned the most perfect first wife he could ever have wished for, chose to stain his own reputation— and ours—to save a *saloon girl*?"

"Dorothy!" Reverend Holden's outraged exclamation surely rivaled the lowest note Charles Wesley had ever written into a hymn.

"No, please, it is all right. Please do not fall out on my account." Genny tucked her hand beneath her and pushed herself up from the chair. "After all, what she said is not far from the truth. But I can promise you, I'll do all I can to ensure the stain is not permanent." She owed Jesse that much.

She walked out of the parlor on wobbly legs. No doubt, the only reason Jesse's father didn't follow her was to further scold his wife. Their hushed voices resumed as Genny mounted the stairs. She was after pen and paper. She had a letter to write to Miss Mattie's sister in Pendleton.

CHAPTER 20

$\mathcal{A}$s dawn broke on Friday morning, Genny placed the last of her possessions in the leather satchel the maid had given her and fastened the top. Her heart squeezed when she thought of the songbird Jesse carved for her. She'd left it at Wade's cabin because she'd not realized she wouldn't be returning. Fitting...considering she'd left her desire to sing there too.

She took one last look around the lovely room that had been hers for the past week. Funny to think, her father might have been pleased for her to end up here. If only Jesse's mother were a different sort of person. But then, Jesse would be different too. Without his hardships, he might not have become the man he was—a man with a servant's heart like his father's. And then she might not have fallen in love with him.

But Mrs. Holden was not the only problem. The real issue was the fact that Genny could not stay with a man who didn't know if he really wanted her, and who could not love her with his whole heart. Because Jesse's heart was not healed any more than hers was. Despite that, she couldn't regret coming here. Reverend Holden had taught her that she possessed intrinsic value and worth in God's eyes, and that God would go with her even if she must walk out of here alone.

Genny tugged the satchel from the bed and squared her shoulders. A glance at the coverlet and she smoothed out the wrinkle. Mrs. Holden should be relieved to find her gone without a sign she had ever been there. Except...she left a note on the dresser with the address where they could contact her to sign whatever papers she needed to sign to annul her marriage. That the notion left her hollow as a gutted fish did not weigh into matters. By the time Jesse contacted her, the in-name-only arrangement would have served its purpose. He would have addressed the grievances of his past, freeing him to go to Mississippi.

She would not be his second Emma and hold him back.

Voices in the Holdens' bedroom assured her the couple was not down to breakfast yet. Clanking and humming from the kitchen indicated the cook was hard at work. Monday, the maid had proven herself trustworthy when she posted Genny's letter to Miss Mattie, letting her know Genny would be taking the Friday stage to Pendleton if Mattie could confirm that she would communicate with her sister. Genny had received a concerned reply in the affirmative yesterday. So now she could ease down the stairs and let herself out onto the street—as yet uncrowded with morning workers and shoppers bound for the square.

A breath of nighttime's cool lingered with the morning dew as she exited through the gate in the picket fence and set off toward downtown. She had spied the stagecoach office when Mrs. Holden had taken her to the modiste. A cut-through on a side street past the butcher's and tanner's shops would see her there most directly.

Genny paused before crossing the street, glancing back at an enclosed carriage that pulled from a driveway opposite the Holdens' and headed in her direction. Some distance back yet, the driver waved for her to go ahead. Returning the gesture, she did so. The side street lacked a boardwalk, but she'd just made it to the far side when jangling hardware and horse hooves swiveled her head. The same conveyance turned behind her. Eyes widening, Genny darted for the overhang of the butcher's shop. Would they run her down?

The carriage door flew open. A man in dark clothing and hat leapt out right next to her.

"Excuse *me*—" Genny's indignant protest cut short as the man grabbed her—a man with a bandana over the lower half of his face. Just like the one who had chased her outside Auraria! She drew breath to scream.

He hooked one arm around her waist and with the other, he shoved and held a bandana in her mouth. *No!* Genny struggled, her cries trapped in her throat, but his arms gripped her with the tenacity of a bear trap. Her bag fell with a thud.

Her feet dragged, then left the ground as the man jerked her into the carriage after him. He released her mouth to grab the door.

"You idiot!" A woman's voice spoke as Genny thrust the cloth from her mouth and sucked in air to cry out.

Thwack! Something hard as steel struck the back of her head, and the dark interior faded into even deeper blackness.

～

"Mind if I stop off at the post office?" Jesse jerked his head toward said location as he and David Taylor rode into Auraria Friday around one. "I'll join you at the assayer's in a minute."

A malfunction with the pulley system of the vertical shaft delayed their departure, and the foreman was already grumpy, but this might well be Jesse's only chance to complete his errand in privacy. Miles had been correct—Larry wanted to meet the mine's newest hire. Thus, Jesse was tapped to accompany David on this week's delivery. Which made it all the more imperative that he hear from Wade about what to do next.

Jesse had snuck across the river twice this past week to spy on the activity at the bark hut. Tuesday, the brown stallion had been picketed outside, and a small cart—the type you could pull behind a horse—sat beside the house. On his second visit yesterday, the horse was gone, but a second cart had been delivered. If there was indeed gold behind that bolted door the tunnel led to, they were about to move it somewhere.

David frowned over at him. "Best hurry. Larry doesn't like to be kept waiting." He spoke above the plunking of a piano and a bawdy ditty pouring from the open doors of a saloon they passed—miners getting an early start to the weekend.

Jesse tipped his hat and turned Perseus toward the old Nuckolls inn where mail was still sorted. In the dark interior that reeked of whale oil, cigar smoke, and burnt lard, he headed for the postal window. When the postmaster who had replaced Robert Ligon handed him a dirty envelope from Gainesville, Jesse's heart leapt. Stepping out into the light, he slit the flap and brought out a small piece of paper containing a few sentences of Wade's slanting scrawl.

My cabin, 3 p.m. Saturday. With preparations for the Brown trial, it's the earliest I can get there. We'll plan for a raid. Peace, brother.

The signature ignited a burning in Jesse's chest. Yes. Together, they'd bring about peace—a resolution of the failure that had haunted them since the past year. He folded the missive and tucked it away in his inner waistcoat pocket. Just knowing his friend—who still thought well enough of him to call him *brother*—would soon be here to formulate a plan kicked his pulse up a notch. Soon this would be over, one way or another. Then he could decide—

"Hey!"

Jesse whirled to find the aproned postmaster in the door, waving another letter.

"Sorry, Mr. Holden. This one was stuck in the bin. Looks important. Public Land Survey System."

Jesse's stomach dropped as the man shuffled forward to hand him the second envelope. Thanking him, Jesse opened it as the postmaster returned to his counter. He quickly scanned the official-looking script. Slots were filling fast as the surveying in Georgia ended. He needed to be there by the end of the month to guarantee his position.

The vice grip around his chest tightened. It could take a couple of weeks to travel to the new territory—not to mention the possibility that he'd need to testify in a trial. He might not be willing to stick around for Brown's, but he could hardly leave Wade hanging if his testimony was needed in Larry's or Charles's. That was...if they could apprehend either of them. What if they couldn't?

And what about Genny?

Panic threatened to pull him under as he untethered Perseus and cut through an alley. He'd pass behind the buildings to the side street the assayer's office fronted.

How was he going to get to Mississippi in time? *It's impossible, God.* He flung the declaration up at the heavens.

Just as quickly, a response popped into his head. *The things which are impossible with men are possible with God.* The verse came from a recent passage he'd read by lantern light in his tent.

Jesse took up the gauntlet. *All right, then. Show me.*

As light spilled in at the end of the alley, a movement to his left drew his eye—a man exiting the rear door of a two-story white frame building. Jesse's feet froze. That was the Boom or Bust. And the tall man, expensively clad, with wavy brown hair, was equally unmistakable—Charles Martin.

Rather than turning the corner, he headed a few paces downhill toward a log storage building in the tree line. Another man moved from the shade to meet him under the shed roof. Larry Jones! Jesse moved back a step to watch from the shadow of the mercantile. And hopefully, eavesdrop, though only snatches of their greetings carried above the street noise behind him.

"...at the appointed spot." Larry offered Charles something —a small pouch or piece of fabric. "Pickup after dark."

"You expect me to go *there*?" Charles's indignant reply was unmistakable.

"We've taken enough risk, acting in broad daylight. Now, pay up." Larry shoved out his palm.

"I'll pay tonight when you take your cut."

Tonight? Jesse's heart hammered. If they were moving the gold this very evening, he would be on his own. And he didn't have the authority to arrest anyone.

Larry posted his hands on his hips, biceps bulging beneath the cuffs of his rolled-up linen shirt. "Now, or the deal's off."

With a growl, Charles reached into his vest pocket and produced what appeared to be a small wad of bills. After Larry took it, he gave a brusque wave. "Go on. Get out of here."

The older man counted the cash, then a grin split his face. "Don't worry. You won't be seeing me again."

Finally, Jesse had evidence, even if it was only in the form of his testimony.

He held his hand to Perseus's nose and backed them into the alley before turning the horse and mounting. Most likely, Larry would head the opposite direction toward the assayer's, but Jesse would take no chance. Neither could he keep his meeting with David and Larry. And not just because he possessed the worst bluffing face east of the Mississippi. He had only one choice—ride to Gainesville to get Wade and hope to make it back in time.

~

*T*he rocking movement slowed. The flashes of light too.

Where was she? The side street in Gainesville...the carriage...

As the motion that had lulled her between bouts of deeper unconsciousness finally stopped, Genny struggled to open her eyes. A sudden rectangular glare made her pinch them closed again with a groan.

Her head pounded. An ache blossomed from the back. And her mouth...so dry. Literally, full of cotton. She had been abducted, gagged. And bound, for a rope bit into her wrists, joining her hands in front of her. The cuff of one of her sleeves was torn, a piece missing. When had that happened?

Genny slumped against someone—a man who smelled of cheap whiskey and sweat. Not Charles, then. She must focus. Must get away, before Charles or Larry made an appearance.

"Quick. She's waking up." The feminine voice that had invaded her awareness off and on rang with command. And why did the harsh whisper sound familiar? Genny slit open her eyes just as the woman's dark form exited the carriage in a rustle of taffeta.

The man at Genny's side turned toward her. Middle-aged, with dark hair poking from under his wide-brimmed hat and stubble shadowing his jaw. A cry died in her throat. The ostler from the livery in Auraria! She shrank into the corner with a whimper.

With a snort, he jabbed one hand behind her and the other under her legs. He dragged her from the carriage and smashed her against his chest while Genny kicked her legs and pushed on him with her bound hands. Late-afternoon sunlight streaked through branches heavy with leaf and pierced her skull. Other hands grabbed her, hauling her up—onto a horse!

Genny bucked and flailed, her screams muffled.

"Now, ma'am." The voice that spoke over her as thick arms came around her was surprisingly gentle and entreating. "It's best you go easy."

She huffed. Growled. And glared into the brightest blue eyes she'd ever seen. This man looked more like a mischievous overgrown boy than a criminal.

Lips encircled by a full, dark beard turned up the slightest bit. "That's right. Don't fight me, and you won't get hurt."

He clicked to his bay stallion, and they set off down a narrow dirt trail. Behind them, leather creaked and hooves clopped as the others mounted on horses this man must have brought, and then followed. Metal jingled and wheels rumbled as the carriage driver drove away.

When her captor turned off into the forest, iron bands of terror tightened across Genny's chest. How would she ever get away from three of them? And even if she did, how would she have any idea where she was?

~

*A*fter a couple of hours of hard riding down the ridge into the Piedmont, Jesse pulled up where Auraria Road intersected the Old Federal Road. The merciless mid-July sun beat down on his shoulders and slicked his stallion's coat. He paused to uncork his canteen, patting Perseus's neck. "Almost to the ford of the Chestatee, old boy, then you can get a drink too."

He'd just swigged and lowered his canteen when his gaze snagged on a familiar rider cantering toward him. His stomach lurched. Wade! Something was wrong, or he wouldn't be here. Not to mention with a brace of pistols riding his hips and a rifle bouncing in a sling on his saddle. Jesse corked the canteen and let it drop by his side, kneeing Perseus to trot forward to intercept his friend.

Wade didn't give him a chance to inquire what was amiss. He started speaking even prior to pulling up on his winded stallion's reins. "Genny's gone! Your parents came to tell me. They found her room empty this morning—"

"Gone?" The word—and the world—exploded in a cacophony of panic. "Where did she go?"

"She left a forwarding address for Pendleton." Wade snatched off his hat and dragged his sleeve over his glistening forehead. "We can only assume she meant to take the stage, but when we inquired at the coaching office, she never arrived."

Never arrived? Then she *wasn't* in Pendleton? "You think someone took her?"

Perseus picked up on Jesse's tension and pranced off the road in a tight circle as a driver and wagon filled with wooden casks rumbled by.

A furrow dented the space between Wade's dark brows, and he gave a single, regretful nod. "My deputy found her satchel on a side street. The butcher said he heard a commotion early this morning, but by the time he got to the front door, a carriage was pulling off."

Charles? Visions of the potential outcome assailed Jesse like angry bats swooping from a cave, and a groan ripped out of his midsection. "How could you let this happen? Didn't you have men watching the house?" As soon as the words were out, guilt stabbed him. If anyone was to blame, it was Jesse himself. His friend wasn't at fault for failing to guard Genny's person when Jesse had not guarded her heart.

What a nightmarish echo of the past this day was becoming.

"As much as I could with the Brown trial coming up. We're stretched thin. There were...gaps." Wade pushed his sweat-slicked hair back and shoved his hat on his head. "I'm so sorry, Jesse. I should have stayed at your parents' house."

"No. No one is more to blame than I."

"Well, your mother, maybe." Wade grimaced.

"Why...what did she do?" Despite the question, Jesse's voice lowered with each word.

"Apparently, there was some incident with parents of a former pupil of Genny's. All you need to know now is, Mrs. Holden feels horrible."

"As well she should." He ground out a sigh and stretched in the stirrups. "We're wasting time. Where do we look?"

"The fox's lair." One of Wade's brows lifted. "Where else?"

Jesse drew his reins tighter. "The Boom or Bust it is." Right back where this all started.

"But Jesse...?" Wade held out his arm. He waited until Jesse looked at him. "I need your agreement that we do things my way. According to the law."

Jesse hesitated only a second and then nodded. He'd come to find his friend, the sheriff, because he couldn't do this without his help. And precious hours had slipped away since Genny was taken. He must find her before Charles secreted her someplace and Jesse lost his only real chance at redemption.

No...his chance at real love. His reaction to Wade's news proved the truth he'd been trying to deny for weeks. Retribution on Charles, apprehending thieves, the job in Mississippi—none of it mattered. Only Genny.

CHAPTER 21

Cicadas sang from the trees and the evening light glittered through the leaves like liquid gold by the time Genny's captors pulled up outside a bark hut hidden in the forest. Two small carts sat outside.

The dark-bearded man mounted behind her patted her hip with his hand free of the reins. "Now you behave while I hand you down to Clive."

She narrowed her eyes and glared at him the best she could around the gag.

He chuckled. "Got a little fire in you, don't you? I can see the appeal. Too bad you're already spoken for."

His comment shot panic through her, fueling the fire of indignation that burned steadily brighter as they traveled through the forest. How dare these people treat her this way? As though she was a commodity to be traded to the highest bidder, a possession...a worthless piece of chattel. No more. She would fight for her freedom no matter the cost.

The ostler, Mr. Simms, came over, and the bearded man grasped her beneath her arms to ease her down to him. Simms lifted his arms to receive her. Genny took her chance, bringing her knee up with as much force as she could muster into Simms's groin. With an *oof*, he bent double. The bearded man burst out laughing.

Genny ran for the trees, stumbling without the balance of her arms. Yes, the man on the horse would follow, but they'd passed a mountain laurel thicket near the river where she might could lose him.

The hammer of a gun clicked behind her.

"No!" Simms gasped out the command. "Larry said not to harm her."

Genny darted around a stand of pines—and almost ran broadside into the third rider who had not dismounted yet. Yards of blue taffeta foamed over the withers of a black mare. A leather-gloved hand trained a small pistol on her. And above that, a familiar face twisted in disdain.

"Don't try me. I don't have a problem leaving Charles a wounded songbird. In fact, it would serve him right to find you dead—which you already would be if these two dunderheads did their job right the first time."

Miss Mattie? She had been working against her all this time? Apparently, from the moment Genny fled Auraria, Mattie had assured she did so with her help.

Tears filled Genny's eyes. The manager of Charles's saloon girls had remained far enough behind during the ride that Genny never glimpsed her face. Betrayal writhed in her chest, trust dying a painful death. "Why?" She managed to enunciate the word past the gag with enough clarity that understanding dawned in Mattie's features.

"Why?" A harsh laugh burbled from her throat. "You really have to ask?"

As large hands clamped onto Genny's elbows from behind, shock weakened her limbs so that she couldn't resist. Mattie tucked her pistol in her pocket and slid from her horse. She stalked closer, surveying Genny with disgust. When Genny attempted to form a plea, Mattie reached for the gag.

"What are you doing?" With a shuffle of leaves, Simms hobbled up next to the younger man who held Genny. "The camp's just over the river. What if she yells?"

"It's Friday night." The voice of Genny's guard rumbled against her back with a touch of mirth. "The men will be livin' it up in town, including the foreman. He thinks he left me on guard."

Mattie leveled a steady look at Genny. "Screaming will do you no good. Understand?"

Genny gave a single nod, and Mattie lowered the gag. Genny ran her tongue around her parched mouth but found no moisture. "I thought you were my friend." Her words came out raspy, pitiful.

Mattie hooted. "Your *friend*? Are you blind as well as stupid? Did you truly have no idea that you took the only man I ever wanted? Since the moment you showed up with your father, all sweet and innocent with your pathetic aspirations to become a diva, Charles never looked at me again. Nothing would do but you. Well, he's getting you—and let's hope he prizes you more than his cut of the gold." She snickered.

So Larry had been working with Charles all this time— with the intention of betraying him?

"No! Please, Mattie. I never wanted his attention. You know how hard I tried to get away." Genny rushed her words in case they stuffed the gag back in her mouth. "You can't give me to him. You said yourself what a dangerous man he is."

"Doesn't matter. He wants *you*. And he paid Larry a hefty sum for you. Soon as he gets here with our payment, we'll load up the gold and be gone, leaving you to wait for your *suitor*." Mattie said the last with a sickening smirk. "Maybe if he gets you alive rather than dead, he won't come after us and the gold." She turned toward the hut, speaking over her shoulder to the men. "Take her inside."

"No! Please." Genny struggled against her captor. "I'll leave, go to the new territory. My husband is a surveyor. I can convince him to take me with him." If that was the price of her freedom, they could pay it and work out the details once they were far from this place.

"A surveyor?" When the man holding her spun her around to face him, Genny almost fell. "What's his name?"

Genny blinked at him. Could any further harm come to Jesse if she spoke it?

"C'mon, Miles. What does it matter?" Simms popped his conspirator's arm with the back of his hand.

Miles didn't spare him a glance. Instead, he shook Genny. "His name."

"J-Jesse. Jesse Holden."

The flash of emotions over the young man's face—Miles's face—drew Genny up short. Was that regret? "You...you know him?"

Just as quickly, something akin to horror seemed to dawn on him. He shoved Genny toward the hut and said to Simms, "We've got to load the gold. Now. We can't wait on Larry."

"Why? What's the problem?" Mattie had stopped and turned back.

"Jesse Holden hired on with Rupert Hanks two weeks ago. He's been in the mine with me ever since. If he was the guy who rode up to the cabin when we tried to grab her last month, the one I didn't get a good look at when the stupid dog chased me..." His blue eyes flashed. "Someone's onto us."

〜

When Jesse and Wade pushed through the doors of the Boom or Bust, Jesse wanted to roar against the rumbling of the early-evening crowd competing with the plunking notes of the piano across the way. But Wade simply slid his badge across the bar to the older man wiping glasses on the other side. "Wade Coulter, Hall County sheriff."

A few men at the closest table looked their way, but Jesse didn't take his gaze off the barkeep.

"Walter Shoemaker. What can I do you for?"

Wade slipped his badge back in his waistcoat pocket. "I need to see your boss. Now."

The man surveyed Wade and Jesse, both of them sweat-soaked and wound tight as poked rattlers. "He's not here." His creased forehead indicated he was probably leery enough of them to be telling the truth. "He left twenty minutes ago."

Jesse stepped forward. "Where did he go?"

Walter raised a brow. "You his deputy?"

Jesse balled his fists. Genny had said this man, Larry's replacement, had been kind to her, though she'd never trusted him fully. "You could say that."

"Sorry. Don't know." Walter shrugged. "I've been behind this bar the whole time."

Helplessness burned through Jesse's patience like a fuse on a powder charge. "Miss Mattie, then. We'll talk to her." Maybe the woman who had helped Genny flee Charles would know the man's whereabouts.

Walter set a glass on the counter. "You won't be talking to her either. She left last night, and I don't reckon on her coming back."

Wade exchanged a glance with Jesse before leaning over the bar. "Seems awful convenient they're both gone and you don't know where. It would behoove you to cooperate."

Walter draped his towel over his shoulder. "Soon as you tell me what I'm cooperatin' *with*."

Wade hung his thumb in Jesse's direction. "With finding this man's wife, who was abducted from Gainesville this morning. We have reason to think your boss is behind it."

Some of the ruddy color bled from the man's face. "Abducted?" His gaze swung to Jesse. "You're wife's not...Genny Gillbard, is she? The Songbird of Auraria?"

Jesse snapped off a nod. "Genny Holden now."

"By George, he's gone and done it." Walter took a step back and palmed his neck, his gaze going unfocused.

"Done what?" Jesse moved closer, barely restraining himself from grabbing the man by his stained apron and shaking the truth from him.

Walter's attention darted to him, and a guarded expression shuttered his features as he lowered his hand. "Whatever I suspected, I took no part in it."

Wade held his hand out, calmly entreating. "Whatever foreknowledge you had can be forgiven ...if you tell us what you know now. Choose not to, and you'll be considered an accessory to whatever crimes your employers may have committed."

The man's Adam's apple bobbed. "I didn't know they were gonna take the girl, I swear. I wasn't even sure about the gold, but Larry Jones, who worked here before I did, ran off at the mouth a time or two, braggin' about how he would skip town with a cut of Rupert Hanks's stash. I thought he put it behind him when he was made manager—maybe figured a steady income would be better. If he was siphoning off a bit here and there, it wasn't my business. I hear a lot of things, workin' here. Can't believe all of them, and you guard your back by not gettin' involved." His tone had grown defensive.

"Was Larry acting on his own?" Wade clenched his fist on the counter. He wanted evidence against Charles. Jesse just wanted to stop the talking and find Genny, but the stoic barkeep had found his tongue.

"He pretended he was mad at Charles for firing him when he roughed up Miss Genny." Walter slid an anxious look toward Jesse. "But I would bet they was workin' together the whole time. Only, Larry planned to double-cross him. He always resented Charles, said he'd been born with the silver spoon in his mouth and treated everyone like they were beneath him. Took what he wanted with no regard to others."

Jesse slammed his hand on the counter. "You think Larry abducted Genny *for* Charles." All along, Genny had been uncertain which man sent the trackers after her, but if Larry had orchestrated the search for her on Charles's behalf, they were looking at one group of criminals, not two. As a new confirmation struck, he let out a scoffing breath.

"What?" Wade nudged him.

"That payment I saw behind the Boom or Bust...I think it was for Genny, not Larry's services in procuring the gold." Jesse's pulse surged in his ears and sudden certainty through his veins. "Wade, they have her at the bark hut. We've got to ride there *now*."

"The thing is..." The barkeep's untimely intrusion drew both their attention. "I don't think they acted alone."

Jesse couldn't stop the shaking of his hands, but he did his best to focus. "Yeah, someone on Hanks's crew had to get the goods out. I suspect Verne Marshall who always guarded the gold." Or David Taylor. Just because he'd ridden into town with Jesse this morning and therefore couldn't have snatched Genny didn't mean he hadn't helped Larry by transporting Hanks's gold.

"Not him." Walter shook his head slowly and lifted an index finger to the floorboards above. "*Her*."

Jesse's heart bottomed out. "You think Mattie was in on it?"

If the woman Genny trusted was involved the whole time, it explained how the men knew when and where to accost her. Genny had thought the woman cared about her. What a betrayal.

Walter extended his callused hand, palm up. "Awful convenient, her packing up all she owned and taking off last night. And in a hired carriage."

Wade's wide gaze latched onto Jesse's, then he asked the barkeep, "You have access to their rooms?"

"Miss Mattie had the only key to hers." A smirk turned up the man's thick lips. "But I can break down a door."

Jesse angled himself between the two men and pinned Wade with his most entreating gaze. "We don't have time for that. We should ride to—"

"We're doing this my way, remember?" Wade's gravelly tone reminded Jesse he was a lawman first, a friend second. "If there is evidence of other conspirators, I need to know that going into a confrontation. Jesse, I have to do things right this time."

Wade's need for redemption thrummed in his tone, but Jesse ground his teeth. He couldn't take on at least three armed criminals alone. But Wade's determination to bring them in according to the law could cost Genny her virtue...or her life.

~

Genny huddled in absolute darkness, fighting terror. Though her captors had left her mouth and feet unbound, it did her little good. There was no one to hear her if she screamed and no place to go if she ran.

After the thieves moved a pair of small trunks from the cellar into the carts outside and hitched them to two of their horses, Larry pushed into the hut to wish her well. And then, with a cruel grin, he removed her gag long enough to smash his mouth against hers. Likely, only Mattie's urging for them to hurry up and leave spared Genny further abuse. Even now, she wanted to spit as she recalled the sour taste of his saliva on her lips. Then he'd lowered Genny into the space under the hut left vacant of the trunks.

Before they closed the trap door over her, the lantern light from the hut's interior had revealed another door, one that must lead to an adjacent chamber or passageway hacked roughly out of the clay and rock. But when she'd managed to stand as far as the low ceiling allowed and lift the bolt, the door hadn't budged. Maybe a similar board held it in place from the opposite side. They had planned this carefully.

What hurt worst of all was that Miss Mattie, the one woman who should have understood her desperation to evade Charles's grasp, was leaving her to him like bait in a trap.

Had she any hope of rescue? She had dropped her satchel when they took her off the street. Would someone have found it? Would they surmise foul play even if they did? And then, would they contact the sheriff or merely take her possessions home with them?

As for Jesse's parents, she should expect no intervention from them. Mrs. Holden had probably read her note with rejoicing. She would assume Genny had boarded the stage and would have no reason to tell anyone she had gone until Wade called again—whenever that would be. Last he'd visited her on Tuesday, he'd heard nothing from Jesse. Who knew if Jesse had made any progress in solving the gold theft? The lack of information seemed to confirm her decision to leave for Pendleton rather than waiting for a resolution that might not come. If Jesse couldn't find the evidence they sought, why wouldn't he simply leave for Mississippi?

Now the desperation of her circumstances acted as a filter to her motives in the same way the screen in Jesse's sluice box separated sediment from gold. She'd told herself she was taking the high road, being noble in putting his desires ahead of her own. In truth, she'd still been reacting from the wounded pride that poisoned her system after his rejection, then his mother's. She should have spoken with Wade before leaving, checked for any updates, and surrendered her personal feelings to his professional judgment. She'd been too determined not to rely on a man.

No. She'd trusted a woman, and look where that had gotten her.

What's more, had she stopped to pray ahead of firing off her letter and then setting off on her own? Indeed, she had failed to ask the only One whose guidance was inerrant.

Genny blew a breath out that barely stirred the tendril of hair sticking to her face. Was it too late to start now? She wasn't very good at this, obviously. *God, please send someone—anyone— who isn't Charles.*

Now what? She shifted in vain search of a more comfortable position against the dank ground. Sweat trickled down her breastbone beneath her corset. She didn't know much Scripture, but the verses of the hymns her mother had sang to her— many of them hymns by Charles Wesley that Reverend Holden also favored—had lodged in her mind for years. She started with the most familiar, drawing a soft breath and singing quietly into the darkness. "'Rock of Ages, cleft for me...'"

As she sang, the darkness did surely recede. Warmth filled her chest, and the cellar seemed less a prison and more an embrace, for she no longer felt alone.

She was on her third hymn when a noise outside—a bigger rustle than the creatures of the forest might make—dried the words in her throat. A flood of cold awareness followed by prickling goosebumps washed over her. Had someone arrived? Had they heard her?

Instinctively, she stumbled to her feet, though she could

only stand hunched over, taking short, quick breaths and straining her ears. Yes, above her, the door creaked, and booted steps thudded on the flooring concealed by the rudimentary hut. Her heart raced, and indecision tore her mind as viciously as two curs fighting over a bone. Should she call out...or remain silent? Had help come...or her greatest harm?

CHAPTER 22

For a few moments of complete silence, Genny held her breath. Then wood scraped, and with a wrenching sound from above, the trap door opened. Genny's heart almost failed. The weak golden candlelight framed a familiar figure...Charles.

His eyes rounded with apparent horror. "Genny! What have they done to you?" He leaned over the opening, gesturing to her. "Come here. I'll lift you up."

Remaining in a hole in the earth when no one else knew she was there was hardly a consideration, and yet she couldn't bring her legs to move. She blinked moisture from her vision. *Oh, God, what should I do?* This was not the rescue she prayed for.

"You're in shock. Wait..." Charles straightened and looked around. He moved out of her line of sight but returned a moment later with the short wooden ladder Larry had drawn up earlier and left in the hut. He lowered it into the cellar, muttering. "The miscreants! Wait until my men catch up with them. They'll never again see the outside of a jail cell."

Genny shuffled aside as he descended, her brows winging

down. She'd expected anger, yes, but about the missing gold. And yet he hadn't even mentioned its absence. Hadn't even appeared to have looked for it in the cellar with her. He must have surmised the truth of the situation when he arrived to find no horses outside and an empty hut. But if that was the case, he was a master actor, all righteous indignation and solicitousness.

Stepping from the bottom of the ladder, Charles turned to her and pulled her against him with a huff of relief. Too stunned to react, Genny stood stiffly. The familiar scents of peppermint and aftershave momentarily overrode the dank earthiness of the cellar and brought a swirl of confusion. "Thank God you're all right." He put her away from him suddenly, grasping her elbows. "You *are* all right, aren't you?" He snatched her gag down. "Did they hurt you? Did Larry dare..." The darkening of his countenance was visible in the dim light from above.

She shook her head. "No." Even articulating the brief denial past her swollen tongue took effort. "Water..."

"Of course. Let's get you out of here. I have my canteen on my horse just outside. But first..." He slid a knife from his riding boot. "Hold up your hands."

Genny complied, though her arms trembled. She would take as much freedom as he would give her, then she would run with it. Charles cut through her bonds and replaced his knife in its hidden sheath.

He started up the ladder as he spoke. "Let me go ahead of you in case you need help at the top." More likely, he aimed to prevent her from darting to the door.

When Genny reached the top rungs, he held out his hand, but she planted her own on the floorboards and scrambled up without his assistance. Any sense of accomplishment promptly disappeared as her legs collapsed beneath her and she sprawled on the floor. Charles was beside her immediately, his arms wrapping beneath hers, tugging her up, against his chest.

His hand smoothed her disheveled hair. His voice murmured against her ear.

"Oh, Genny, my Genny. I'm so sorry you went through this. When I found the note Mattie left me, I couldn't believe it. I—"

"Water." She had to stop his rush of words. They bent and scattered in her head, bringing into question the reality she'd been so sure of. Not to mention, the false promise of security offered by his embrace twisted time back on itself.

"Right. Sit here." Charles supported her over to one of two spindly chairs in the room, next to a tiny table where her captors had left a candle burning. He hurried to the open door. He'd left his mount right outside. Could she reach the horse in time? But he returned almost immediately, closing the door behind him, uncorking his metal canteen, and handing it to her.

Genny hesitated a moment, staring at the spout. She'd have to put her mouth where he had placed his, but thirst overpowered her objections. She tipped up the canteen and drank deeply of the cool water, then capped it and handed it back to him. He laid it on the table and reached over to wipe a dribble that had escaped onto her chin. Genny shrank back, and his eyes darkened.

"Are you sure they didn't harm you? Tell me the truth. I won't let them get away with it."

"No." Finally, she could speak clearly, though she rubbed at the chafe marks on her wrists. "I think they feared that very thing. They hoped you would be pacified to have me unharmed rather than the gold."

"What gold?" Charles blinked, his supple lips parted slightly.

Reality bent again as Genny stared at him, reaching for solid thoughts. Could it be that Larry and Mattie had attempted to leave Charles holding the proverbial bag when all along, he'd known nothing of their misdeeds? What evidence did she truly have against him besides their word? The word of criminals? No. It couldn't be. "You know what gold! You paid Larry to siphon it off from Rupert Hanks, and then he double-crossed you."

"Genny, I have no idea what you are talking about." He shook his head.

She spluttered a moment. "But Mattie said…"

"And she's proven trustworthy?"

"Then how did you know to come here?"

Charles reached into his vest pocket. "Because of this." He held a folded page out to her.

Genny opened it and read. *If you want to see your lady love alive again, you can find her at the miner's hut across the river from the Hanks Mine. I hope she's worth it. Mattie.*

She sucked in a tremulous breath. That did look like Mattie's handwriting. The paper fluttered to her filthy calico skirt.

"I found that in my room when I got back from Lumpkin Courthouse today. Mattie was gone, along with all her personal items. Walter said she left last night."

"Why would they kidnap me and leave me here for you if you didn't order it?"

Charles opened his hands in a helpless gesture, then scooped up the note and tucked it away. "I can only assume in hopes of getting me arrested for kidnapping. And to turn you against me. They know…" He let out a heavy sigh and sank into the chair next to her. "They know nothing would pain me more."

"It's long past time for that, Charles, and you know it."

"Will you never forgive me, Genny?" He leaned forward, face intense. The candlelight played off the sheen of his shot-silk vest. "I had no choice about my marriage, but it's no more than a sham. She cares nothing for me, nor I for her. I have to play the dutiful heir until I can make certain arrangements, but my father can't keep us apart forever."

Genny's stomach clenched. "What arrangements?" Did he really expect she would be his mistress, or was he speaking of something far more sinister?

He went on as if he hadn't heard her. "I know you feel the same. You had to leave when you heard Larry threatening to take you. Mattie told me that much. But I know you cared, how you stayed in hopes I could marry you, and that even after you ran away, you wanted me to find you."

"I didn't....no..." She rose on shaking legs. Things were becoming more convoluted by the second. Could she get to his horse before he did?

"Why come to the Fourth of July celebration if you were trying to hide from me?" He stood too.

"I had no idea you'd be there! And you sent those men to the cabin to find me. Clearly, I didn't wish to be found then."

"What men? What cabin?" He made a scoffing sound. "Do you mean that made-up story about you being married?" He moved between her and the exit, looming over her. "You knew that would twist the dagger, didn't you? After all I've done for you, that you could be so cruel..."

She was cruel? Genny shook her head, loose hair from her bun tumbling over her shoulders. "It's not a made-up story, Charles. You've deceived others for so long, you believe your own lies—and expect others to lie too. I really am married. And so are you. You have to let me go. Take me to town. We can go to the sheriff and tell him about Mattie and Larry."

"Oh, I'll take you." His fingertips grazed her cheek, and she flinched away. "Back to the Boom or Bust where you belong...at least until I can get my new hotel built. Then you'll have the finest suite of rooms in the place, and our—*your*—fame will spread far and wide. We'll be so rich, Genny, we can go anywhere. Do anything."

"And what of your wife?" She eased around him. "And my husband?"

"What husband?" He grabbed her elbow and squeezed. "Tell me this man's name."

"Jesse Holden!" She flung it like a slap in his face.

He recoiled, then laughed. "I know no such person. A figment of your imagination. Or at least, he soon will be."

What did that mean? Genny snatched her arm back, but he held on. "Oh, he's very real. In fact, you met him. He's the man who came to my aid when you wouldn't, the first night I sang at the Boom or Bust."

He spluttered a laugh. "*That* boy? He wouldn't know what to do with you."

Despite the jab of that implication far too close to her heart, she lifted her chin. "He made me his wife to protect me from you. He ended your guardianship of me. And he's onto you—he and his friend, the Hall County sheriff!"

Charles's eyes widened, and he shook her arm. "What did you tell them, you little minx?"

At last, the real Charles. "*Everything*. And they were already looking for an excuse to settle the score for you shooting Wade's sister...Jesse's first wife!"

There it was—that moment when shock slackened Charles's expression...and his grip. Genny lunged for the door. Booted steps thumped after her. She grabbed for the latch. Charles grabbed her waist and Genny screamed.

"Oh, no, you don't. Not after all I did to have you." His hot breath rasped against her ear as he dragged her back.

She managed to hook her fingers around the latch, the backward motion pulling the door open a crack. "Let go. They'll be looking for me!"

He flattened one hand against the wood, slamming the door and her body up against it. "It's just you and me, Genny. No one is coming. No one knows we're here." His moist mouth pressed against her neck.

A hard shudder passed through her, and bitter liquid rose in her throat. "No!" She jabbed her elbow back into his ribcage. When he grunted, she clawed for the handle.

His arm swept out, pinning hers to her side. He whirled her and dragged her toward the ticking mattress on the other side of the hut. Genny pushed, writhed, and kicked, but he wrapped both arms around her in a crushing grip. She whimpered as Charles lowered his mouth to hers and claimed her lips with a crazed fervor that left her weak with terror.

When he lifted his head, she let out a sob. "You can't get away with this."

"Can't I?" He gave a breathless laugh, his eyes dark, glittering. "I got away with your father's *heart attack* and with making you my ward."

In the moment that shock rendered Genny passive, Charles pushed her onto the mattress. Her arms and legs flopped like a ragdoll's.

Her father. He hadn't abandoned her. Charles had...killed him? And even now the monster was lowering himself over her to take the last thing he hadn't yet stolen from her. Revulsion and rage shot through her, and Genny lunged for the knife in his boot.

∼

Half an hour earlier...

$\mathcal{J}$esse rode Perseus hard down Auraria Road with the swatch of brown calico he'd found in Charles's room in his pocket and a prayer on his lips. *Please, God, don't let us be too late.*

Presumably, the scrap of material was what he'd witnessed Larry pass to Charles behind the Boom or Bust—proof he had

Genny. They'd also found a trunk of what Walter identified as Genny's belongings in Mattie's room, confirming her involvement. A letter postmarked from Gainesville on Monday lay on top—Genny's request to Mattie to let her sister know she'd take the Friday stage to Pendleton. The traitor. The woman deserved to be clamped in the jail cell and then tried right alongside the men.

Jesse took the lead when they turned off the main road. He didn't know a more direct approach to the hut than accessing it the only way he ever had, from the Hanks Mine across the river. After they clambered up the bank on the other side, Wade let out a soft whistle.

"Hey. You have to slow down now."

Jesse nodded. "I know a spot we can dismount out of sight of the hut."

It took all the restraint he possessed to keep Perseus to a walk. Even the horse seemed to sense the tension, tossing his head and snorting. Jesse ran his hand down his neck to soothe him. "Easy, boy." It was imperative they not alert anyone at the shelter to their approach.

The forest was far too quiet as they drew up behind the chestnut tree, near the mountain laurel stand. No breeze rustled the treetops. No birds called, and no animals scurried through the brush. The half moon hung low in the sky like a jewel riding the fear neck of wispy clouds.

Wade held the horses while Jesse peered around the giant of the forest. His breath hitched. "There's one horse out front." One he didn't recognize. "And a light around the door. Whoever it is must be inside. But the carts I saw earlier are gone."

"We may be too late." Regret rasped in Wade's reply.

"For the gold, maybe. Not for Genny." Jesse had to believe that. He leaned against the tree, facing Wade. "What's our plan?"

"You said the tunnel opened into the cellar?"

"I said it ended in a bolted door that must be the cellar."

Wade looped the horses' reins around a low-hanging branch and crouched next to Jesse. "If they've taken the gold, chances are fair they left it unlocked. Chances are also good they bolted the hut door after them. I'm thinking one of us should go through the tunnel while the other tries the front."

Jesse grimaced. Wade had said "chances" one too many times. "What happens if both are bolted?"

His friend slid the double-barreled French pistol he was so proud of out of its holster. "I've got twenty rounds. I can shoot my way through if necessary. I'll take the front."

Jesse tensed. "No. I will." He'd lose his mind making the agonizingly slow crawl through the tunnel—likely to terminate in disappointment. "Even if I can access the cellar, how am I supposed to get through the trap door?"

"Chances are—"

"If you say one more thing about chances!" Jesse's voice rose louder than he intended.

Wade shushed him with a slicing gesture.

Jesse suppressed a groan. "She's my wife, man. And every minute we sit here talking…"

"I know." Wade clamped his hand over Jesse's shoulder. "And rest assured—I'll die before letting you lose another. But only one of us can come through that door at a time. And only you know the way through the tunnel. It could give us the element of surprise, which we may need if…"

If Wade got shot. Jesse bowed his head.

"Take this." Wade felt on his belt and handed Jesse a small hatchet.

Jesse palmed the handle with his brows winging up. "Where'd you get this?"

"Walter gave it to me when you were getting the horses. May be that it comes in handy." His teeth flashed in the moonlight. "Especially seeing as how you've got only one shot with that antique of yours."

"Fine. Give me fifteen minutes." Jesse tucked the hatchet in the back of his suspenders. "What's the signal?" He'd need to know when to bust out of the cellar.

"I'll yell like a Cherokee on the warpath. Might startle them more'n a whistle."

"If you say so." Jesse clasped Wade's forearm and looked him in the eye. "God go with you, brother."

Wade's fingers tightened. "And with you."

Jesse scrambled off toward the river. In the faint moonlight reflecting off the water, he knelt on a rock near the twin boulders, pulled out his pistol, and reached into his cartridge box for a pre-measured twist of powder which he poured into the pan. It would be too dark and narrow to do so in the cave. He holstered the weapon he'd barrel-seated earlier with powder, patch, and ball with a prayer he wouldn't have to use it. But he'd do what he must to protect Genny.

What if they had taken her with the gold and whoever was at the hut was merely there to clean up? No. He couldn't entertain that thought.

His boots splashed in the shallow water that lapped the bottom of the boulders, then squished in the sand at the tunnel entrance. Down on all fours, weapons tucked away as securely as possible, he forged through the darkness. His fingers sank into slimy clay. Dirt fell onto his head from above. He kept his face down, praying and moving as quickly as possible.

When he'd gone about fifty yards, he paused. Voices? Yes. He was getting close. And more than one person was in the hut! Jesse started crawling forward again, faster. Up ahead, did light filter through the cracks in the door, or were his eyes just seeing what he wanted them to? Definitely light. But that meant the door was closed, possibly bolted.

A feminine voice raised—and raised his hopes. Genny or

Mattie. Then footsteps pounded, followed by the sounds of a struggle. A scream!

"Genny." It must be her. Jesse's heart thundered, and he all but flung himself the last ten yards to the door. *Come on, Wade.* Surely, his friend would make his charge now.

"They'll be looking for me!"

It *was* her! Breath laboring, Jesse groped at the wooden barrier. A board lay across it. He shoved it upward, and it fell with a clatter that was lost in Genny's cry. "No!"

Jesse pushed. The door opened! He almost fell over the board on the other side, stumbling into an empty cellar as he pulled his pistol. Light flooded from above. A ladder led out. He grabbed it and hauled himself up with the weapon in one hand. Someone cried out in pain.

As Jesse's head cleared the floor, a man bent over a woman's form on a cot in the corner, clutching his side. The weak light of a candle revealed his twisted features. Charles.

A blood-curdling whoop rang out, and the hut's door banged open. Wade charged through the entrance, weapon in hand. Simultaneously, Charles whirled, jerking a gun from its holster on his hip.

Jesse aimed for his shoulder and fired. The pistol dropped from Charles's hand as he howled in agony. He toppled over, and the woman gasped as his weight crushed her. Jesse discarded his smoking gun and leapt through the trapdoor at the same time Wade rushed forward. Jesse let his friend roll a moaning Charles off the cot. He only wanted to get to Genny.

She stared at him with her eyes huge in her pale face. A bloody knife glinted in her left hand.

"Genny. Oh, thank God." He reached for her, but she lay stiff as a poker, making him dizzy with fear. "Are you hurt?" Jesse patted her from head to torso, looking for rips in her clothing or blood. She was silent—too silent.

Instead, Wade spoke as he handcuffed Charles. "Don't

know about her, but she poked him a good one. He's bleeding from his side."

"And you shot me! You..." A tangle of curse words spewed from Charles's lips. Ah, strip away the mannerly veneer, and that was what was inside.

"Shut it." Wade jerked his arms, now bound behind his back, eliciting a strangled cry and the end of the profanity. "You tried to shoot *me*, you ingrate. Although, I guess I'll have to bandage you up."

He could bleed out for all Jesse cared right now. His desperation for a sign Genny was all right fairly strangled his chest and throat, yet she gave no sign of recognition. What had transpired before they got there? He tamped down his panic and spoke gently.

"Here. Give me that." Jesse reached for the knife. When she only clutched it tighter, he cupped her face with his hand and stared into her unfocused eyes. "Genny. It's over. You're safe. Let go of the knife."

Her fingers splayed, and the blade fell to the mattress. She lunged forward, flinging her arms around his neck with a shuddering cry that worked loose his own emotions. "Jesse!"

"It's all right. You're safe." Gently, he clasped her shoulders, afraid to hold her too tightly until he grasped the extent of potential damage. "Are you hurt?" He repeated the question with a different meaning now. When her head shook against his shoulder, his heart nearly burst from relief. They were in time, then.

"I thought you wouldn't come. I thought I had to kill him. When he said he killed my father..."

What? Jesse jerked back for a view of Genny's stricken face. Wade looked up from tearing a strip of Charles's fine shirtsleeve to bandage the gushing hole in his upper arm.

Charles exploded in protest. "I never said that!"

"Yes, you did. You liar! You are like your father, the father of lies." Genny turned her face away as though she couldn't bear to look at her former guardian. Instead, she focused on Jesse, speaking as though she needed to convince him. "He deserves to die. I would have killed him too. I would have. I would." Her words dissolved into sobs, and he wrapped his arms around her back and rocked her. It would seem their arrival not only spared Genny from assault...but from possibly killing the man.

Thank You, God.

"I'm here. I've got you."

Yes, he clasped Genny in his arms, but after all she had been through, could he convince her to stay there?

CHAPTER 23

Oh, how tenderly Jesse held her atop Perseus as they rode to Wade's cabin. He'd insisted on taking Genny straight back there while Wade escorted Charles to the jail. What a surprise the Lumpkin County sheriff was about to receive! But would Charles only get the man on his side by spinning a similar tale blaming the others as he had done with her?

Genny shivered. Would she ever be free of the man? Ever feel completely safe again? How close she'd come to being indelibly branded by his evil.

Though, with no one to gander at her ankles, she rode astride, Jesse's arm kept her tucked against him. Twice or thrice, he leaned in so close, his nose bumped her shoulder or neck. When his breath fanned her cheek, it was all she could do not to turn her face toward his and seek his mouth in the dark. Because as deliriously grateful as she was to be in his arms, as much as his affection might have purged the pain of her abduction, his silence gave her no clue how he felt.

'Twas almost a relief when the cabin door opened and Toby

barked from the porch. She jumped as Jesse called out from right behind her. "Ho, the house!"

She'd forgotten about the miners Wade had hired to guard the land. Apparently, they'd taken up residence inside in their absence, with or without Jesse's invitation. A bulky silhouette appeared in the doorway, waved, and lowered a rifle. Jesse waved back, but the notion of interacting with strange men made Genny's muscles tighten up.

Jesse squeezed her. "It's all right. I'll ask them to leave."

He still read her with astonishing sensitivity. "No, that would hardly be fair—"

"Shh." He patted her leg, and her tension drained away. When he pulled her from Perseus a few minutes later, she fairly puddled in his arms. "Wait here." He murmured the directive against her ear, then went up on the porch to speak to the men.

Toby skittered down the steps and jumped up on her.

"Oof!" Her heart squeezed with joy even though he almost knocked her over. "You big lout. I'm the one needs holding up tonight." But she sank onto the bottom step and pulled the Irish setter close as he curved his wagging body around her knees, huffed, and licked at her face and hands. She laughed and soaked in the doggy goodness as the men murmured behind her, the cicadas droned from the trees, and the stars twinkled above. The moment infused her with a sense of belonging and security she hadn't felt since she left. "I missed you, old boy."

"Looks like he missed you too." Jesse chuckled from the top step. "But he's going to camp with these guys tonight."

Genny ducked her head against Toby's as the men tromped down the steps carrying guns and bedrolls. "Evenin', ma'am," they both said respectfully, without a hint of resentment. She could bring herself to do little more than peek up at them and nod. If she spoke, she'd apologize and embarrass herself. What had Jesse said to them? Even more, why was he sending Toby away when he knew the dog comforted her?

Her stomach knotted. He'd always gone silent when he was angry. And he had good reason this time. If she hadn't run away from his parents' home like a pouting child, she never would have been abducted.

One of the men called the dog, and Jesse told him to go. Reluctantly, Genny released Toby's neck, and he trotted after the miners toward the tents still pitched at the tree line.

"I'm sorry." The apology popped out of her with a will of its own the moment she stood when the men were out of earshot.

Jesse took the steps quickly and ran his hand down her arm. "What are you apologizing for?"

"For making you rescue me...a third time." She grimaced and couldn't meet his eyes. During her time here, she had learned to stop taking blame for things she wasn't guilty of, but this apology was surely in order.

A laugh rumbled in his chest, though there was a tightness to it she hadn't heard before. Almost as if he was...anxious. Nervous. "Well, you know what they say about the third time..."

She chanced a look at him. "You're not mad?"

He huffed a sigh. "I'm a lot of things right now, but I'd just as soon not discuss them out here. Will you come in?"

"Gladly." She laid her hand on the rail and took a step up, but her legs wobbled.

"Whoa, there." His arm slid around her waist. "Need some help? You're fair done in."

Genny nodded and raised her hand to his shoulder, expecting to lean on him, but he swept her up. She gasped as he carried her up the stairs. "It occurs to me you had to do this the first time I came here."

"Had to. Now I want to."

Her heart fluttered as he set her down in the middle of the

floor. While he returned to bolt the door, she went to sit at the bench on the near side of the table. He hung his gun belt with his hat on the peg by the door. Jesse came back with the pitcher and two cups which he filled and set before them, then he took a seat across from her.

"Thank you." She sipped her water while he leaned forward with his arms folded on the board and stared at her. Her mouth went dry despite the liquid.

"You want to tell me why you did leave?"

"It was stupid." She placed her hands before her and lowered her gaze. "The family that got me dismissed from Mt. Olivet showed up at your father's church service. Your mother... she already disapproved of me. Their reaction tipped the scales."

"You left because they looked down on you." His flat tone implied his disapproval.

"I did." Genny sat up straighter with a deep breath. "I let what they said get in the way of my better judgment. I should have talked to Wade first, but I thought the investigation was stalled and it would be better for everyone if I left."

"Better for everyone...including me?"

He wasn't letting her off the hook, not with his questions, and not with his gaze. Why? Did he want her to grovel? Fine. He could have been shot tonight, defending her. She could grovel.

She folded her hands. "Yes. I thought if I was out of the way, you and Wade could do what you needed to do, then you would be free to go. I left an address where you could send papers for me to sign."

"I know." Definitely disapproving.

Genny hurried on. "But if I hadn't acted rashly, I never would have put myself in danger or forced you to come after me without the benefit of planning, so I can't say how much I regret..."

Her apology halted when he reached across the table and put his finger over her mouth. "I forbid you to say you're sorry one more time, Genny Holden."

She blinked, as effectively silenced by the use of her married name as by the finger. He lowered it and grabbed her hand.

"If anyone ought to be apologizing, it should be me. For leaving you with my mother when she acted so inexcusably. But even more, for leaving you with an uncertainty about the future that made you think I wanted you gone."

"Y-you don't?"

Wrapping both hands around hers, Jesse slowly shook his head.

Her throat worked, but she couldn't swallow past its sudden constriction. The way he was looking at her, so intensely... "But Mississippi..."

"...will still be there when I get there. Or if not, some other territory. I can't say as much for you. I was almost too late today, Genny." His fingers tightened on hers. "When I found out Charles had you..."

"How did you know?" She could've kicked herself the minute the question came out, for it broke his train of thought and his grip on her hand. What had he been about to say?

He sat back and pulled a scrap of fabric from his waistcoat pocket—a piece of brown calico.

Genny gasped and extended her arm. Jesse laid the material in the gap on her sleeve, where it fit perfectly. She pressed it into place. "They must have torn it right after they took me in Gainesville—once they'd knocked me out. But where did you find it?"

"In Charles's room when Walter helped us search. He's the one who clued me in to Mattie's involvement. I'm so sorry about that. I know how that must have hurt." His face twisted with sympathy.

She nodded and lowered her gaze again, laying the fabric scrap on the table. "I'm afraid I wasn't the only one betrayed by someone I trusted."

Jesse tensed. "What are you talking about?"

"You know how Wade wanted to go after the robbers before we left the hut, but he had to deal with Charles first?"

"Yeah." Jesse tipped his head to one side.

"While you were getting the horses, I told him who else was there besides Mattie and Larry." Genny curled her fingers. "It was the ostler from the livery we used, Clive Simms. That's how they followed me so fast when I first left the Boom or Bust. And also someone from the Hanks Mine."

Jesse sat forward. "Middle-aged, dark-haired? The silent type?"

She shook her head.

He blew out a breath. "Then it was David, after all." When she frowned, he explained, "The man who came up here when I was panning that day, saying he was looking for work. I called him Red then, on account of his coloring. But I came to think I could trust him in camp. He was the foreman." Frowning, Jesse rubbed his chin with a light rasping sound. "But he would've had to have showed up later because he was with me earlier in the day."

Genny caught her lower lip between her teeth. "I'm afraid it wasn't him either. It was a young man with a dark beard and blue eyes they called Miles."

Jesse seemed to deflate, slumping on the table. "Miles...I can't believe it. He was my partner in the mine. And I didn't see it. Not once. He disappeared so much, the men teased him about his sensitive stomach." He drummed his fingers. "But how did he get access to the gold when Verne always held the key to the storage shed?"

"Could he have taken it at night, perhaps?"

"Possibly, while he slept. But the day I found you at the creek, the man tracking you rode a dapple gray. David's horse was the same type, which was why I thought...." Jesse shifted his jaw back and forth. Suddenly, he thumped his fist down. "Blast! What an idiot. Miles didn't have a horse of his own."

"Stop." Genny touched his arm. "You can't beat yourself up. That we believe people are who they present themselves to be is a sign of goodness, not stupidity. We might get some answers in the coming days, but other things, we may never know. And I think we have to be all right with that. After all, God will have the final justice."

His brows winged up. "Such faith. Where is this coming from, if I may ask?"

Genny chucked. "The time with your parents wasn't all bad. Your father and I had several talks, and he reads the Word aloud every night, as you do."

"I'm glad. If God has become more real to you through all this, that makes everything worth it. I know He has for me. More than once, I was at a total loss of what to do next. If He hadn't led me to that tunnel..."

"But He did." Genny patted his arm. "And then you found this." She pointed to the scrap of fabric on the table between them. "So it seems He was definitely leading you."

He fingered the fabric. "I also saw Larry hand it to Charles this afternoon, and Charles paid him. Both times, I'd prayed, asking for God's help."

Her chest squeezed. Hadn't she felt God's nearness, too, there in the dark cellar? Then giving her the presence of mind to deal with Charles and his lies?

Jesse grimaced. "Although it was more a demand borne of desperation. Still, He honored it."

"He knew your heart. And it was no accident that you showed up just in time tonight. But ..." Genny lost her breath for a second as she stared at the fabric. "That means Charles *knew*. He knew Larry had me."

"Of course he knew." Jesse's brows drew together. "That's what the payment I witnessed must've been for."

"But that's not all. Mattie told me Charles expected a cut of the gold."

"Walter said he suspected as much."

Genny's eyes widened. For her, that was even more convincing. "And yet when Charles came to the hut, he acted as if he knew nothing about the gold. He didn't look for it. Didn't ask about it. He just seemed concerned for me. He said he knew where to find me because of the note Mattie left in his room."

Jesse scoffed. "What a load of bunk."

"No, he showed it to me. He has it with him." She opened her hand on the table. "Jesse, he's going to tell the sheriff the same thing, and that man was in his pocket. What if they believe him? He could get off scot-free." She pushed back the bench and rose on trembling legs. "We have to warn Wade. We have to take him this." She picked up the scrap of cloth and waved it at him. "You see? This is evidence he was involved."

"Genny...slow down." Jesse stood and crossed over to her. He took the material and set it on the table, then ran his hands down her arms and wove his fingers through hers. "The sheriff isn't in Auraria anymore." Gently, he shook her hands for emphasis as he spoke. "He's in Lumpkin Courthouse, remember? There's no way we can ride there tonight."

"Oh..." All the helplessness of the past several years leaked out on that one syllable.

"Everything will be fine." Jesse stepped closer and ran his hand along her cheek and jaw. "Charles is not going anywhere. Wade will take care of things, and he promised to stop by in a day or two with an update. All right?"

"All...all right." She fought the urge to lean her face into his palm. She'd mistaken his comfort for affection before. Her heart couldn't take any more bruising and battering. "And you...will you leave for Mississippi then?"

Jesse held her gaze. "I reckon we'll need to stick around for Charles's trial. And maybe if we get lucky, they'll catch the others too. Wade still wanted to send riders after them once he got Charles locked up. But yes, eventually, I would like to see if that job is still available..."

"I see." Genny dropped her arms to her sides and turned away. He'd be leaving, just as she feared. She couldn't hide her feelings from him anymore. But where could she run? The pain was so intense, it was all she could do to hold in a sob, and the exhaustion so heavy, it would be a miracle if she made it to the bed, where she just wanted to crawl under the quilt and cover her head. Despite her best efforts, a whimper slipped out past her clenched teeth.

Jesse grabbed her hand and spun her so fast, she stumbled against his broad chest. His warm exhale brushed her face. "I want you to go with me, Genny. As my wife."

She gasped. "But you said..."

"I said a lot of stupid things. I've always been a wanderer, and I reckon I've got as much healing to do as you do, but I was thinking..." He dipped his forehead to hers. "Maybe we could do it together. That is, if you don't mind not putting down roots for a while."

Had she heard him correctly? Genny's hand fluttered to her mouth, then to his shoulder. "I...I've never been much of one for roots. I'd much prefer a fresh start."

The smile that broke over Jesse's face like to stopped her heart. Slowly, he nodded. "Then a fresh start, it is, Mrs. Holden."

"I like the sound of that," she whispered. The name, as much as the promise. And if she was Mrs. Holden for sure and certain, then she could be bold. Take a risk. "Now's as good a time as any." She drew his head down until his lips met hers in a kiss that was the perfect combination of tenderness and passion. Finally, she had found the one who desired her for who she was. With him, she could make a home anywhere, even if it was under the stars.

When he led her to the bed she'd spent so many nights alone in and pulled her down beside him, she finally understood why he'd sent the dog away.

~

Only a little more than a week had passed since Genny's rescue, yet it seemed a lifetime ago. The peace of this place healed her heart. She could almost wish... But this was Wade's land, not theirs. They had yet to find their home somewhere to the west.

She looked up from filling her big Cherokee-made basket with roasting ears. Genny squinted in the August sun despite the shade of the bonnet Jesse's mother despised. Somewhere in the adjacent field, Jesse was cutting the wheat. There he was. *My...* She parted the cornstalks for a better view and smiled. The mere sight of her husband shirtless and glistening with sweat, his muscles rippling as he swung the scythe, made her pulse tick up.

With Charles in custody and Larry fled, the guards had been dismissed, affording Genny and Jesse more of the privacy they craved. If only the demands of the late-summer harvest didn't keep them so busy. Genny could happily spend every moment at her husband's side, soaking up his attention, secure in his obvious admiration—because to finally have someone who loved her unconditionally, as God did, was most healing of all.

It also mended a corner of her heart to learn her father had not willingly left her in Charles's care. Whenever she allowed herself to think on it, questions about exactly how Charles had carried out his twisted plan to claim her plagued her. She had to remind herself of the words she had spoken to Jesse about releasing certain mysteries to God and entrusting His justice because doubtless, Charles would never confess to such a crime, and it would be his word against hers.

Toby, who had been chasing butterflies from the Queen Anne's lace at the edge of the field, drew her attention with a sudden bark. He trotted toward the lane where a rider approached. Wade's muscular form sat his stallion with expertise, his hat pulled low. But a certain slump to his broad shoulders tugged at Genny's heart as she lifted her basket to her hip and called to Jesse that his friend had arrived.

Did Wade bring them more bad news?

~

Summoned by his wife as Wade rode up the lane, Jesse used his bandana to dry off prior to donning his shirt. A break from the blistering sun and back-breaking work would be welcome no matter the cause, but he'd been anticipating this visit with a mixture of hope and trepidation.

The part Jesse played in rescuing Genny and the healing power of the love that now bound them had gone far to help salve the wound of his failure with Emma. Still, no one shared Wade's desire more than Jesse that justice be meted out to Charles Martin, especially after he had hinted he'd caused the death of Genny's father. The blood of at least two people stained the man's hands. Jesse had done his best to conceal from Genny exactly how much he wanted vengeance. She had only begun to walk the long road of healing, and forgiving

Charles would be part of that process. He wouldn't be the cause of setting her back.

While Wade dismounted, Jesse met Genny at the front steps and dropped a kiss on her rosy cheek—flushed from his attention as much as the sun, or so he'd like to think. He'd taken great delight in every aspect of his bride this past week.

"Wade, welcome." Jesse extended his hand to shake his friend's.

This wasn't Wade's first visit since Genny's rescue. Two days after, he'd brought Sheriff Jones to take their statements and inform them that the manhunt for the gold thieves had come to naught. They had been tracked as far as the Alabama line, where they scattered.

And now Wade's grim countenance foreboded more ill tidings. "You may not feel that way when you hear what I have to say."

Genny squared her shoulders. "We'd best sit down, then. I'll get us all some lemonade." She started up the steps, Toby on her heels. "Is here on the porch all right?"

At least here they'd have the faint hope of a breeze. Jesse nodded. "Sounds fine."

He and Wade sank onto the bench while she went inside to fetch drinks.

"How goes married life?" Wade removed his hat and balanced it on his knee.

Jesse patted Toby's head as the dog settled at his feet. "Better than I ever thought possible." He shot a glance sideways. "We're staying together, Wade."

"Ah, you made it permanent, then, did you?" The sight of his friend's grin was almost worth the embarrassment as Wade elbowed him. "I thought so the last time I was here. I got the feeling neither of you cared near enough that the whole gang of thieves had gotten away. You could hardly tear your eyes off each other."

"I admit to being a bit distracted of late." Jesse smirked and rubbed the back of his neck. "But it's been a welcome distraction. For once, I'm looking forward rather than backward. I might finally be able to put the past in the past."

"I'm glad to hear it. I really am." Wade patted Jesse's knee. "That you came out of this finding love at least brings me some small measure of comfort."

Jesse grimaced. "Wade..." How could he verbalize his regret over how he'd treated Wade's sister? That he'd given up so quickly on trying to find love in his heart for her, leaving her vulnerable and in danger?

"No." Wade held up his hand. "We don't need to go back over that ground. I know you regret what happened and would do things differently now. I also know Emma wasn't the right match for you—for anyone, really. She wasn't ready to be married. I should've seen she would pull you under."

"You can't blame yourself." Wasn't that what he'd been trying to convince Genny of too?

"But I do...then *and* now. It was my job to prevent a public confrontation, and I let it get out of hand. It was my job to bring in these criminals, and I failed. Shoot..." He ran his hand over his face. "If you hadn't nailed Charles with that antique of yours, I'd probably be six feet under, clutching my fancy double-shooter atop my best vest." Despite the jesting in Wade's voice, his chagrined expression revealed his shame.

Jesse shook his head. "You said going in it might take both of us and the element of surprise. If we had done things my way, Charles would've gotten his shot off for sure." He bumped Wade's shoulder with his own. "The important thing is, we got him."

Wade let out a lung-deflating sigh. "But we didn't."

"What's that?" Genny stood at the door, holding three tin cups of lemonade that were already perspiring in the heat.

Wade looked up at her, then quickly away. "We had to let him go today."

"What? No!"

The way her shoulders sagged, Jesse feared she might drop the drinks. He sprang up to help her, distributing the tin cups and guiding her to the bench in his place. He remained standing, leaning against the post. His knuckles tightened around his cup handle, but he fought to keep his voice even when he spoke. His wife was already distraught, and his friend defeated. "What happened?"

"I consulted with a lawyer—Mrs. Paschal's son—and Sheriff Jones, but we didn't have enough evidence to hold Charles Martin. Not to mention, his father retained a powerful Atlanta lawyer." Wade bolted back his lemonade in a hard swallow as though it was liquor and clanked the empty cup on the bench. "He's gone back to the city to recuperate."

That might at least buy them some time to get out of the area without looking over their shoulders, but surely, this could not be the end of the matter. "What about Walter's testimony?"

Wade ruffled a hand through his dark hair, leaving it sticking up in sweaty spikes. "When he saw the way the wind was blowing, he withdrew it. At least, the part about Charles. He told me privately he suspected Charles had hired Larry to swindle Rupert Hanks but that he possessed no actual proof. Can you blame him? If he had pressed matters, he'd leave himself not only out of a job but in fear for his life. That leaves Larry and Mattie holding the bag." He paused before speaking again, his voice bitter. "Only, they aren't, because they got away."

Genny ventured a query—softly, as if sensitive to Wade's self-recrimination. "And the fabric from my dress? Didn't that count for anything, along with what Jesse witnessed behind the Boom or Bust?"

"Charles is claiming it was enclosed in the note Mattie sent him, which he produced for Sheriff Jones. He says he never met with Larry or paid him any money since the man left his employ."

"But he's lying!" Genny threw her hands up, causing Toby to lift his head and look at her. "Just as he's always lied."

"Of course he is." Wade cast her an anguished glance. "But his lawyer would take you and Jesse apart on the stand, even if we had a strong enough case to try." His gaze shifted to Jesse, entreating. "He would claim we implicated Charles from a desire for revenge because of what happened to Emma...and romantic rivalry over Genny. It would be his word against ours, and wealth and power always win."

Silence reigned a few moments, each of them absorbed in their own thoughts. His head on his paws, Toby let out a mournful sigh that seemed to embody all their feelings.

Jesse moved away from the post, set down his drink, and laid his hand on Wade's shoulder. "Nobody blames you, man. We know you did all you could."

"But it wasn't enough. That's why when I get back to Gainesville, I'm tendering my resignation. I wasn't cut out for this job."

Genny gasped. "No, Wade!" She rose as Wade did and Jesse took a step back. "That's not true."

"How?" He looked her in the eye. "Tell me how it isn't true. I failed Emma and I failed you. It was Jesse who rescued you. And not one criminal in this ring is behind bars. I wouldn't be re-elected even if I wanted to be. No, it's best this way..."

She started to touch his arm but seemed to think better of it, and her hand fluttered down into the folds of her skirt. "But what will you do?"

"I don't know yet. Maybe I'll go to work for my father."

Jesse almost choked on a scoff. "You'd be no better at that than I."

Wade shrugged and settled his hat back on his head. "We'll

see. I'm glad you've found your place here, though, that you're happy. As I said, it brings me comfort. If you feel safe enough with Charles at large, I'd like to sell you the lot. I'll give you a good price."

"Actually, I have a better idea." Jesse moved behind his wife and rested his hand on her waist. "Genny and I have decided to go to Mississippi. I had an offer to resume my work there, and now we won't be delayed by a trial." He cast Genny a quick glance. The flare of life in her eyes showed she'd welcome the opportunity rather than remain mired in fear or resentment.

She voiced her agreement firmly. "The sooner we leave, the better."

"Really?" Wade looked between them with a faint stirring of hope on his shadowed features.

"Really." Genny stepped forward and wrapped her arms around Wade's neck, clearly stunning him as well as Jesse with her tender gesture. But he could hardly be jealous given the way his friend hung his head, so obviously in need was he of grace and comfort. "The place is yours, but we thank you for the use of it, and we pray that one day, you will be happy here. This we ask in Jesus's name."

As her words settled like the prayer they were, like a benediction, bringing a holy hush to the hot afternoon, Jesse's heart squeezed. This was a woman to build a life with. He wanted the same for his friend...his brother. Jesse put out his hand and squeezed Wade's shoulder. "Amen."

Wade made a show of adjusting his hat as he stepped back, but Jesse suspected the move was designed to cover a surreptitious wiping of his eyes. "Well, then, I'd best be on my way. I'll return in say...a week?"

Jesse clasped arms with him. "That should give us enough time. We'll lay your corn by and take the wheat to the mill, and Genny will put up the garden produce. You should be set for fall."

"And ahead of the autumn planting. Some hard work will do me good."

"I pray so." Jesse had to pause when he choked up. "I reckon we won't see each other for a while, but we'll stay in touch."

Wade nodded, then his brows flew up. "Speaking of staying in touch, I almost forgot I brought you this." He pulled an envelope from his waistcoat pocket.

Jesse blinked as he recognized his mother's flowing script on the front, but his friend offered the letter not to him, but to Genny.

"For me?" She laid her hand over her chest.

"Well, you're Mrs. Jesse Holden, are you not?" Wade winked at her.

Reluctantly, Genny took the missive and tore it open. Jesse looked on with equal misgiving. What further damage might his mother inflict now? Maybe he needed to suggest Genny read it later when he could better comfort a bout of tears.

But the little gasp she issued was one of amazement, not offense.

Jesse angled closer. "What does she say?"

Genny's lashes fluttered as she glanced up at him, then back down to the letter. "She says she is deeply sorry for any pain she caused me, is greatly relieved to receive word of my rescue, and wishes to offer a wedding present as a gesture of apology."

"What kind of wedding present?" Fear stirred that his parents might attempt to lure them back to Gainesville with some offer of a house or job.

"Your parents want to finance our travel west...and see me established in a safe place while you begin work."

Jesse let out a huff while Genny blinked as though still in disbelief herself. "Well," he muttered. "Maybe there is hope for her, after all."

Wade cleared his throat. "In that case, I'm glad I could

deliver some good tidings, at least. And on that note, I'd best be going."

Before he could turn and head off the porch, Jesse hooked him into a rough embrace. "Take care of yourself, my brother."

"I will. You do the same...and take care of this fine woman you've found." Wade thumped his back, then abruptly moved back and clambered down the steps.

Both Jesse and Genny were wiping their eyes as Wade waved and rode away. Toby barked his farewell. Genny dropped her hand to the dog's head. "Do you think he'll be all right?"

Jesse let out a sigh. "All we can do is pray and leave him to God." He turned to face her. "And you? Are you certain *you're* all right with this?"

"Oh, yes." She nodded enthusiastically. "I take your mother's letter as a confirmation of all we've decided here, don't you?"

He chuckled. "It does seem only a wee bit short of miraculous. But there's one thing we haven't discussed."

"And what's that?" Genny tilted her head and smoothed back his sticky hair under his hat. Her warm, assessing gaze said she found his nearness as distracting as he did hers, but this topic was important to him. He didn't want her sacrificing her dreams for his.

"Your singing. You once told me you wanted to make your own way in life, using your voice." He frowned. "Where we're going is wilderness. There won't be towns—much less, big cities. I imagine opportunities for vocal performers and instructors will be quite limited."

Surprisingly, the corners of her mouth tipped up. "The thing about wilderness is that it will grow. Maybe I'll be singing to the rocks and trees—and you and God—for a while. I'm fine with that. Besides, I no longer have to prove anything. My father loved me. He did not abandon me as I thought he did. And neither did my Heavenly Father."

Jesse captured both of her hands in his and brought her knuckles to his lips. "I'm so glad you have peace about that now."

She nodded. "That's mostly thanks to you. I'm not worried, Jesse. God has put everything in order thus far, and now He's given me something to sing about. He's restored the years the locusts have eaten."

Jesse tipped his head. He still found it surprising—but quite appealing—whenever his wife quoted Scripture. "When did you read that?"

Genny laughed. "Something your father told me."

"And if you were picking a song for today, what would it be? One of Wesley's?"

"Why, of course. Hmm..." She laid her finger to her lips a moment, gazing out toward the mountains. Then she started to sing with a joy that showed she serenaded the most important audience of all.

> Christ, whose glory fills the skies,
> Christ, the true and only Light,
> Sun of righteousness, arise,
> Triumph o'er the shade of night.

After she fell silent and dipped an adorable little curtsy, Jesse drew her against his side. She tipped her head up, and he kissed her rosy lips—so soft and yielding against his own.

"I love you." How he had not said it already? "I love you forever."

Genny's eyes went wide. "Ha! Thought you'd never say it."

He cocked a brow. "Oh, really? So are you going to leave me hanging, Mrs. Holden?"

She giggled. "Truth is, I've been in love with you ever since I heard you play your fiddle. Or maybe it was when you read your Bible to me. Either way, I heard the message you weren't able yet to say." She pulled his face down to hers and offered him a kiss that promised all her tomorrows.

Funny to think how he'd feared marriage like a prisoner feared shackles when the idea of a lifetime at her side now brought the headiest sense of adventure.

~

Turn the page for a sneak peek of The Mountie and the Maiden, the next book in the Twenty-Niners of the Georgia Gold Rush series!

OCTOBER 16, 1837

"Sergeant Edwards, you're needed for a mission of the greatest urgency."

The youthful yet earnest voice outside his tent had Gage pulling up his suspenders and pushing aside the canvas flap without so much as his waistcoat to break the early-morning chill. A mission the day after Buffington's Company of Georgia Mounted Militia arrived in Cherokee County? Before morning muster? It must be important. And that was why he was here—a chance to prove himself and to help his step-grandmother's Cherokee people.

He found the new acting assistant quartermaster planted on the other side of the front tent post. The man was just as stiff and about as lean as the post. "What is it, Private Wood?" Gage slipped his arms into his woolen vest.

The youth snapped off a salute, which Gage returned. "The corn we hauled from New Echota has to be taken to the mill." He swiveled to wave toward the parade ground. "The sacks are still in the wagon. The ostler is hitchin' the team as we speak."

Gage slid the last pewter button of his waistcoat through its hole. "*This* is the urgent mission?"

John Wood shrugged. "Men have to eat, sir. That corn's the army's gold."

"Then why aren't you taking it, Assistant Quartermaster Wood?" The question sneaked out of him like a minnow through a fish trap.

"I'm helping set up the meal tent. Besides, Captain Buffington wanted an experienced military man to take the shipment...in case there's trouble. He has a particular interest because he supplied the corn himself."

Gage frowned. "Is trouble expected?" If so, he'd request Donald McCleary ride shotgun. He trusted the no-nonsense Scotsman to be cool under fire above any other private in the company.

"Nothing beyond what might be expected for soldiers of an occupyin' army." Wood's chortle drew Gage's brows even closer together.

"We're not here to occupy, Private. We're here to protect."

"Right, sir. Whatever you say, sir." Wood shifted impatiently. "In any case, the captain specifically asked for you."

He did? Gage weighed that information, sliding his forefinger over the slight bristle that covered his chin. He'd been with the Gainesville Dragoons in the spring campaign against the Seminoles last year, but did Captain Buffington know his record? Was that why Gage was chosen for an assignment the drummer boy could carry out?

When they'd been stationed at the Cherokee capital where they'd received their training, he'd not been chosen to accompany Lieutenant Clayton to pursue the murderer of a native man in Walker County. Or to investigate the depredations against Cherokees in Paulding County. The rising fear in his gut that he'd been enlisted as a sergeant as a nod to his father's military renown battled with the humility his faith and his godly mother had instilled in him. Who was he to think he deserved anything? He'd have to earn a chance to prove himself. And he could start by driving the corn to the mill.

He dropped his hand and gave a brief nod. "My apologies, Private. It will be my honor to carry out Captain Buffington's request. Just where is this mill located?"

Private Wood gestured to the Alabama Road—deserted and barely visible in dawn's gray haze—where it ran near their camp, which would soon enough be Fort Buffington. "'Bout a quarter mile west toward Canton, you'll find a lane running south to Mill Creek. Walker Mill sits on Walker Creek, a tributary. Should be signs. Now, if I can beg your leave..."

"Of course. Thank you, Private Wood." After the assistant quartermaster returned his salute and skedaddled back toward the cooking tent, Gage let out a sigh and re-entered his temporary lodgings to finish dressing.

Ezekiel Buffington was right to safeguard the corn. His company could hardly be expected to build a palisade, barracks, stables, and blockhouses on empty stomachs. Fort Buffington was to be the supply depot for the westernmost encampments in a chain of over a dozen forts established under General Wool. The mounted troops manning the forts operated under his orders to protect the lives and property of the Cherokee people until the deadline for their removal next spring.

Many good citizens protested the plans of the government —pushed by the greed of settlers seeking gold since its discovery in these parts eight or so years prior—to move the peaceful Cherokees west to Oklahoma Territory. To take land that had sustained them for decades. The notion was especially egregious to men like Gage's father, who credited the victory at Horseshoe Bend against the British-allied Creek Indians to the Cherokee Regiment he'd been honored to fight alongside during the War of 1812. Which was one reason Gage's opportunity to serve here was so vital. After what had happened in Florida, Gage owed his father a debt that reached beyond the grave.

Though a trip to the mill would likely offer little of interest besides viewing the machinery, Gage would dedicate himself wholeheartedly to whatever he found there.

By the time he'd shaved and donned his boots and overcoat, the musician had sounded reveille. The low hum of male voices permeated the camp as men prepared for their first roll call on land owned by local farmer Moses Perkins. The clank of metal indicated that their farrier and blacksmith was somehow already at work despite the lack of an established forge. Gage slung his cartridge box over his shoulder and reached for his musket before exiting his tent. He found the wagon loaded and waiting as Private Wood had described.

The smoke from campfires mingled with the lingering morning mist as he pulled the team onto the Alabama Road and headed west minutes later. Gage unwrapped his biscuit and jerky to consume his morning meal as he jounced along. He'd little distance to go before the turnoff onto what was likely to be a narrow lane requiring both hands on the reins. This land was not so different from his home. Gainesville was more rolling, to be sure, with deep woodlands, gold-rich rivers, and ridges that stunned one with unexpected mountain vistas. Easy to see why the Cherokees would be loath to leave.

Clouds of tiny white and lavender asters lined the road while stalks of goldenrod studded the fields. When he made the turn to Walker Mill, the forest in its autumnal glory enclosed him. Russet dogwoods and golden poplars and maples competed for his attention like ladies parading on a boardwalk. The pokewood stalks and berries had purpled, and the mimosas dangled rustling leather pods over the lane. Not to be outdone, the sourwood and blackberry leaves glowed like a red woolen petticoat flung amongst the underbrush.

As he neared Walker Creek, a few homesteads broke the heavy forest canopy—dew on the pumpkins, stalk leavings in cornfields, and neat log cabins and outbuildings set in dirt clearings. Bottle gourds attracted nesting martins as they stood like sentries over gardens with pale-style or woven cane fencing. Some homes had potato houses on high ground and springhouses near the creek.

Gage shook his head. Despite their European design, most of these spreads probably belonged to Cherokees. Just another travesty of this scheduled removal was the fact that the tribe had adopted many ways of their white neighbors, down to their own newspaper and legal system. Missionaries had long been at work among the people, starting schools and churches.

Sudden unease clenched in his gut. He hadn't considered that the mill might be owned by Cherokees. How would they feel about grinding corn for the army?

Troops had been stationed in the area for years—mostly east of here. If he remembered correctly, they'd been near the inn owned by Jacob Scudder, a white man considered a blood brother to the Cherokees. But while some of the native population appreciated the protection from gold-hungry winners of the lottery designed to divvy up their land, others saw their presence much as Private Wood had described...as that of an occupying force. A reminder that, should the efforts of Cherokee leaders fail to convince Washington to help, the same soldiers would be called on to forcibly remove those who had not already chosen to depart for the West. Gage had every intention of mustering out before that happened.

The music of the creek trilled above the creak and jingle of the wagon as the lane widened into a dirt yard that supported the mill complex, which included a log cabin and outbuildings much like those he'd just passed. Gage drew the team to a halt to admire the picturesque view. Walker Creek had been partially dammed above a natural shoal. A box raceway using a gate system channeled the flow to the top of a massive wooden overshot wheel attached to the back of the two-story frame mill building, and currently sat silent.

Sight of another wagon in front of the mill and two men standing before the half-open Dutch door spoiled Gage's hopes that he might be the first customer. He parked alongside the other vehicle and set his brake. Only then did the raised voices reach his ears.

"You can't deny me service! I got the same rights as any customer." Shadowed by a thin younger man, a stocky middle-aged man whose battered black hat covered most of what his grizzled brown beard failed to conceal shook his fist at two boys who stood behind the lower portion of the door.

"I can deny you service if you bring less than the required portion." Emotion made the reply of the youth in an equally floppy hat more than a bit unsteady as he tipped his head toward the small bag the man held. And judging by the tenor, the owner of the voice wasn't much older than the boy who hung back just behind him, his head just reaching the older one's shoulder.

If the boys found the courage to stand up to two full-grown men, there must be a good reason. Gage climbed down and reached behind the seat for his musket.

The irate customer lowered his arms to his sides. "Where's your father?"

That's what Gage wanted to know.

"At a meeting. If my terms don't please you, you can try the mills at Sixes or Scudder's." The youth squared his shoulders. White, then, judging by the diction and the lack of nasal sound that Cherokees often had when speaking English—though the slighter boy who watched the exchange with wide eyes had the tawny look of a half blood. Hired help, perhaps?

"Yeah. Maybe we should go, Uncle Isaiah." The younger man with shoulder-length blond hair and a rangy height spoke for the first time. He ventured a nudge to his companion's arm.

The one called Isaiah threw him off with an explosive curse. "I ain't goin' miles outta my way when we got a mill right here." He stepped closer to the building. "Or maybe it only serves *certain kinds* of customers."

"Is there a problem here?" Gage moved into the man's line of sight so he could no longer be ignored.

Finally, Isaiah shot him a look. "Sure is. Can't get no service at my own local mill."

"This is the third time he's come with below the portion we require to run the machinery." Disgust roughened the voice of the miller's son, whose face flashed in Gage's direction, although he still stood in the shadows as though ready to turn away at any moment. "My father let him get away with it the first two times because he didn't want trouble. But there won't be a third."

The blond turned to his relative. "Is that true, Uncle?"

The older man ignored his nephew as he spluttered his

indignation. "Oh, there won't, will there? We'll see what you have to say when—"

"Isn't the machinery running at all hours in harvest season?" Gage moved closer to the miller's boy.

The wearer of the black hat gave a brief nod. "But he bets on the fact that my father won't charge a toll if he's under the amount. Everybody knows Isaiah Thompson's a cheat."

"Why, you..." Thompson lunged forward, reaching over the top of the Dutch door and grabbing the boy by his muslin shirt before Gage could react. Thompson shook the youth, bumping him against the doorframe. The boy's hat fell off, revealing two long, dark braids and the prettiest features Gage had ever laid eyes on.

The miller's son was...a woman?

Did you enjoy this book? We hope so!
Would you take a quick minute to leave a review where you purchased the book?
It doesn't have to be long. Just a sentence or two telling what you liked about the story!

Love Christian Historical Romance?
Looking for your next favorite book?
Become a Wild Heart Books insider and receive a FREE ebook
and get exclusive updates on new releases before anyone else.
Sign up for our newsletter now.
https://wildheartbooks.org/newsletter

AUTHOR'S NOTE

Dear Reader,

My first series, The Georgia Gold Series, touched on the Georgia Gold Rush, though it focused more on the early days of prospecting in Habersham County, the Cherokee Removal, the Civil War, and Reconstruction. In the ten years since its release, I've written novels set in the Revolutionary War, the War of 1812, the Civil War, the Gilded Age, and contemporary times. The period of the 1830s is one largely untouched in American history by fiction writers, but for Georgia history, one of great importance. I always knew I might revisit that decade in more detail. Thus, The Twenty-Niners of the Georgia Gold Rush was born.

Gold was first discovered by white men on Coker Creek in 1827. But it wasn't until fall of 1828, when Benjamin Parks found a nugget as he returned from filling his cattle's lick log west of the Chestatee River, when the mining industry exploded in North Georgia. The area was flooded by prospectors of all nationalities and walks of life who clashed with the native Cherokee people. The land was soon taken away from the Cherokees and divvied up in a lottery of ninety-two districts of nine miles square, with farming plots set at a hundred and sixty acres and gold lots at forty acres. By June of 1832, almost six hundred surveyors from across Georgia were hard at work.

Auraria, located on the mountain ridge between the Etowah and Chestatee rivers, was one of the boom towns that lingered into the twentieth century, although now only a few abandoned buildings remain. Nathaniel Nuckolls erected the first hotel, which was later purchased by Agnes Paschal and her son, as indicated in the story. "Grandma" Paschal was a well-known healer who helped fight typhoid, scarlet fever, and various other illnesses with more natural methods. She swore by red peppers on the feet and her special red pepper tea. She also helped found Auraria's Baptist church and was instrumental in the erection of the first log church building, although it fell down the first winter. While her interactions with my characters were, of course, fictional, I strove to depict her as accurately as possible from my research, including the book *Ninety-Four Years* by her son, George W. Paschal.

The murder of Robert Ligon was reconstructed from court records of Jesse Brown's August 1833 trial—except to fit the timeline of my book, I had the incident occur in May instead of early June. Same for the theft of two horses from Auraria. Jesse Brown was convicted of murder and sentenced in February 1834 to five years in the penitentiary.

The debate over the location of the Lumpkin County courthouse also transpired as described, including the dual Fourth of July celebrations. At that time, the town of Dahlonega, which will be featured in book three, *The Schoolmarm and the Miner*, c. 1839, was still known as Headquarters, Licklog, and Lumpkin Court House/Courthouse. Despite the location not being named Dahlonega until October of 1833, the erection of the courthouse there spelled doom for the town of Auraria. One by one, businesses relocated north to the new county seat, especially when the beautiful brick courthouse (now the gold museum) was built in 1834 and a U.S. branch mint (on the current location of Price Hall on the University of North Georgia's campus) was completed in 1837.

The city of Gainesville, gateway to the mountains, was founded about two hundred yards north of the boggy ground surrounding Mule Camp Springs and grew apace with the Gold Rush. The mention of the first Methodist circuit-riding preacher being ridden out of town occurred in 1830. Rev. J.W. Glenn began a congregation of about fifteen individuals in a local house soon after, and in 1834, they purchased the old log courthouse for a hundred and fifty dollars and began First Methodist Church.

I hope you found the healing journeys of Jesse and Genny inspiring as they drew strength from the Lord and began a healthy relationship after suffering mental and emotional abuse at the hands of those who should have protected them. The ability to pen this story while coming out of the greatest trial of my own life is a testament solely to the goodness of God. I'm claiming that promise with my characters that He will restore the years the locusts have eaten. For those of you walking through hardships, I pray you will do the same.

We left another character badly in need of healing at the end of this novel—Sheriff Wade Coulter. Hang on, readers. His chance for redemption is coming. But first, things have to get a whole lot worse as the settlers push out the Cherokees in order to claim the gold lands. Look for *The Mountie and the Maiden* in about six months.

I'd like to thank the team at Wild Heart Books—including my publisher, Misty M. Beller; my editor, Janyre Tromp; Sarah Erredge and Sherri Wilson Johnson—for their skill and vision in helping me bring this story to my readers. Also my launch team, especially my beta readers— Gretchen Elm, Catherine Patton, and Jennie Webb. And you, my amazing readers, who love history as much as I do and support me as an author so well. Remember, find Denise Weimer books under Denise Farnsworth, my new married name, now!

If you enjoyed *The Songbird and the Surveyor*, your reviews let publishers know my stories are worth continuing to publish. I notice and treasure each one. I'd also love to connect with you online.

Newsletter signup: https://webs.us19.list-manage.com/subscribe?u=16c561f75e5036405879c9836&id=b58acc62a5

Website: https://denisefarnsworthbooks.mailchimpsites.com/

Facebook: https://www.facebook.com/denise.farnsworth.books

Twitter: https://x.com/denise_farnsw

ABOUT THE AUTHOR

North Georgia native Denise Weimer, now Denise Farnsworth, has authored around twenty traditionally published novels and novellas--historical and contemporary romance, romantic suspense, and time slip. As a freelance editor and Acquisitions & Editorial Liaison for Wild Heart Books, she's helped other authors reach their publishing dreams. A wife and mother of two wonderful young adult daughters, Denise always pauses for coffee, chocolate, and old houses.

You can visit Denise at https://www.deniseweimerbooks.com, and connect with her on social media.

Monthly e-mail list: http://eepurl.com/dFfSfn

If you love historical romance, check out the other Wild Heart books!

A Winter at the White Queen by Denise Weimer

In the world of the wealthy, things are never quite as they appear.

Ellie Hastings is tired of playing social gatekeeper—and poor-relation companion—to her Gibson Girl of a cousin. But her aunt insists Ellie lift her nose out of her detective novel long enough to help gauge the eligibility of bachelors during the winter social season at Florida's Hotel Belleview. She finds plenty that's mysterious about the suave, aloof Philadelphia inventor, Lewis Thornton. Why does he keep sneaking around the hotel? Does he have a secret sweetheart? And what is his connection to the evasive Mr. Gaspachi, slated to perform at Washington's Birthday Ball?

Ellie's comical sleuthing ought to put Lewis out, but the diffident way her family treats her smashes a hole in his normal reserve. When Florence Hastings's diamond necklace goes missing, Ellie's keen mind threatens to uncover not only Lewis's secrets, but give him back hope for love.

~

A Counterfeit Betrothal by Denise Weimer

A frontier scout, a healing widow, and a desperate fight for peace.

At the farthest Georgia outpost this side of hostile Creek Territory in 1813, Jared Lockridge serves his country as a scout to redeem his father's botched heritage. If he can help secure peace against Indians allied to the British, he can bring his betrothed to the home he's building and open his cabinetry shop. Then he comes across a burning cabin and a traumatized woman just widowed by a fatal shot.

Freed from a cruel marriage, Esther Andrews agrees to winter at the Lockridge homestead to help Jared's pregnant sister-in-law. Lame in one foot, Esther has always known she is second-hand goods, but the gentle carpenter-turned-scout draws her heart with as much skill as he creates furniture from wood. His family's love offers hope even as violence erupts along the fron-tier—and Jared's investigation into local incidents brings danger to their doorstep. Yet how could Esther ever hope a loyal man like Jared would choose her over a fine lady?

If you love historical romance, check out the other Wild Heart books!

Rescue in the Wilderness by Andrea Byrd

William Cole cannot forget the cruel burden he carries, not with the pock marks that serve as an outward reminder. Riddled with guilt, he assumed the solitary life of a long hunter, traveling into the wilds of Kentucky each year. But his quiet existence is changed in an instant when, sitting in a tavern, he overhears a man offering his daughter—and her virtue—to the winner of the next round of cards. William's integrity and desire for redemption will not allow him to sit idly by while such an injustice occurs.

Lucinda Gillespie has suffered from an inexplicable illness her entire life. Her father, embarrassed by her condition, has subjected her to a lonely existence of abuse and confinement. But faced with the ultimate betrayal on the eve of her eighteenth birthday, Lucinda quickly realizes her trust is better placed in his hands of the mysterious man who appears at her door. Especially when he offers her the one thing she never thought would be within her grasp—freedom.

In the blink of an eye, both lives change as they begin the difficult, danger-fraught journey westward on the Wilderness Trail. But can they overcome their own perceptions of themselves to find love and the life God created them for?